APOLLO
DISCARDED HEROES: SCIONS

DISCARDED HEROES: SCIONS

ATLAS

APOLLO

ACHILLES

DISCARDED HEROES

NIGHTSHADE

DIGITALIS

WOLFSBANE

FIRETHORN

LYGOS

APOLLO

DISCARDED HEROES: SCIONS

RONIE KENDIG

SUNRISE PUBLISHING

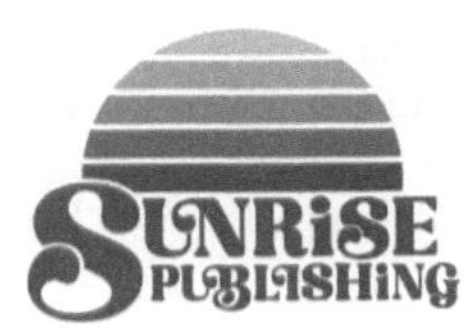

Apollo
Discarded Heroes: Scions, Book 2

Published by Sunrise Media Group LLC

Print ISBN: 978-1-966463-53-5

This book is a work of fiction. Names, characters, places, and incidents are either products of the author's imagination or used fictitiously. Any similarity to actual people, organizations, and/or events is purely coincidental.

For more information about the author please access her website at roniekendig.com.

Published in the United States of America.
Cover Design: Sunrise Media Group LLC

To my amazing Rapid-Fire Readers, the true guardians
of this world: may you find the courage, joy, and love
contained within these pages.

A NOTE FROM RONIE . . .

After fifteen years and forty-plus books, I am always looking for something new and unique to spark story ideas. As you might have read in ATLAS, I asked my husband to pick three unique and not-normally-written-about locations for the SCIONS. He chose Armenia, Saudi Arabia, and Yemen, so I started digging into each country's history to find something new and fascinating to bring to light in the stories. Before I dive into that, let me note that in APOLLO, I created a fictional Central Kingdom, so that I could have my way with the story and royals of that kingdom, and not reflect poorly on any real institutions.

Now . . . back to the tale that grabbed my attention. Research led me to a shocking true story about the Vanishing Princesses of Saudi Arabia. Back in the mid-nineties, an American doctor from Texas was called upon to treat a princess in the country in which he worked, Saudi Arabia. That was his introduction to a daunting, horrific tale that seemed too incredible to believe: four princesses were being held virtual prisoners by their father-king. Their mother, who had fled to escape the king's cruelty for not producing a male heir, was trying to save her daughters from afar. The doctor learned the princesses were being dosed with a medicinal cocktail of drugs that essentially left them pliable and immobilized. For years, the doctor advocated for them, tried to help them escape. The princesses even made contact with journalists at one point in an attempt to get word out about their plight. However, after the king died, contact with the princesses abruptly stopped. It is said that at least two of the princesses ended up dying of starvation-related health problems and the long-term drugging. The others were never heard from again! Truly, it's such a heartrending story, so I found great solace in giving a fictional Saudi princess a happy ending that never came about for those who inspired her story.

If you would like to read more about the vanishing princesses, check out this article or Google it for yourself!

https://www.newyorker.com/news/a-reporter-at-large/the-texan-doctor-and-the-disappeared-saudi-princesses

He has shown you, O mortal, what is good. And what does
the LORD require of you? To act justly and to love mercy
and to walk humbly with your God.

Micah 6:8 NIV

ONE

Two Years Ago
Sterling, Virginia

DEPOSITING HIS SEVENTY-POUND RUCK JUST inside the foyer, Owen Metcalfe kicked the door shut behind him. "Mom?" He shed his backpack, never slowing as he aimed for the kitchen. "Mom, you here?"

Lights out, fridge humming noisily like always, the kitchen offered little welcome as he slid his truck keys onto the island. He checked the living room and hall for signs of life but came up empty. Huh. Where was she?

The rumble of his gut had him tug open the fridge and eye the contents. He grabbed a piece of leftover pizza. It wasn't the on-the-fly fast-food kind that he'd had too many times on his last rotation, but the mom-and-pop, legit Italian place that was a Metcalfe staple. Folding the slice in half, he grabbed a paper towel and headed to the stairs. "Mom?" He stuffed half the pizza into his mouth and chewed, waiting for her response before ambling to the sliding glass doors that led to the North Forty backyard. The place his aunts and uncles had played many a game growing up. Nothing.

"So much for a 'welcome home,'" he muttered and took another bite. Back in the kitchen, crust sticking out of his mouth, he snagged the last slice. "Serves you right for not being here—"

The heavy thrum of the garage door rising reverberated through the house. He tossed the last piece back in the box and headed into the garage bay. Over the roof of her silver SUV, he saw Mom step out and move to the rear hatch. "Need help?"

His mom's brown head and eyes swiveled his direction. She gave him a broad smile. "Hello, handsome." Retrieving a satchel, she walked over and waved him into her arms for a hug as the hatch shut. "I thought you weren't getting released on leave till tomorrow."

He bent down to accept the embrace and kissed her cheek. "Got things tied up quicker than expected." *Please don't ask if I'm okay. Or about the future.*

"I'm glad." She eyed him with an assessing look, then started into the house. "I take it you already raided the pizza."

"One slice."

"Dad left it for you, so have at it."

His phone buzzed, indicating a text, and he eyed the screen.

Sophia
____

Glad you're back. Bonfire at the ranch. 8pm. You're my date.

With a sniff, he shook his head, hit the garage door button, and stepped inside. "Soph's having a bonfire again."

Mom nodded. "The twins' graduation party."

Dude, already? "Oh, right."

His mom turned as she drew a glass down from the cabinet and arched an eyebrow. "You going?"

"Apparently I'm her date, so I guess so." He opted to snag the last slice after all.

"Will you two ever make it real?" Mom asked as she filled her glass with filtered water from the fridge.

"Negative," he chortled, biting back the laugh at the way his mom gave him a concerned look. "She's my sister."

"*Tala* is your sister," Mom corrected. "Who's doing great, by the way, not that you asked."

"Tala is always okay," he said. His half sister had gone off to New York to pursue a career in art and never looked back other than to provide occasional updates so Dad didn't track her down and get in her face about communication and familial bonds.

"But Sophia Neeley is *not* your sister." Hair down past her shoulders, Mom looked smart in a blouse and slacks. Had she been to an appointment? "There is no biological connection there, and—"

"Like I need you to tell me that." Owen sagged beneath her blinding flash of the obvious. "That dog will never hunt. She's *always* been the kid sister I never had. And Scions have a strict no-dating rule. Too weird." He grimaced and shuddered. "With Soph, I run interference for her at parties. Dudes are always in her face, asking for a date."

"It wouldn't hurt you two to—"

"Nope." He waved a hand in the air and nuked the pizza. "Not doing this. I've got another year on my contract, and nothing happens till then." Though he had hoped to make Selection and go career with the Rangers, that hadn't happened. And now failure hung over his head like an anvil.

In two large bites, he finished off the pizza and went for a protein bar from the pantry. The Spidey sense said Mom was about to unlock "mom mode" and start drilling him with questions and lectures, so he needed to beat her to the gate. "You look nice. Last-minute meeting?"

"Nice diversion," she said with a wry smile. "I was visiting Uncle Stone."

"Cool, how's he doing?"

"He and Brighton are expecting again," she said, shaking her head, clearly aware he was still diverting.

"Isn't he, like, too old for that?"

She arched an eyebrow. "He's only a few years older than your dad."

"Exactly." Owen knew Dad was sensitive about his age. "Uncle Stone'll need a walker to get to his kid's graduation."

Mom yanked a towel from where it hung on the oven handle and snapped it at him. "You menace."

Laughing, he held up his hands. "Seriously," he said around a laugh. "I'm glad he's happy." He remembered the brooding Uncle Stone too well, and the tension radiating through the family after the scandal broke. "So, was it just a casual chat or was this about the trafficking shelter?"

She nodded, peeling an orange. "He asked if I could work my connections on the Hill to make some more headway on improving anti-trafficking laws."

"Yeah?" He wolfed down the bar and pitched the wrapper. "You going to do it?"

She drew her hair into a ponytail, a sure sign she was getting down to business. He'd need to bug out before it got tense in here. "Not sure. I know it needs to be done, but I'm not sure I have the time in my schedule to do it justice. Agreed I'd look into it." And then, just like that, she folded her arms and launched her heat-seeking missile. "So, you're home. Since Rangers didn't work out . . . what're you planning?"

What little air was left in his chest deflated. "Mom, c'mon. I'm home ten minutes and—"

"I know you, Owen Navas, and the longer you think about something, the worse it gets. You're like your father—a man of action. Sitting around doesn't help."

That was the thing of it—he *wasn't* like Dad. God knows he'd tried to be. Believed that same tough mettle was in him, but Uncle Sam disagreed. Selection board disagreed. "Just let a guy breathe, 'kay?"

Quiet settled between them, but that blaze in her eyes said she wasn't going to leave it alone. "You're not a failure."

Bam—right for the heart. "I, uh . . ." He aimed for the living room. "Gotta get the rest of my gear from the truck and grab a shower before heading to the ranch." He kept moving, not looking back. Avoiding the Mom look. Mom guilt. She was an expert at it.

<hr>

Later that night, he made his way out to the Neeley ranch. Long before turning off the county road, he spotted the raging bonfire. That and the fifty or so cars lining the gravel driveway. "What in blue blazes . . . ?" he muttered as he lumbered past the many vehicles. Finally found a place to park his Raptor, cut the engine, and stared out beyond the hood that even now caught the firelight in the reflection.

The old barn had been converted into a wedding and party venue, staying pretty busy. Soph had helped her mom with the business and had a good head and eye for it. Light and music filtered out from the buzzing barn, spreading its revelry toward the riding corral. A lot of people—way too many, in his opinion— loitered there.

For a half second, he wondered if sitting at home and getting an earful from Mom might be less painful than this. Probably.

A lone figure striding toward him squelched the idea, especially when she waved at him. Soph. Wearing jeans, boots, and a plaid shirt, she let her hair loose in waves down past her shoulders. She looked pretty.

Abandoning the thought of bugging out, he exited the truck and met her halfway.

She leapt at him, wrapping thin arms around his neck, and laughed. "You made it!" Her blonde hair smelled of smoke from the bonfire. "About doggone time."

"You didn't give me much warning," he said, releasing her.

She swung around behind him, caught his shoulders, and hiked up on his back for a piggyback. Arms looped around his neck, she rested her face near his. "Someone didn't tell me he'd be coming home. Or I would've had it all planned, the million ways you can save me at the party."

"Huh. Wonder why he didn't tell you . . ."

She lightly popped the other side of his head. "How long you here for?"

"Couple weeks." Arms hooked behind her legs, he hoisted her into a better position. "Ben or Dill here?"

"Ben, yes, but as usual, he's ticked at Dad and pouting in some corner, no doubt. But Dillon . . ."

At her tone, he angled to look into her eyes. "What?"

"Your parents haven't told you?"

He frowned and let her down, considering her seriously. Had a bad feeling about this. Dillon had been in communication on and off, but that wasn't unusual. "What's happened?"

"He vanished two months ago after an argument with Auntie Syd."

Slowing, Owen huffed and looked at the night sky, guilt haranguing him.

Soph gaped at him, those green eyes piercing. "You knew and didn't say a thing? Even to the Scions?"

"I didn't think he was serious," he balked.

She slapped his shoulder. "Usually, thinking is your strong suit." She clucked her tongue, looped their arms, and resumed walking. "Apparently, he told Auntie Syd he was going to find his dad."

"Holy . . ." He swiped a hand over his mouth, still unable to believe Dillon really thought he could resurrect the dead.

"Nobody's heard from him since," Sophia said as they neared the barn and pulsing music. "Because he's an adult, local authorities can't do a single thing."

"Maybe I need to try to reach out."

"You know he won't tell you anything. Of the Scions, he's always been the most stubborn."

"Says the girl who held her breath till she passed out when she didn't get her way."

Her green eyes widened. "I was four!"

"Uh-huh." He jutted his jaw to her feet. "How long you hold out for the boots?"

She frowned, but it was fake and surrendered to a smile that she topped with her nose up in mischief. "Not long at all. Daddy's so proud I got into Carnegie Mellon, I could've asked for the moon and he'd have roped it for me."

"Think Jimmy Stewart already did that." Scanning as they entered the barn, replete with the smells of the country—hay, animals, and BBQ—he followed her to the refreshment table and grabbed a bottled water.

"Owen!"

He pivoted and spotted Sophia's parents arcing out from behind the food table. "Ma'am, sir."

Uncle Colton pulled him into a hug. Patted his back like he was providing life-saving measures. "Good to see you, son."

"Thank you. Same, sir."

"Has your dad talked you into Special Forces yet?"

Heat-seeking missiles apparently ran in the Scion family. Did everyone know? "Not yet." He took a swig of the water. "But I'm sure it's coming."

The barrel-chested guy laughed. "You're bred from good stock, so I'm sure you'll find the right MOS."

Stretching his jaw, Owen searched out his charge. Found Sophia in a huddle of girls and spotted some guys homing in on her. "If you'll excuse me, Uncle Colton . . ."

"Appreciate the way you watch out for her."

"Family," he said with a cockeyed nod. "We protect our own." With that, he strode toward her but slowed his roll, suddenly realizing he was legit out of place here.

Most of those partying were from the twins' graduating class, so only a couple years younger than him, but with three years of Army under his belt, he felt a decade older. These people were just getting started. Hadn't felt the sting of failure like he had.

"Sorry, Corporal. We just didn't see what we need for the Regiment."

As he reminisced that day, he slowly grew aware that he was staring at someone. Not intentionally, but his gaze had inadvertently locked with brown eyes. Olive complexion. A breeze swept through the barn, swaying the string lights crisscrossing overhead, and rustled her long, dark hair. Light hit her eyes and turned them caramel. She held his gaze for a second, then focused on her friends and lifted a red cup, which she sipped from. Smiled at something a friend said. Those caramel eyes found his again. And like that tiny zap of a hot socket, he felt the connection.

"Owen!"

He twitched at Soph's shout and pivoted her way.

"C'mere!" she said, lacing her arm through his and drawing him into the huddle. "Look who it is."

Owen grinned at the dark-haired guy she pointed to. "No way!" He pulled him into a one-shouldered hug and shook his hand. "Khalon Russell." He patted the guy's shoulder. "How's it going?"

Two years younger, Khalon Russell had always been a like-minded individual. They'd met when the guy had joined the private academy the Scions attended, then Principal Hamrick chose Owen to mentor Khalon through his first few weeks. They'd struck a solid friendship.

"Good." Khalon gave a slow smile and nod. "Glad to finally be done with school."

"What about college?" Owen asked with a laugh, and something in his periphery lured his focus away.

Her. Red-Cup Girl was drifting closer, trailing a bunch of rich kids who didn't really seem Soph's speed. Or RCG's speed. In fact, she seemed to hold back. Was that because of him, or the company she was keeping?

"I'm going to spend a year in Nigeria with my godfather," Khalon said. "Then . . ." He shrugged. "We'll see."

Huh. That sounded a lot like Khalon had things to work out. Once again, they were on parallel paths. "You'll figure it out."

Khalon gave him a speculative look. "I thought of joining the Army. Any tips?"

"Yeah, *don't*." Owen snickered, telling himself not to look at the girl now hovering to Soph's ten o'clock. "Nah, seriously—if it's what you want, do it. What's your dad say? And your uncle?"

It'd been a hot minute since Khalon's uncle was president, but former presidents wielded a lot of influence. Could get his nephew into any school he wanted.

Even as the guy answered, Owen noticed RCG shift into view over Khalon's shoulder. When her friend leaned into her, she again lifted that cup to her mouth—used the thing like a shield as her friend nodded to Owen and whispered something, turning RCG's gaze his way.

Yeah, not needing that complication, he refocused on Khalon, whose mouth was still moving. Shoot. What had he missed? No idea because his ears were straining to pick up whatever RCG's friend said that caused them to laugh hard over the din.

RCG stood about five-six, had an athletic build, and by that outfit, had a good sense of style. Yet, while she hung out with the rich crowd, there was something . . . different about her. She didn't look relaxed or comfortable here. Was it the barn? The country atmosphere?

It seemed more . . .

Her friends were laughing and likely had something else in their red cups other than the punch the Neeleys were serving. Her, though? Straight-laced. Alert. Those pretty brown eyes searched the crowds more than once. And they weren't just looking for him or a good time. It was . . . *awareness*. But something else too. Maybe vulnerability? Cloaked in . . . wariness.

"Hey!" Soph punched his bicep.

"What?" he balked, flinching as he protected his arm. "What was that for?"

"I was talking to you!" Soph's furrowed brow lifted, then smoothed when she saw what had distracted him. "Oh." She let out a huff and faced him full-on. "You *don't* want to get involved with that."

He arched an eyebrow at the way she said "*that.*"

"No, trust me, Owen. She's Holland's older sister."

"Holland?"

"The girl who threw herself at you when we went to prom last year—she was *lit*, and I don't mean in the good way. I know how you feel about stuff like that."

Fair. He'd seen too many friends wreck their lives with substance abuse. "Oh."

"Yeah. Don't waste your time—with any of that crowd." She sniffed. "You're way above all of them."

Was Soph sure about that? Because the beauty seemed light-years beyond him.

RCG looked away, pretending she wasn't trying to avoid him, but she was close enough to have heard Soph's comments. He'd already told himself once he didn't need the complication.

Yet like a riptide that yanked him from shore, her presence

demanded his attention. Sucked every bit of common sense out of him. And somehow he found himself heading in her direction.

A weight plowed into his back. "Metcalfe! What's up, dude?"

Owen turned to find Ben Neeley in a big black Stetson. They clapped hands and drew each other in for a one-shouldered hug. "Congrats on not failing too many classes to get flunked."

Ben's green eyes sparked at the taunt. "Dude, that is so wrong." He thrust his pointer finger up. "What matters is I got the stupid diploma. Now, I think I'll trail Khalon to Nigeria."

"Don't think so," Khalon said with a smirk.

Even as the group started chatting again, Owen felt a seismic shift that sent his gaze to the girl shrouded in mystery. Wondered at the strange thing plucking at his conscience that said to protect her.

"You must be really into the older sis to stare at her like that."

He glanced at Soph. "Jealous much?" he teased as he combed the crowd for RCG, but she had vanished, leaving him with the haunting sense that she was in danger. A lot of it.

TWO

Present Day
Sterling, Virginia

THAT LOOKS TO BE ABOUT IT, CORPORAL. Now, to make it official." The balding civilian behind the desk spun a stack of papers toward Owen. "Give this a quick look-see to be sure we have the correct info and put your John Hancock at the bottom. Then you'll be cleared and officially separated from the Army."

Un-freakin-believable. He'd never seen this happening. How had it come to this?

Black ink pen in hand, Owen stared at the DD214. Palming the desk, he let his gaze drift over the information. Five years and this was all he had to show for something he'd intended to do for over two decades, for his career?

"Problem?" the guy asked around a bite of a greasy fast-food burger.

"No," Owen grunted and scratched his name at the bottom, huffed, and tossed the pen down. Slid both back to the civil service member in charge of out-processing. Unceremonious and anticlimactic.

"Okay, you're officially no longer a slave to the US government." The guy grinned, burger stuck between his teeth, before slurping soda from a straw. He printed some copies, then handed over a file of his records.

"That stuff will kill you," Owen muttered as he hiked his pack onto his shoulder and stepped back.

"That's the plan," the guy said, unrepentant. "Have a good life!"

"Right. Yeah." Owen backstepped again. "Thanks."

What on earth was he thanking the guy for? For *officially* telling him he'd come up short again?

Owen pivoted on his heels and stalked out of the building. Headed to his truck and climbed in. Got heading west, back toward his parents' house. The road noise and blaring rock music did little to drown the voice screaming in his head that said he wasn't good enough. Wouldn't ever be good enough. Twenty-two years old and he was going back home to live with Dad and Mom.

So much for being a prodigy.

He was a prodigy all right—at always missing the mark. Falling short. Ears hollowed by the vacuum that had become his life, he had no idea what was next. Whack, how his entire career trajectory disintegrated.

"Call from Pike Auberon," intoned Siri through the truck's dash console.

"Yeah, right," he muttered, then added, "No, thanks."

"You haven't even heard the question."

Owen jerked straight, nearly veering into the right lane as he realized Siri had answered the call. Shoot. "I . . ." His brain dropped out of adrenaline mode, and he reminded himself what this guy wanted. More of the same. "Yeah, not interested."

"You realize who you're talking to?"

"Arrogant much?"

A sniff carried through the speakers. "Just want to be sure you didn't think I was calling to offer lower interest rates."

Owen nearly smiled. "Sorry, sir. Not—"

"Heard you separated today."

Glaring at the system as if Pike could see him, Owen had no idea how the chief already heard. "Knew you were well connected, but I didn't realize you were hardwired into the security cameras."

"There's a lot you don't know about me. Or what I'm offering."

Walked right into that one. "Look, I appreciate it—"

"Do you?"

"—but I don't think this is my jam." Couldn't stand the thought of signing on only to find out he couldn't cut it there either. Dad knew these guys. Didn't need more humiliation—or to malign the Metcalfe name or Dad again.

"Don't make a mistake, Apollo."

Dude knew everything, even his Scion callsign. That wasn't cool—it was straight outta Creep City.

"Haven't you heard? That's all I'm good at." Owen ended the call and slumped back in the seat as he hit the toll road.

There'd been a sour taste in the mouths of the Scions about Omen because Uncle Max had been killed working OTG. Besides, Owen wasn't interested in discovering he wasn't cut out for ops, though that had been the career he'd wanted since he was a kid. But missing out on Rangers tempered his risk-o-meter.

Despite the hour-long trip back home, Owen knew he didn't want to face Mom or Dad, get drilled with questions. So, he detoured off the toll road and hit a burger joint. He planted his backside at a booth farthest from the door and sat, staring at the menu.

What was he supposed to do with his life? What good was he to anyone? He'd graduated a year early, went into the Army with his entire career path plotted out. Despite Dad's connections, he'd ended up . . . exactly nowhere. Unlike pretty much every forebear he had. It was a long line of patriots, military heroes: Dad, General Lambert who was his grandfather, all his Scion uncles.

And I'm what?

Out after serving five years.

"You okay, hon?"

Owen blinked and looked up. "Sorry, what?"

The waitress wore black jeans and shirt. Easily as old as Mom but stick-thin. Curly hair framing her small face. "You've been here an hour, staring at that menu."

"Oh." He eyed the plastic sleeve in his hand, seeing the words for the first time. "I . . . uh, a burger. Bacon and cheese. Mayo and tomato."

"Fries?"

"That stuff will kill you." His words from earlier rang in his head. "Absolutely."

She winked at him. "You look like you got some things to work through, so I'll bring you double."

He tried to smile, but his lips just refused to take the curve. No idea how long he sat there, but at some point the food had showed up and he'd chewed his way through it and the hollowing emptiness called his life.

God, just show me . . . Show me what do. He'd never felt so lost in his life. So . . . directionless. Adrift. But he knew God was a master planner—he'd redeem this. Just . . . no idea how. God had his work cut out for him with Owen's life.

After finishing the food, he paid for the meal and got back in his Raptor. Only as he cranked the engine did he realize darkness had fallen over Northern Virginia. Was it really that late?

Pulling into the long drive fifteen minutes later, he eyed the clock on the dash. After nine. House should be pretty quiet. Mom was probably watching her favorite historical drama. A luxury import was parked in the drive, and he pulled alongside the sleek sedan. Who was here this late?

Owen climbed out and made his way up the sidewalk, concerned. His parents weren't night owls. And that car did not belong to any

Nightshade team member as far as he knew. Though, it had been a while since he'd been home. Maybe—

A noise filtered from around the side of the house and slowed him. He frowned, craning his neck in that direction. Heard voices . . . Dad . . . Who was he talking to?

Diverting toward them, Owen followed the path around to the back, to the North Forty. When he spotted two men sitting by the firepit about twenty feet from the back deck, some heightened instinct told him to wait. Not sure if he was intruding—why would they be outside, talking in the dark?—he strained to listen.

Why were his nerves on end?

"She and Yasmina were shopping when she was taken," a man said in a thick accent, his words grave, heavy. "Broad daylight, with hundreds in the center. She went to try on clothes and never came back."

"And you think it's the royals."

Royals? What the . . .

"I know it was. I went there." The guy's accent sounded Spanish, but wasn't *Yasmina* an Arabic name?

The question drew Owen closer, but he used a crepe myrtle to conceal his presence.

Face lit by the firelight, Dad frowned and leaned forward, posture and tone filled with tension, mild alarm . . . and disappointment. "You went there?" he balked.

"Do not judge me too harsh, Midas."

Whoa. Dad's old callsign went way back. He'd shed that name after Owen was born, as much as he could. Was that how this man knew him—from . . . *before?*

"There are many parts to this. Nobody knows Nouri is my daughter, or so I thought. But when I surveilled the palace of the Central Kingdom to find a way in, I noticed this man." A blue halo of light bloomed in the night as he showed his phone to Dad.

"Should he mean something to me?"

"You recall Nesto Bruzon?"

Dad punched to his feet. "Are you kidding me, Navas?"

Owen hauled in a breath at that name, but quickly, deliberately, swallowed it. Retreated deeper into shadow, pulse jackhammering. This man . . . *this* was the man he'd been named after. The mercenary who'd saved his parents in Venezuela. Saved Dad from prison. Dad had always said giving Owen that name was only the beginning of what they owed this man. That really, they owed Navas a life debt.

"The general's brother and son have built an empire down there," Navas went on. "They want to hurt Nouri to punish me for what I did, helping you get Danielle to safety."

"Holy . . ." Dad hung his head and ran his hands over his hair.

"You know I would not be here if there was any other way," Navas all but hissed. "I have a plan—we embed you into the palace—"

"No. I can't." Dad looked at the mercenary—*is he still a mercenary?*—and seemed grieved. Alarmed. "I'm not that man anymore. I—"

"Nouri has been in Faruq's hands for months. He believes she is *his* daughter."

With a groan, Dad tightened his expression, and Owen felt himself shifting forward.

"If Bruzon tells Faruq that she is mine, he will kill her—or worse, and I do not have to explain the things they dream up to torture women." He threaded his hands in a praying gesture. "Please. I must get her back and cannot do that without your help."

Owen felt a thrumming in his veins at the man's pleading request. No way Dad could turn him down.

"Navas . . . I can't. I retired for medical reasons—my spine. And I'm out of practice. I would not be a help—I'd put her life at risk."

Man, Owen couldn't fathom Dad saying no, but he had given up working with teams long ago because of his back. Still . . .

"Do you expect me to just leave her there? They will kill her! The risk is too great to not only Nouri, but Yasmina and myself." He stepped closer and tapped Dad's chest. "You owe me this, Midas. I saved your lover, now you help me save *mi hija*."

"It's not that easy," Dad complained. "The sun set long ago on my skills. We need someone young. I could talk to—"

"No, I do not want some stranger who would not care about my daughter. It must be someone with skin in the game. This has to matter to them or Nouri is as good as dead!"

"I'll do it." Only when their heads swiveled in his direction did Owen realize that had been his voice. Speaking aloud.

Dad was on his feet, scowling. "You shouldn't—"

"I'll go," Owen insisted. Hadn't he just been begging God for direction? Might as well own it. He stepped forward, the back porch light streaking over him, as if to amplify his volunteering. "Let me—"

"No, you have no idea what's happening here. You—"

"Dad." He regretted the bite to his words, but he was tired of being told no. "You just said you need someone young…" He held his hands out to the side, offering himself up to them. "Here I am."

Navas angled his head and moved toward him. "You are Owen."

Heart thudding that this mercenary knew not only of his existence but his name, he nodded. "I am."

Nodding, Navas looked to Dad, then back to Owen. "This could work."

"Hold up." Dad held up a staying hand to Owen along with a severe expression that warned him to stand down. "He's never seen combat. His entire five years have been training."

Hearing Dad spell that out, disqualify him … hurt more than both non-selections. More than being handed his DD214 this morning.

Pursing his lips, Navas didn't look deterred. "He does not need combat experience—this is a palace. What he will need is *instinct*." His teeth bared beneath that word. "Do you have that?"

"It's in my blood." At least, Owen hoped it was. Who could

explain why he'd qualified Rangers *and* Special Forces but didn't get selected for either? Maybe it was for this reason. To save some chick in a palace. "I can do this, Dad."

"Owen, *think*," Dad ground out. "This is a girl's life."

"Do you really think I don't get that?" He considered his dad for a second. Frowning, he was suddenly back on that peewee baseball mound all over again when he saw that look in his dad's eyes that said he didn't measure up. "You don't think I can do it." Disbelief chugged through his veins.

"*I think* it's in a foreign country. Do you know how to get in and out of there on your own?"

Miffed at how deep his dad's rejection cut, Owen exhaled and held his ground. "They taught us that in Ranger school. I might not have been selected, but I qualified."

Dad shouldered in, eyes lit with challenge. "You go in there and get caught, it won't just be you who pays the price. Besides, getting in is one thing. Getting out—that's a whole different game. You have to get both of you out. *Alive*."

Had to admit a wad of hurt lodged in his throat that Dad seemed to think so little of him. Guess after two failed launches it was par for the course. "This is just like what you did with Mom." He'd grown up hearing that story over and over. That mission to Venezuela to rescue Mom from General Bruzon had been the same one in which Owen had been conceived.

"Owen," Dad said, frustration in his voice as he landed a hand on his shoulder. "I was a combat medic. With multiple deployment stripes on my sleeve before Venezuela. This isn't just a thing to do, a notch in your tactical belt."

Those words punched his gut. "Do you really think that's what I'm doing?" But . . . wasn't he? After all, purpose dangled before him, taunting him. Yanking out of reach with each word Dad spoke.

He refused to be thwarted. "I may be lacking in a lot of areas, but not in grit and determination. Metcalfe blood is raw and ready—you taught me that. So stop doubting me. Believe in me."

"It's not—"

"You are young." Navas gripped Owen's bicep and squeezed. "Strong and agile. You are a good fit. It can be done." He sized him up, apparently by a very large measuring stick—Dad. "Have you ever killed a man?"

Owen took a steadying breath, begging Navas not to disqualify him now. "No."

"Are you prepared to, if needed?"

"Life is precious. But I wouldn't have joined the Army if I hadn't been willing to defend the innocent with violence of action."

Jeddah, Saudi Arabia

Concrete walls soared three stories tall, surrounding her on all sides as if keeping her captive in a well instead of a tiny courtyard. Was this how Joseph from the Bible felt when his brothers threw him down into a well, then sold him off? It was a distant, though not entirely inaccurate, parallel. Sun high overhead, its bright rays pushed down into the dull hollowness that consumed her.

Leighton Kingslake peered up, grateful the guards had been delayed in returning her to the cell. This lapse in their duties afforded her a rare moment in true sunlight. Not just ambient light that trickled through the opening above. Eyes closed, she savored the warmth on her face. Time had lost meaning with each day being spent in a concrete room with nothing but a pillow and blanket. No bed. No electricity. No pictures. No books.

If you don't make sacrifices for what you want, what you want becomes the sacrifice.

That could not happen. So, she must do this, maintain her quiet vigil to keep Ummi—her biological mother—safe. To keep herself safe.

A creak above made her eyes fly open. Connect with a beautiful woman whose thick, black hair formed a curly halo around an olive complexion. Much darker than Leighton's. The eyes too. Her heart jarred, realizing *who* that was!

Giggling, Princess Daria dropped something from the upper terrace. Laughter drifted down with the object—a pink flower petal. It alighted on the nearby stone pavers, delivering a subtle joy to Leighton. The petal, a stark, elegant contrast to the dark stone, seemed a symbol of hope.

When she glanced back up, Leighton too late understood her folly, for the princess had been replaced by a fierce man. The princess's fiancé, Hassan.

Startled at the sight of the mean Arab, Leighton yanked her gaze back down, the ache of her last beating—for daring to meet the eyes of the crown prince—all too fresh in her mind and body. It would not surprise her if Hassan punished her for looking at the princess.

"Keep your eyes to yourself or they will be gouged out!" Hassan shouted.

Hugging herself, she hurried into the cold, solitary embrace of the shadows. Fearing the guards might hear Hassan's shout and return her to the cell, she moved deeper into the nook, not ready to be forced back to that concrete coffin. The cold of it made her bones and joints ache for the warmth she found here. And she appreciated the fresh smell of the plants and trees.

"Nouri!" a voice barked into the quiet of her solitude.

Flinching at the sight of her guard, Asim, she noticed he had not yet located her behind the trees and shrubs. Yet, hiding would only incur more wrath and physical punishment. She shifted into the open.

Asim's gaze rammed into her, and his mouth tightened. "Inside."

Moving toward the voice, she trained her eyes on his boots as she reluctantly obeyed. Her slippered feet hit the marble floor of a long passage inside the palace. When he banked to the right, she faltered but didn't slow. Why was he going that way? The dungeon lay in the opposite direction. She looked toward the other end where her cell waited.

"Now!" he snapped. "I do not have time to wait on you!"

That was literally *all* he had to do, but she dared not raise his ire. Only then realizing she'd stopped, she scurried to close the ten-foot gap between them. Followed him past—*great mercies*—the grand salon! Stunning and masculine, the décor reflected the king and his more modern tastes, lightly accented with historical flavor. Distinctive for the Central Kingdom, its opulence and luxury left her breathless. In Virginia, she had lived in wealth, but nothing like this. This was extravagance at its peak.

When he veered toward an arced staircase and started climbing the stairs, she had to force herself not to hesitate. What on earth was going on? She itched to ask where they were going, but the men in this palace did not tolerate "nagging." Maybe he'd forgotten she was still with him and was inadvertently leading her to the wrong place. Asking if he'd made a mistake wouldn't go over well. At the top, she tensed, dread coursing through her. Months they had beaten it into her that she should neither be seen nor heard. If she continued, surely someone would see her.

"Keep moving." His growl was lazy but still loud this time.

Nerves had her skipping a step, but she nearly careened into him when he stopped at a door. Flicked it open. "In."

Leighton faltered for only a second, fearing that look in his eyes. But that was all it took for him to smack the back of her head. "Now!"

She pitched herself across the threshold. Inside, she peripherally noticed the plush rug that padded her steps and relieved the ache in her knees and ankles. Amazing! Never thought she would so appreciate *carpet*, but here she was.

Behind her, the door closed with a thud. A definitive *shunk* sounded.

Not surprised they'd locked her in, she glanced back as if she needed confirmation. Yep, door locked and—shocker—no knob. Wondering what was going on, she glanced around the room, but knew better than to move. She'd made that mistake once before, and guards had manifested seemingly from the walls themselves to beat her into submission.

Fisting her hands, she waited. Wondered why he'd brought her up here. Whose room was this? But when her legs started tingling, she fisted her hands. Braved another look. Then a quiet call. "Hello?" She cringed at how loud her voice felt in this empty room, how it echoed over the marble floor of the bathroom to her right.

Slowly, she traced every shadow and cornice. Bathed in creams, golds, and powder blue, the room was simple compared to the lavish overkill throughout the palace. A queen bed dominated the open space and sat between dark, wood end tables with lamps. Flanking the bed, Middle Eastern scalloped arches set off a gilt floor-to-ceiling mirror on one side and an inset settee on the other. A chair sat nearby, almost within reach of her right hand. Beyond the bathroom door and shower within, there seemed to be a closet back there.

Whose room was this? *Why am I here?*

As the minutes fell away, so did restraint. Her imagination took over, working through what she'd change. Not much—the décor was tasteful and pretty, though . . . extravagant still. That mattress seemed as high as her waist.

Oh, the thought of sleeping on a real bed nearly tempted her across the room. It must be glorious. The pillows looked dreamily soft. Her aching body begged for a reprieve.

But she dared not.

Except, after what felt like hours, she did—well, not the bed. But she allowed herself the nearby chair because her legs were growing numb. The relief was acute as she perched on the edge, ear trained on the door and marble floor beyond—anxious for the clip of shoes on the marble—ready to bolt to her feet again when they returned.

Had Asim forgotten her? With the passing minutes, she began to sag. Yawned.

"Get up, girl!"

The smack across her face jolted Leighton awake. She shot upward, her legs tangling in the thick fog of sleep. She landed on all fours, but scrambled back to her feet with a hurried apology.

"You mongrel—what are you doing?" Hands on her hip, the woman seethed.

"Waiting, ma'am," Leighton murmured, limbs trembling from the rude awakening.

"Waiting for what?"

"For . . . whoever stays in this room to come."

The woman barked a laugh. "It's your room, *ya hamar*!"

Leighton started. Her head came up—but she remembered herself and studied the carpet. "I think there is a mistake, ma'am."

"Save the ma'ams and sirs for the royals. I'm Zayna." She motioned Leighton into the bathroom. "Come in here. I need to fit the abayas to you."

Though she complied, Leighton expected a trap. Her steps across the room were silent and tentative. When no more punishment came, she peeked to the side where the woman had vanished. She'd been right—there was not only a closet but a dressing room through there.

"On the dais," Zayna snapped, pulling out two brown, beaded garments. "Wear the abaya over the pants. Keep your head covered at all times, unless you are in your room. Understand?"

Leighton nodded, her mind racing. But, no . . . "I don't understand."

"What don't you understand about keeping your head—"

"No, I—" Frustration twisted her words and thoughts. "I mean the room . . . the clothes . . . Why? I do not live here. I—" She better not say she was a prisoner, though it was true. "I do not have a room—not like this one."

"Thank Princess Daria for changing that. She's especially gracious now that her wedding plans are in full swing."

Shock rooted her to the floor that the princess had *any* say in how Leighton was treated or where she stayed. Why would the king listen to a woman? Especially about a prisoner?

"She has decided you are a part of the wedding party."

"Me?" Leighton squeaked. "I don't—how—why?"

"That does not matter. You will attend and remain silent. Speak only when asked a direct question." Zayna began stripping the smelly clothes off Leighton, then produced a tape measure from a pocket in her dress and measured her. "You are painfully thin. I'll need to adjust everything." She clucked her tongue in disapproval. "And if I were you—which I am not, thank Allah—I would keep every answer simple. I warn you, while she might see you as a pet now, Her Highness bores quickly and easily. You are a novelty today; tomorrow, an annoyance. Yes?"

Leighton nodded.

The rest of the fitting continued in silence, then Zayna ordered Leighton to shower. Once cleaned and changed into simple clothes that still bordered on luxurious, Leighton emerged from the bathroom to find the woman tidying up.

Zayna went to the round table in the corner and tapped a pad of paper. "These are all the royals and their names. Learn them. Memorize them. After this great gift you have been given in having a room up here, the last thing you want is to insult them by not knowing their names."

Right. Because this was her idea of fun, being kidnapped and held hostage by ultra-rich royals. And yet, she recognized this gift of a clean, dry room with access to a bathroom—not a hole—and shower.

"Food will be delivered as it was in your cell. Stay away from the windows or they will board them up." Zayna gathered the dirty clothes and towel. "Now—anything else?"

She's asking me?

Zayna huffed when she did not answer. "Do you need anything, child?"

Yes, my home! My parents! My freedom!

But . . . for Ummi . . .

Positive those answers would earn a slap, Leighton had no idea what to say. But when the woman remained there, expression growing more angry, Leighton knew they'd never give her a phone or device, but perhaps . . . "May I have some books to read?"

"Books—*tsk*." Zayna stalked to the door and gave it a distinctive rap—apparently to signal Asim—as she looked at Leighton. "I will bring the Salat. That is all you need." When the door opened, she stepped aside.

Asim entered with a food tray and dropped it noisily onto the small round table next to the list of names. His gaze struck her. He scowled. "Cover your head!"

Heart pounding, she ducked, looking for a covering.

Zayna tossed one at her, then left with the guard.

Nerves flailing, Leighton jerked at the loud clap of the door slamming. Then flinched at the lock. And mercies, she hated it—hated being a prisoner. Hated how every little thing sent her nerves into overdrive. She dropped onto the chair and cried into the headscarf. *How long, God? How long must I do this?*

It was hard. So very hard. Yet . . . if it kept Ummi alive, so be it.

THREE

Loudoun County, Virginia

THERE MUST BE SOME UNWRITTEN RULE THAT covert ops had to be planned under cover of darkness, because they didn't meet at the airstrip until well after sundown the next day.

Owen strode behind Dad and Navas across the tarmac to the waiting jet. Somehow, bringing up the rear felt a lot like being six years old when he'd followed Dad into work. Feeling like the afterthought, the spectator. Not the one responsible for carrying out the mission.

Took everything he had to shake that thought as they climbed the metal stairs up into the cabin of the plane. This wasn't a standard private jet—it had a long open center with an anchored table and walls covered in screens. Chairs hugged the table. The chemical smell of the A/C rankled his sinuses. Beyond the central Command area lurked a seating group and a long gangway with several doors.

Impressive.

Someone rose from a chair and turned.

A sense of rightness hit him as he recognized the guy. "Dante!" Owen squeezed past Dad and Navas to greet his Scion brother.

"Bro." Dante gave him a shoulder hug and patted his back. "You good?"

Question of the year apparently. "Yeah."

Dante sniffed. "Liar."

With a shrug, Owen eyed the cabin. "You know how it is."

"Living in our dads' shadows?" Dante nodded with a wry grin. "Yeah, know all about it."

Change the topic. "How's the wedding coming?"

A slow, content smile spread across Dante's face. "Not soon enough."

"You do know you're violating the Prime Directive." The unwritten rule that Scions didn't date each other.

"So sue me," Dante said with a smirk.

Owen laughed. "Nah, I'm glad for y'all. Mickey's carried a torch for you long enough. About time you shouldered that burden." He checked for Legend but didn't see the tall mountain of a man. "What're you doing here?"

Dante gave him a strange look.

"Your dad's not—" Like lightning, it struck Owen. "Aw man…" Cold chugged through his veins as he remembered Dad saying he knew someone who could handle coordinating the effort to save Navas's daughter. "Omen." He exhaled heavily. "This is Omen's op."

"See?" Dante backhanded Owen's gut. "Knew you had more than air behind that pretty face."

"You find me pretty?" Owen couldn't help the comeback but focused on his frustration. "I told Pike I wasn't interested."

As if on cue, the cabin interior darkened beneath more shapes moving through the hatch. A half dozen men crowded the table. Including one Master Chief Pike Auberon. The man he'd told to take a hike.

"Oh man. I'm dead."

"No, it's *O-men*." Brandishing a wry grin, Dante clapped him on the shoulder. "Welcome to the afterlife, bro." With that, he headed toward the chief.

Swallowing his pride—what else could he do?—Owen hung back, letting the meet-and-greet happen without him. Avoided Pike's gaze. Just had to lie low and pretend—

"Y'all know my son, Owen," Dad announced, motioning to him.

Yep. Thanks, Dad.

In a blink, Pike was up in his personal space, challenge glinting in his steely eyes. "Owen Metcalfe."

"Present and accounted for, sir." Holding the man's gray gaze took every ounce of feeble strength Owen could muster. Noticed the guy stood a couple inches taller and had a similar build to his own—athletic, bordering on muscular. But there was no doubt that this operator could kill him before Owen even knew what hit him.

"How's that mistake working for you?" Three lines at the edge of Pike's eyes crinkled as he studied him, unflinching. The man knew who was in control, and it sure wasn't Owen.

But it'd be a cold day in—

"Welcome to the team, Apollo. Quick intros," Pike said, then gave a laundry list of names—Brick with the red beard, easy enough. Luther who reminded him of an actor that played a character by the same name. Crow looked Native American or Latino, and the medic . . . whose name he'd already forgotten.

Unbelievable. He resented that Auberon basically owned him now. Had a preternatural ability to make people feel two inches tall.

"Heard you volunteered to go after this girl."

Owen tried to read the former master chief. Was he impressed? Ticked? "It's the right thing to do."

"In other words, you thought it was better than coming on with OTG."

Acutely aware of his dad watching the whole encounter, Owen was not going to cower. Never had been one to yield easily. "Your words . . ."

Eyes locked on him, Pike angled his head to the side. "Midas, your boy has a mouth on him."

"Metcalfes call it like they see it," Dad said without a hint of embarrassment or disappointment. "Fortunately, he also has his mom's common sense to balance it."

Pike's gaze bored down into Owen. "Look forward to seeing some sense."

Oof. Dude didn't pull any punches—that comment implied he hadn't yet seen any sense. The dig was intended to fray Owen's nerves, but he had known walking into this that he'd be closely monitored to ensure he had what it took. Maybe he'd already messed up by rejecting Omen.

The speaker overhead crackled with the captain's announcement that it was time to get underway.

"Nonactive personnel need to vacate the plane now." Pike shook Dad's hand and said something to him, then moved on.

Dad reached over and patted Owen's shoulder. "Stay true."

Owen nodded, aware of too many gazes assessing him as a cabin steward secured the door.

"Grab a seat." Pike indicated everyone to the table. "Fourteen hours to put a working plan in place. First things first—Tariq." He nodded to the Middle Eastern man, who drew something from a kit. "Apollo, Tariq is going to embed an intermittent transmitter in your neck. It'll put off a signal only when active, which we'll do at random intervals to reduce the likelihood of detection. With this, you can communicate with us. You won't be able to activate it on your own, to lessen the chance of a blow bringing it online."

A bug in his neck . . . ? Impressed with the advanced tech, Owen nodded. "Shelf life?"

"About ten days."

Nodding, he understood the implication. "So, I have ten days to get her out."

"You have ten days to communicate with us," Pike corrected. "If your situation needs more time, communicate that to us. We'll work it out."

Owen tensed as the guy aimed a device that looked like a gun at his throat.

"You'll feel a sting," Tariq said, doing the work as he described it, "then tugging, followed by another sting to seal it."

Owen winced through the sensations, hoped this thing wasn't connected to a T-1000. "Scarring?"

"A scratch." Tariq turned back to his kit, putting away the gear.

Resisting the urge to touch the spot, Owen adjusted in his chair.

"Bueno," Navas said, glancing around the table. "Now can we work on saving my daughter?"

"Light it up, Luther," Pike ordered.

The OTG logo filled the screens as Luther's system synced with the plane's.

"Let's show Apollo what he's gotten himself into." The chief indicated to a face that splashed onto the wall screen. "This is your objective: Nouri Al-Shaheen."

A jackhammer hitting Owen's heart wouldn't have shocked as much as the face staring back at him. His mind threw him back to Soph's graduation party. To her—RCG.

"Here in the States, she's known as Leighton Kingslake." Pike paused, studying him. "You know her."

Trying to smother his reaction, Owen knew he'd failed. "Yeah, sort of."

Navas's gaze whipped across the table to him. "How?"

"I . . ." Dumbfounded still, Owen struggled for a clean breath.

How was this possible? "Met her at a party." When that earned a glower from Navas, he clarified. "Not like that—it was the graduation party for Sophia Neeley. Leighton was there with a . . . sister? Friend?" He angled to the mercenary and frowned, trying to sort the facts hitting his stunned brain. "How is Leighton your daughter? How would she live in Virginia, go to Liberty Academy . . . ?" The night the merc had talked to Dad assailed him. "You said your daughter's name was Nouri."

Jaw tight, lips pressed into a line, Navas furrowed his brow. "Did you talk to her? At this party?"

Owen scowled, feeling the jet barreling down the runway. "You didn't answer—"

"Did. You. Talk?"

Owen had never been one to fall in line just because someone said to, but he also had to pick his battles. Wouldn't look good to be oppositional with men who'd be covering his six. "No."

As the jet left the ground, Navas stared at him hard, unconvinced.

"She bailed almost as soon as I saw her." That's when he noticed everyone studying him with strange looks. "What's the problem?"

"The problem," Pike intoned solemnly, "is if you know her and she recognizes you when you insert, she could blow your cover and this op fails before it can get traction." He narrowed his eyes, pressed his fingertips to the table, and leaned in. "Tell us exactly what happened at that party. Every detail. *Don't* leave out anything."

Not liking that they made him feel as if he'd done something wrong, he exhaled slowly before launching into a play-by-play about RCG. Now known as Leighton Kingslake . . . Nouri Al-Shaheen . . . the daughter of Navas, the guy who'd saved his dad from prison. "And . . . that's it."

"You were attracted to this girl?" Pike asked, his tone flat.

Son of a . . . Owen had an inkling Pike was a human lie detector. "Yeah. She was pretty, but that's not why I remember her." Every word mattered here, and he had to be sure he didn't make himself sound lovestruck. "I saw something in her face, her expression. Like she was . . . scared."

The barrel-chested guy with a red beard barked a laugh. "Yeah, had nothing do with her pretty face or blue eyes."

"They aren't blue."

The big guy busted out laughing and high-fived another operator, who was also laughing.

Realizing how easily he'd fallen into that trap, Owen scowled.

"I think we're clear to proceed," said Luther, Pike's apparent right hand. "They didn't talk. It was relatively dark."

"He just admitted they were eyeballing each other," Dante countered, slicing a hand toward Owen.

Traitor.

"But come on," Crow said, "do you remember every chick you hit on?"

"It is too risky," Navas decided gravely. "If she recognizes him, she will react and give him away. Faruq will kill them both."

As they continued debating the efficacy of going ahead with the mission, of cutting him from the op, Owen stared at the face that had distracted him that night. Recalled the undeniable fear haunting her brown eyes. That made him wonder how long she had been captive—hadn't Navas said something like *months*? What would happen to her if they *didn't* go through with this?

Owen wasn't going to let that happen. "You said your enemy is or was at the palace where she's being held." Amid his interruption, he realized he'd missed some conversation that died, the cabin falling quiet as eyes turned to him. "You said Bruzon knew who Leighton is. Right?"

The mercenary stared at him, and his dark eyes held little distinction between appreciation and hatred.

"Look, we're already in the air," Owen pushed forward. "There's no time to find another monkey for this mission. And from the distress I heard in your voice last night while talking with my dad, she might not have time for further delays."

Navas's gaze darkened.

Owen looked at her picture again. Recalled her deftly avoiding him. "Look, I doubt she'd remember me." Did that sound as desperate to them as it did to him? "There's an active threat against her life if Bruzon is near that palace or able to gain access. I don't know if this guy is holding back because he wants to draw you out or what, but we can't risk assuming that. Because if we're wrong— she pays." He gave a cockeyed nod. "So, I'm still in. Let me do this."

"Chief." Luther sounded distracted as he eyed the laptop. "Incoming video call from London."

"That will be Yasmina," Navas said, nerves radiating off him like a solar flare.

Who was Yasmina?

"We'll table the convo about Apollo till after." Pike indicated to a screen. "Put her on the wall."

An attractive older woman in a coral kaftan and soft brown hair appeared, her dark eyes searching the screen. "Hello?" Her finely drawn brows tugged together as she leaned in.

Navas stood and moved to the middle of the room so his face was front and center where the camera hit. "Princess."

Yasmina drew back as recognition slid through her olive skin. "Juan," she breathed, her entire visage relaxing beneath a smile.

"Yasmina," Navas said, his tone tender, sweet—entirely contradictory to the known and wanted mercenary. How had a guy like that ever leveled up enough to rate a *princess*? "Good to see you."

"And you." She brushed a wavy strand from her temple. "Does this mean you are going to find Nouri?"

"We will get her back, Yasmina." Conviction coated his words as Navas bobbed his head toward the team. "I pulled in some favors."

Pike adjusted to the merc's right and folded his arms over his chest. "Ma'am. Pike Auberon, CEO of Omen Tactical Group. Can you tell us exactly what happened the day she was taken and what you know so far?"

"Of course," she said quietly.

Owen definitely saw the likeness between Leighton and her mom. Still kinda jacked with his brain that they were both legit princesses. A princess had been in Soph's barn, a few meters from him. Whack.

"We were out shopping," the princess began, "Nouri—Leighton—went to try something on and never came back. Nobody saw her leave. We searched everywhere for her, but could not find her in the shopping center. We had security footage pulled, but the cameras in the storage area and back alleys were not working."

"That right there is what I call convenient," muttered Brick.

"It is proof of who did this," she said gravely. "The al-Zahranis are the second richest royal family in the world—trillion-dollar worth. Unlike the Northern and Southern kingdoms, the Central Kingdom is notorious for throwing money around and controlling industries. They think they can buy anything—even people."

"They sort of can," Brick said under his breath, earning dark looks from Pike and Navas.

"I still have connections at Omnia Palace," Yasmina went on, "and they confirmed Nouri is being held there. Like a prisoner in a cell."

"You have connections?" Pike unfolded his arms. "Think they could—"

"No," the princess said emphatically, then softened. "Sorry. My title afforded me a modicum of respect, however, asking anything more than a simple question—like is Nouri there—puts them at risk. If they are discovered doing *anything* for me, not only will they die, but their families will be slaughtered for betraying Faruq. It is a price I will not ask of them."

Pike didn't like that but seemed to process and proceed. "How long has she been gone?"

"Eight months," Yasmina said.

Pike frowned at Navas, and even Owen could read the disappointed inference—how had a man let his daughter go missing for eight months before trying to get her back?

"Do not blame him," the princess said. "It was several months before I could even confirm she was there. Of course, I asked immediately, but at first, they could not find her."

"And then, I wanted to confirm for myself," Navas explained. "Took weeks to work myself into a position to get actionable intel. When I saw Nesto Bruzon leaving the palace, I knew help was needed."

Staring at the man, Pike rubbed his jaw. "What's their endgame?" Next to the table, he hiked a leg and perched on the edge. "Why are they even interested in her? I get Bruzon has a vendetta against Navas, but . . . a young college student?"

Yasmina exhaled heavily and looked aside—at someone offscreen, it seemed. "Me. Faruq would punish me for fleeing him and Omnia Palace."

"Why'd you flee?"

"It is a long story," Yasmina said somberly, then took a sip from a teacup. "My mother, Queen Saffiyah, had given birth to three girls and was quickly losing the favor of then-king Nasir, despite modern science proving it is the man who determines a baby's gender. But they are cruel and relentless at Omnia. Too stressful. My mother feared for her life. So she took all three of us girls to Tahiti for a year, hoping distance would cool his temper."

"And it did not . . ." Pike supplied.

"No," she said with a sigh. "For all four of us girls, that time in Tahiti was life-altering. One night while there, some missionaries invited us to a tent revival. We went, more out of curiosity or to mock than to hear about their faith—which shames me to admit—but as I listened . . . what they said made sense. I felt something deep in me burning. My mother said she heard Jesus calling her." She motioned to her ear. "We were at the revival every night, and they gave my mother a Bible when she asked Jesus to forgive her sins. At our condo, we read from it every night."

"Bet Nasir loved that."

She laughed, giving the same tilt of head that Leighton had done that night in the Neeley barn. "I do not know how he learned about it all, but he was *furious*. What we had done was unforgivable," she said with an airy laugh. "He ordered us to return to Omnia and even sent guards to bring us back. There in the receiving room, him on his throne, we were forced to our knees. Ordered to renounce Isa or he would kill us."

Disappointment lurked at the back of Owen's mind. The woman was alive, so . . . she had denied Jesus?

"Something else happened while we were in Tahiti. I met and fell in love with a man. We were going to run away together, but Nasir's guards showed up to take us back before I could. When I was returned to Omnia, I was already pregnant," she confessed quietly. "I had always been the king's favorite, so there on my knees, when I faltered, still new in my faith but also keenly aware of the life I harbored in my womb, the king assumed that I, his youngest, had been coerced by his errant wife. To protect my child, I let him believe that. So while he let me live, he did not forgive me. Imprisoned in the palace, I was not allowed to leave. Allowed no visitors. And I endured it for the sake of my baby. I hid my pregnancy, gave birth in secret, and with the help of my maid, arranged for an American family to take my daughter. A year after she was safely out of Omnia, I escaped and fled to London."

That was an incredible, daunting story. Yet . . . "Am I missing something?" Owen cursed himself for drawing Pike's gaze again. "If you spirited her out of the palace and fled, why would they come after Nouri? They don't know she exists. Or again, did I miss something?"

"No, you are correct. I . . . I was trying to protect myself by only telling certain parts of this story, but that will not work," Yasmina said gravely. With her head down, she continued. "Shortly after our return from Tahiti and being granted mercy by King Nasir, I was raped by my stepbrother—the king's eldest son."

"Faruq," Luther Landry said, rapping his knuckles on the table. "As in the current ruler of the Central Kingdom: *King* Faruq."

Yasmina inclined her head. "After my escape, they tortured my maid. Learned about Nouri, but she had been very clever and refused to know where Nouri or I ended up. But they still knew I had given birth to a daughter."

"King Faruq thinks Nouri is his daughter?" Disbelief colored with dread filled Brick's words.

"So *that's* why he's keeping her," Owen muttered.

Yasmina shuddered a breath. "If they discover she is not his daughter, that I was already with child when I returned from Tahiti—"

"She's as good as dead," Owen said quietly. What Navas had told Dad confirmed all this.

"Faruq believes he has his daughter, that holding her will force my return—he wants to punish me for stealing his father's affection, for supposedly bearing his child and giving her away. But he is . . . evil. And if he discovers any of this, Nouri will die. *Please*," she pleaded, despair pushing tears down her face, "you must get her out of there before they uncover the truth. Even Juan mentioned that his enemies have discovered her existence as well. It is clear, is it not, the danger she is in? I have only just gotten her back. I cannot lose her."

"Nobody will lose her, Yasmina," Navas vowed. "She will be back in your arms soon. I swear it."

Dabbing a tissue at her eyes, she managed a small smile. "I am surprised you are not breaking down doors yourself."

Navas swiped a hand over his mouth. "If I had a few less gray hairs . . ." Then he indicated to Pike. "He will need as much information from you about the palace and family as you can remember. We are even now en route, and our timeline is short." Then he motioned to Owen. "This is the young man we will insert."

Craning her neck, she seemed to be straining to see him. "What is your name?"

Owen eased into full view beside Navas. "I am—"

"Apollo," Pike interrupted, inclining his head to the screen. "For operational security, we won't use his given name."

"Of course," Yasmina said, her gaze shifting. "Apollo, Nouri has it ingrained into her to be wary of strangers. She will not trust you. To gain her confidence, say this: 'religieuse may be your favorite, but it is not the best pastry.'"

Owen faltered, no idea what that meant. "Religious . . ."

"*Religieuse*." Yasmina gave a triumphant nod.

"It's a French pastry," Luther said, and when the rest of the team gaped at him, he held up his hands. "Just because you heathens are uncouth doesn't mean I am too."

"By that, she will know you are there with my blessing," Yasmina continued. "And once you say that, she will trust you."

Owen wasn't sure what to say to the princess's instruction. A pastry was supposed to save him?

FOUR

ONE SINGLE HAIR COULD UNDO EVERY EFFORT here. If King Faruq learned she was not his biological daughter, he would kill her, then track down her mother and kill her. Maybe even kill her adoptive family. Thus, Leighton put forth every effort to keep the room as sterile—and lacking any means by which they could extract DNA—as was humanly possible. Granted, they could simply hold her down and swab her mouth, but she must nurture their belief that she was Faruq's daughter and was integrating into their world. Do everything in her power to convince them she did not mind being here.

Leighton inspected the pillow—surprisingly comfortable—and scanned for hair. Then she checked the bathroom for the same, poured some of the sugar-laced mouthwash—oh, the irony—into a glass and set her toothbrush in it. That wouldn't necessarily eliminate DNA evidence, but she knew from some TV show she'd watched ages ago that it would degrade and make a clean extraction or analysis difficult.

And I'm all about difficult if it means my family is safe.

After one more vigilant check, she stood in the center of the room, drew in a steadying breath, and smoothed a hand over the brown abaya that was more like a paper sack than a dress. Nerves thrummed—she had been instructed to be ready at eight o'clock for dinner with the royals. Guess they were short on servants to beat tonight.

But seriously . . . Why? No idea, save that ominous warning from Zayna about Princess Daria. But Leighton had a terrible feeling she'd forgotten something. This attire was all new to her, yet she loved its comfort and the whisper-soft fabric against her skin. Running a hand over her hair—

Hair! She'd forgotten the headscarf!

Heart in her throat, she bolted to the dressing room, snagged the black one, and raced back to the bedroom. No sooner had she returned and wrapped her head than the click of the lock sounded.

Asim pitched open the door and stepped in. Glanced around as if she could've possibly snuck someone into the room. "Let's go," he gruffed.

Swallowing, she stepped out, noticing an ominous quiet in the cavernous, columned marble passage. She took in the long hall that spanned right and left, with many elaborate arches and an endless array of plants and chandeliers. For the first time since being relocated to the bedroom yesterday, she realized she'd not heard anyone coming or going. Or talking. Only her guard and Zayna.

Asim stalked away from her. "Stay close," he barked and banked right around a corner.

No windows or doors lined this narrow stretch of hall that led to a thin set of stairs leading down three levels. Servant's stairs, she guessed by the lack of ornamentation and simplicity of design.

Once on the main level, he turned left and headed down a long passage. A few minutes later, they pushed through a door into a grand foyer that presented itself with the luxury expected of a royal palace. Ahead, twin staircases of white marble and bannisters trimmed in black and gold—literal gold—swung around and over a passage to another hall.

Asim strode beneath the flanking staircases. At double-arched doors, he veered toward the right one. Voices haunted the hall as they passed a dozen or more. A din of conversation grew and came to a crescendo, leveling as Asim stopped before a set of doors and tugged one open in a way that kept him out of sight.

Leighton glanced inside. Her heart climbed into her throat at the sight—the crowd. Roughly twenty people in there . . . Princess Daria, the bride-to-be, laughed hysterically at her fiancé, Hassan, who had an inch-wide beard that traced his jaw and upper lip.

Leighton felt her stomach tighten, recalling his barked command to her in the outer garden. She swallowed, her gaze colliding with Prince Nasir, whose eyes were sharp as daggers. He stood with another, taller man who seemed somehow more casual in the thobe and ghutra, which was held in place with the black igal. She did not recognize the tall man, though she guessed him to be one of the princes of the Central Kingdom. It was impossible to keep them all straight, and she could never learn all of the Saudi Arabian princes' names since there were over fifteen hundred!

Stiffening as conversations fell away and all gazes found her, she felt a poke in her back, urging her forward. Even as she entered and shifted aside, she heard the door whisper closed behind her. Being painfully aware she was out of place forced her to lock her eyes on the intricate design of the cream-colored carpet with red-and-black foliage. Slowly, chatter rose, their Arabic not quiet. Clearly they assumed she did not speak the language. Fighting the urge not to react at the epithets and slurs hurled about her, she did not budge.

"Ah, Nouri!" cried Princess Daria in dramatic excitement. "You are here at last."

Leighton shivered in the icy silence, only then detecting in her periphery that the princess was crossing the room, her shoes padding determinedly on the rug.

Daria clicked her tongue. "What in the world have they put you in?"

Gaze skidding around, Leighton allowed it to streak over the kohl-lined eyes of the one before her, relieved to find the princess peering back at the other royals.

Daria turned, took her arm, and drew her from the anonymity of the wall. "Family," she said in English, dragging her into the fray. "This is Nouri. She's . . ." Her near-black eyes assessed her, then swung to the gathered with a breathy laugh, "our cousin."

A stern man in a white ghutra stalked closer and remonstrated the princess in Arabic, said it was inappropriate to call this American family.

Turning her gaze to Leighton, Princess Daria motioned to the man. "Nouri, have you met Maaz?"

The crown prince!

Leighton started, unable to hide her shock from the heir to the throne.

"Come, Daria," another man—the only one without the ghutra but still in a long tunic and slacks—said with a laugh. "You are embarrassing the poor girl."

"Rayan, that's absurd!" the princess objected, taking Leighton's hand and drawing her toward the table.

"If it is embarrassing to be with us," hissed the princess's fiancé in Arabic, "she should not be here."

As if I had any *choice.*

"Personally," the man continued, "I count it an honor—"

"Enough, Hassan," Daria groaned. Rolling her eyes, she turned to a woman next to her, who looked even younger than Leighton and wore a very flattering tan kaftan with beads and gems down the front. This could be Princess Aliyah, the youngest of the royal heirs in residence at Omnia, according to Zayna's list.

Murmurs undulated around Leighton as the princess directed her to gilt chairs with brocade cushions.

"Here," Daria said, indicating to one along the side. "You will sit by me and Hassan."

"That is not possible, my sweet," her fiancé said, hovering near his bride-to-be, "as you are seated next to Nasir, and I beside you."

Daria moaned. "You are all being very dull."

"This," said a quiet, deep voice right by Leighton's ear, "is where she bores of you, Hassan, as she does with everyone."

Sliding a glance to the side, Leighton dared not look directly at the man, but without the ghutra, she guessed it to be Prince Rayan. The youngest half brother of the current king, yet closer in age to the king's children due to a late marriage between Rayan's mother and the king.

Tall and dark-haired, he had a kindness about him. He motioned to a far chair. "Your seat, Nouri."

Leighton noted that he spoke English, no doubt assuming the same as most here. And she would not disabuse him—or anyone—of that notion.

Some silent signal must have occurred because, almost as if an alarm had gone off, all the royals moved to their places.

"Come," mused Rayan, still holding his hand toward the brocade chair.

Uncertainty flashed through Leighton. Glancing to Daria, ensconced in conversation with the other royals as they took their seats, she realized she was forgotten and accepted the chair Rayan indicated.

Chatter again filled the hall. As staff wandered beneath the enormous glittering chandeliers, delivering plates of hummus and bread, she felt the isolation of identity close in on her, hearing their snide comments about her, calling her inappropriate words, saying she was plain and bordering on ugly. She'd thought being out of the room and among people would be better for her mental state. But this? So much worse.

For Ummi . . . I do this for Ummi . . .

"Where in America did you live?" Rayan asked as he dragged flatbread through his hummus.

Stomach growling, she twitched. Wet her lips, not entirely sure she should answer, but the last thing she wanted to do was upset those at this table. "Virginia," she said quietly, forcing herself to take the bread and tear a bit off, though she feared reprisal. The chickpea hummus would be good protein but bloated her stomach, so she just tucked the flatbread into her mouth. Chewed.

"I visited there while attending Harvard," he noted solemnly.

"You went to Harvard?" She flinched at her own question, remembering too late Zayna's instruction not to speak unless asked a direct question. "S-sorry."

"You are sorry I attended Harvard?" he chuckled, scooping more hummus and eating it. "I think many would agree with you."

"No," she gasped, "I—"

"I am teasing, Nouri." He gave an encouraging nod. "Yes, I got my law degree there."

Wondering at his kindness, his very different manner to his cousins, she braved another glance at him. "I was going into law . . ." Before she had been ripped from her life. She retracted her gaze as she took a falafel and dipped it in the small bowl of sauce.

"I am impressed." Rayan angled more toward her and considered her. "And who were you wanting to fight for?"

Pulse tripping over his words, she nearly choked on her next mouthful. "What?"

He gave a half-hearted smile. "I find that most people who go into law or medicine want to do so because someone they loved did not get the justice or help they deserved."

Was he serious? "I would think my cause might be obvious . . ."

When their eyes met, she instantly regretted her reply. Hoped he did not resent her or grow angry.

"Ah." Suddenly focused on his food, he switched to the deep-fried balls.

Soon, the staff delivered the main course of a rice mound with meat to each of them. Steam spiraling up taunted her with a delectable aroma, which made her mouth water, even though she did not know what it was. And really, did it matter?—this would be her first full meal since being taken from Ummi in London. She searched the plate for any allergy offenders.

"This is maqluba," Rayan said, clearly seeing her uncertainty. "Maaz would eat it for every meal if we let him."

Picking up her spoon, Leighton appreciated his guidance throughout the meal. Yet, she weighed his generosity. Wondered that he did not see her as an intruder or interloper like the others. Unlike Daria's congeniality, which somehow felt as if there were an ulterior motive behind it, Rayan seemed . . . genuine. Kind.

Raucous laughter erupted from the far end of the table, drawing her attention. Princess Daria and her fiancé were laughing hard, while Crown Prince Maaz sat there, jaw tight.

"Oh, come, brother," Daria chuckled. "You have to admit—"

"You are inappropriate, Daria!"

Silence clapped down on the room, and the princess's merriment faded.

The bite of falafel in Leighton's mouth soured as she slowly chewed. Licked her lips and swallowed.

"What were you thinking?" Crown Prince Maaz spat, his Arabic quick and sharp. "You have lost all sense of decorum. I should have known after you had *her* brought to our table!"

The princess all but preened, apparently proud of the tension she had wrought. "Our father said I could have whomever I wanted in my wedding party," Daria sniped back, "and I want her."

"You cannot—"

"I can," she said with a flourish of her manicured and bejeweled fingers. "It has all been cleared through the king's office. She is to be with me."

Maaz did not erupt in fury as expected, but a clear menace lurked in his expression when he cast his gaze at Leighton. Mouth tightening, he jerked back to his sister. "Do you not respect the memory of *jiddat al-ab*? He is your blood!"

Grandfather . . . ? Oh, King Nasir—her mother's father.

"Of course, I do," Daria hissed quietly. "But she could be our sister, Maaz. You know what Baba did to his own sister!"

Maaz shoved upward. Backhanded her, the sound a loud *crack* in the now-silent dining hall. "Do not speak such evil, or I will cut out your tongue!"

Hassan shot to his feet, arms drawn back, ready to defend his betrothed, but also conflicted as he owed his allegiance and loyalty to the crown prince.

Maaz squared to the challenge, like the alpha in a pack of dogs. The would-be groom lowered his head. Set a hand on Daria's shoulder, clearly bringing her under control.

It was infuriating. Frightening, these men so intimidated by a woman with a mind. Pulling her thoughts and attention back to herself, Leighton tried to steady her racing heart. She did not want or need the crown prince's anger barreling into her. She could not believe he had threatened to commit such violence against his own sister. She certainly could not fathom doing that to Hale and Holland, her adoptive siblings.

A cool breeze swept her shoulders, eliciting a shiver. She glanced there, wondering at the chill, and found Rayan had stood to go after the prince. The others focused on eating. Princess Aliyah sat quietly, chewing the side of her lip, then offered a wan, apologetic smile paired with shrug. Even amid the uneasy quiet, the staff served dessert.

If this was their idea of family . . . no, thanks. The instinct to rush back to her room proved nearly overpowering, forcing Leighton's gaze to the door, hoping Asim would be there. He was not. And she could not move about unescorted, so—

A soft thump sounded beside her, drawing her gaze back. Had Rayan returned? Instead, she found Princess Aliyah adjusting in the seat. She gave a mischievous smile. "It is the special request of Princess Daria that you come with us to Paris for her wedding shopping."

Shopping? In *Paris*? That would be a long way from the concrete dungeon of two days ago. "I—"

"Do not worry." Aliyah touched her arm. "It will be great fun. And after that, we go on safari. For fourteen days!"

Leighton gaped at the pretty princess whose dimples winked each time she laughed. Paris *and* a safari? "I don't understand," she said quietly. "Why me?"

Aliyah giggled. "You are family. Princess Daria insists, so you must go and have fun." Another giggle. "So much better than where they had you, yes?"

Disbelief corkscrewed through Leighton. "You knew?"

"Of course." Aliyah seemed contrite all of a sudden. "Daria was very upset when she saw you in the dirty clothes, walking in the alley. She begged the king for this one favor, to have you with her." She rolled her eyes. "His Majesty would do anything for her"— she leaned conspiratorially and lowered her voice—"though she is quite rebellious." She giggled again, then rasped, "Do not tell her I said so."

There was no explanation for why the princess had chosen her. Incredible to think Daria had even begged the king to remove Leighton from the dungeon. Why? She let her gaze wander to the princess receiving care from her betrothed. When those large, darkly lined eyes slid to Leighton, she gave a slow nod.

In that moment, Leighton understood. Felt it in her bones— solidarity. She returned the nod, hoping to convey her thanks.

After weeks spent in that dungeon, the daughter of her captor had rescued her. Now would take her to Paris to shop. Was this really happening?

Even as she wondered, there rose in her a vibrating sense of caution. Told her to tread softly. Carefully. All was not as it seemed.

Paris, France

If someone had told him last week that he'd be sitting at a café in Paris waiting to save the girl he'd never forgotten about, Owen would've told them to get therapy. The Omen flight to Jeddah had been diverted when word came that a Saudi royal entourage had headed to Paris—and Leighton had been spotted deboarding a private jumbo jet with Princesses Daria and Aliyah.

Owen had suggested they just grab Leighton and run, but Pike showed him surveillance footage that revealed more than two dozen armed, concealed assets on-site to protect the princess.

"Heads up," Crow Rawlins comm'd, watching from the feed of a micro-drone high overhead. "Princesses exiting shop."

"Good copy," Pike replied. "Apollo, visual confirmation on six armed security trailing objective in addition to the two vans and limo." Six out of the twenty-four. Packing kinda light . . .

Owen lifted a cappuccino to his mouth. "Yep." He took a sip, glanced around, and checked his watch, as if he were waiting on someone to arrive.

"En route to you," Crow reported.

"Brick, move in," the chief said. "Tariq, prepare to intercept trailing security."

"Roger that."

"Apollo," Pike said, "on you in five . . ."

Owen eyed the windows of the outdoor shop and saw the four

women in its reflection. He stood and strained his neck, searching for that nonexistent friend again.

"Two . . ."

Tugging down his ball cap so Leighton wouldn't recognize him right off, he looked in her direction. Felt his heart twinge at the droop to her shoulders, the way she kept her head down. Behind her, the burly oaf was barreling down on her.

Two additional operators Omen had recruited intentionally shifted between Leighton and the princesses.

Brick barreled into Leighton, snatching her bag.

"Look out!" Owen bolted forward, partly hating that he was playing a fake hero, but it served a purpose. "Hey!"

As the attacker, Brick hooked an arm around Leighton, eliciting a scream as terror seized her.

That expression on her beautiful face tore at Owen. "Hey!" he shouted again, rushing into the supposed fray. "Hey-hey. Easy, man. Don't do this." He motioned the other princesses away and focused on Brick. "Let her go, man. This isn't worth it."

Leighton was hauled off her feet, and the move made Owen tense. The big buy was going a little rough. *"Easy,* easy!"

When he heard tires squealing a block away and the signal from Pike in his ear for the big finale, Owen threw everything he had into launching at Brick. Pitched the two apart. Clipped the back of Brick's legs. The big guy stumbled backwards, last-minute hauling Owen to the ground with him. Owen dropped hard onto the guy's gut. Heard the hard grunt.

Before he could realize it, Owen found himself on his back. He jabbed a dagger hand into Brick's side. Heard the guy's pained grunt. Hoped he hadn't struck too hard. He'd deliberately gone into the wrong spot to prevent any real damage. But it gave his escape legitimacy.

But the brawny guy was faster than expected—he drove a stiff left hook at Owen's chin. That sucker hurt too, pain ricocheting down his jaw and neck. But even as he stumbled backwards, he was free. Hopped to his feet, landing in a fighting stance. Angled aside and shifted around, searching for the objective.

Mouth open, Leighton stood frozen, bags dangling from her hands. Though she turned, as if to flee, she didn't.

"Go!" he shouted.

Tires screeched in the street behind him, and he looked there, found SUVs barreling at them. He pivoted back to her—still standing there. "Go go go!" Tugging down his ball cap even more, he caught her arm, hurrying her toward the interdicting limo, then turned back as if to deal with Brick. But the guy was gone, as planned, sprinting between buildings.

"Hey! Stop!" Owen took off after him. Bolted toward the alley. Saw people glancing after Brick, then to him. "Move-move-move!" He careened into the wall and used it to redirect his momentum. Darted into the shadowy darkness. Banked left at a concrete wall. In his periphery, he noted Brick duck into a side door, which Owen shot past. He came out the other side, looking around.

"Where'd he go?" he growled to the ambivalent pedestrians. With a shout, he pivoted and glanced back into the alley. Drew around and threw a punch in the air for obvious display, knowing he was likely being monitored by the royals.

He huffed and rubbed where Brick had punched him. "Think he nearly broke my jaw," he complained aloud.

"Had to make it realistic," Brick snickered in the comms. "Besides, I owed you for that kidney strike."

Ignoring the complaint, Owen stalked back to the café to retrieve his drink and lunch.

"They have eyes on you, Apollo," Pike reported. "Nice and steady."

That warning of being watched churned through him and made it really hard to keep his focus ahead. By the time he returned to the café, his food and drink were gone. "You kidding me?" Nursing his bruised jaw, he sagged in defeat and headed off.

"Tails sticking close," Pike comm'd. "You know what to do."

Owen headed to the designated hotel, where he'd been booked with a multiple-night stay. He made his way up to the room. Inside, he went to the small bathroom and checked the bruise swelling across his jaw. Then he ordered room service, turned on the TV, then subvocalized, "Going dark."

"Good work out there," the chief said. "See you on the other side. Go dark."

After flushing the comms device down the toilet, Owen lowered himself to the edge of the bed and waited for the food. Yeah, it'd gone to plan out there, but now it was all on him. On the royals playing into an anticipated timeline of events. Following the logic and obsessive control Faruq was known for. Absently, he touched the advanced tech implant that would afford limited comms with the team, and only on their activation.

So don't screw up. The many reminders that this wasn't just about his life but Leighton's rang in his head. What if the royals didn't play into the trap? Could Pike be wrong? As much as Owen didn't like OTG or its chief, the guy had a reputation for a reason. What if the royals showed up and he was brought to her? Would Leighton recognize him? Or had her attention at the party been his imagination?

Three raps sent his heart into overdrive and pulled him from the bed. The person on the other side of the door announced, "Room service."

I don't believe it—the plan worked! He hesitated, then headed to the door. Since he wasn't supposed to be an operator but an average American who had interrupted an attack, he peered through the peephole, half expecting to get shot in the eye. Instead, he saw a guy with a dome-covered plate in hand. The guy might have a tray, but he could've picked that up from outside any door.

Was this it? Would the Saudis hit him here? What choice did he have? This part was crucial to the endgame. He flicked the lock and opened the door.

The man rushed into him. "Inside, inside," he husked, forcing Owen backwards. The tray of food clattered onto the small entry table even as the guy kicked the door shut and locked it.

"What is—"

Dark eyes met his.

Owen gaped. "*Dillon*?"

Black hair shorn, frame a little lighter than usual, Dillon gave a dull nod. "Hey."

"What are you doing here?" Owen balked, his mind clamoring over what it'd look like if the Saudis found them both here. "You have to get out. Leave! You could blow everything."

Dillon's brow furrowed. "Blow what?"

"I'm on an op."

Something ominous flashed in Dillon's eyes as he looked around the hotel room and frowned. "Omen. Are you freaking kidding me? You know they're connected to what happened to my dad!"

Chagrined that he was working with Omen after the Scions had decided they were bad news, Owen faltered, but more at the venom in his Scion brother's tone. "I'm—"

"Forget it." Dillon went to the backpack on the chair. Tore into it.

"What're you doing?" Owen reached him in two long strides. "Aren't you listening? You can't be here. You have to—"

"You have a phone on you? Credit card?"

"No. I—"

"Bullspit. They wouldn't put you on an op—"

"I *don't*," Owen ground out. "I'm here, waiting for Saudis to come kidnap me."

Dillon slowed, his gaze rising to him, then sliding toward the door with more than a little anger. "You serious—No, you're flippin' stupid! *Saudis?* They'll gut you, Apollo. They aren't anything to play around with. What's the op?"

"I'm not telling you anything until I know what *you* are doing here!"

"Chasing leads. This guy I'm tracking, who was the last person to see my dad alive, is here." He gave Owen a look. "You seriously working for Omen? Thought you hated contract—"

"Dillon," Owen said, weary with arguing. "Get out of here. You cannot screw this up."

Two knocks stilled them both. "Room service for Mr. Apollo."

"Food's already here," Dillon said, indicating to the tray he'd brought in, then he darted to the door.

"What are—"

"It's one guy," Dillon said. "We can take him."

"No!" Owen hissed. "If that's the Saudis, you cannot intervene." He gripped his head "You can't be here. You're going to screw everything up. Whatever you need, take it and go—out the window!"

"Nice to see you too."

"Says the guy foraging for a credit card."

Dillon smirked. "Fair." He ducked into the bathroom and cocked his head toward the door, telling Owen to get on with it.

More knocks. "Mr. Apollo, forgot your drink. Leaving it by the door."

Double-checking through the peephole, he saw exactly what the guy said. He opened the door, called a thank-you, and retrieved the drink. *Why am I exposing myself here?* He ducked back inside and locked the door. "You have to find a way out so nobody will see you," he called to Dillon as he set the drink on the credenza, then grabbed his ruck. When no answer came, he noticed the bathroom door ajar. Eased it open. Empty. No Dillon. "What the . . . ?" He looked over his shoulder and noticed the silver metal food tray lid had been removed. Burger gone. His gaze hit the balcony just in time to see a shadow vanish.

"Twice in one day," he muttered, mourning the stolen burger. At least the fries were still here.

Now that he wasn't fighting for op-sec, he regretted making Dillon leave. Had to admit it'd been good to see the guy who'd been on the lam, searching for his dad the last two years. And still alive. A miracle in and of itself, considering the hard-driving mentality inherent in the thick skull that had just left. The Scions hadn't been sure he still numbered among the living after the long radio silence following his run-in with McKenna in Armenia. Crazy.

Man, had to let someone know he'd seen Dillon. But he was on his own now too, so no phone. No contact. Screw that up and it could mean Leighton's death.

Alone with his thoughts, he sat on the bed and ate the fries. As the time fell off the clock, his doubts grew louder. More persistent. What if this part of the plan didn't work? What if the guards who followed him decided he wasn't worth the effort?

Stretched out on the bed an hour later, he couldn't help but wonder—what if Pike and Navas were wrong? What if all this had been for naught? How long would it take before he knew if this was a no-go?

That would majorly tick him off since he'd suggested to Pike that they just take her from the street. But the innocents and the high number of guards trailing them had been enough justification from Command to kill the idea.

Yawning, he shook his head. Now here he was, hours later, wondering if it wasn't already screwed up. TV droning, darkness falling, he swiped a hand over his mouth. Yawned again. He closed his eyes and pinched the bridge of his nose.

God, pretty sure I could pull this off, if you give me a chance.

He thought of Leighton. Her terror when Brick had grabbed

her, which reminded him of Soph's party when he'd seen that fear on her resting expression. Had she been afraid this whole time? Thinking about her, wondering about her months in captivity . . . Another yawn and he closed his eyes, letting himself imagine what their first encounter would be like. Would she hug him, relieved to see a friendly face? Which would be bad—so how did he stave that off? Not that he'd mind if she was in his arms . . .

Two taps to his temple twitched him awake.

"Do not move," warned a deep, ominous voice.

Awareness flared through Owen—when had he fallen asleep? He froze every muscle as his eyes barely made out the large handgun pressed to his temple and the dark form looming over him. "Easy," he muttered, heart ricocheting, blinking away the fog of sleep. Shocked this had worked. Thrilled this had worked.

"You will come with us or you will die. Which one do you want?"

Yeah, real hard decision. "I'll come."

FIVE

Jeddah, Saudi Arabia

G O, GO, GO!"

The man's urgent words had played over and over again in Leighton's head since that moment on the street in Paris. An hour ago, she and the other princesses had returned to the palace under guard. The princesses had been ushered into the king's reception hall, or whatever they called it. She had been forced to wait a while with Khalil, her new-but-temporary guard since Asim had been injured in the Paris incident.

Finally, Khalil turned to her. "It is time. Do not speak to the king unless he directly asks you a question."

The doors opened and she entered. The long, narrow space had twenty-foot ceilings heavily adorned with plaster and intricate designs. Six chandeliers hung overhead in pairs of two, forcing her gaze straight down the middle of the room to the central couch where King Faruq sat, flanked by his advisors on their own seating arrangements. Couches and tables lined the walls on either side with dozens of men in white kaftans and ghutras.

In the front, right corner, Aliyah and Daria were moving to settees. Aliyah gave her an apologetic smile, but when Leighton's gaze shifted to the king—and connected with his eyes—she remembered to avert at the last minute, but not before seeing him rise.

Oh mercy, she'd angered him already. Pulse stampeding, she stared at the glossy floor, though keenly aware of his black shoes clipping nearer.

Having reached her, he hooked a finger under her chin and nudged it upward.

Still, she looked elsewhere.

"Look at me!" he demanded.

Twitching at the terse command, she popped her gaze to his.

His beard was peppered with gray. Brown eyes studied her. "I see your mother in you . . ."

She hated this man. She shouldn't—it wasn't Christ-like—but he had raped her mother. Out of spite. And she resented having his attention trained on her.

"She had that look too." He pitched her head backwards, then returned to his settee and nodded to his eldest son.

Crown Prince Maaz leaned forward and gave her a hard look. "Did you enjoy the trip?"

Knowing this prince did not approve of her in his home, Leighton guessed the question was a trap. Staring at the inlaid black designs in the marble floor, she made herself offer a benign reply. "It was an unexpected honor to be invited." A smile would be a nice touch, so she put one on her face. "It was my first trip to France."

He stood, and it seemed the very movement stirred a wake of heat toward her. "That is not what I asked," he bit out in irritation.

Dread churning, Leighton knew she had to enter his trap. "Yes," she admitted quietly. "Princess Daria was exceptionally kind to include me."

"She was," he pronounced as he paced closer, treating her as if she were on trial and he the prosecutor. "Many in this House believe she was too kind. That you were treated to an excursion far beyond your right."

Treated? Had he forgotten that she'd been attacked? That a man had nearly strangled her in a botched robbery? Yet . . . his point was valid. Since he had not directly asked a question, she kept her lips pressed together.

"Perhaps," he said with a sneer, "at the hotel, you managed to get hold of the princess's phone. Send a secret message to someone to help you escape."

Leighton started. Mind racing, she frowned that he was accusing her of orchestrating the attack. Outrageous! Ludicrous! But she had no proof of her innocence. Too, arguing with him would only earn his backhand.

"You have nothing to say for yourself?"

Oh, she had plenty. *A quiet answer turns away wrath . . .* She wet her lips as she thought of an answer that would turn aside his anger. "I was never left alone while on the trip, Your Highness." This might be a good time to try and convince him she had no desire to escape, yet she knew she could not bring herself to lie. If she said she did not want to go on the trip in the first place, he would accuse her of being ungrateful. It was an impossible situation.

He stared at her hard as quiet rankled the receiving hall, all eyes trained on her. "The man who put his arm around your neck—do you know him?"

"No, Highness."

"What did he want?"

"He demanded money."

"And did you give it to him?"

"I had none to give," she said plainly. The unfairness of being targeted then and now sent her pulse into overdrive, but she forced herself to remember . . . *If I am here, Ummi is not.*

"And you are sure you did not know him?" Crown Prince Maaz demanded as he stood over her, staring her down with the full weight of the entire royal House.

Leighton started. "Quite sure."

Scratching his beard as he paced around her, he grunted. "It makes no sense when you, an unknown, is attacked and not the princess." He returned to his cushioned settee at the front, next to the king.

"I agree," she said, breathless at the unspoken accusation. When he snapped a glower at her, she remembered herself and fell silent.

"It is suspicious that you arrive here," he continued, "are chosen to go on this trip, and suddenly, my sister—who has never been a source of attacks—is at the center of one."

"Your insinuation cuts me deep. I did not ask to be here or 'arrive here,' but I have never given any complaint or fight, despite horrific treatment, and now I am—"

But Prince Maaz flew off the settee, and struck true and hard, knocking her to the ground.

Even as she caught herself, she saw others coming too. Panic streaked through her chest, and she huddled there, covering her head. Felt spittle land on her arm and clothes. Hands slapped at her head as she curled into a ball. Pain exploded through her side from a kick, making her cry out.

"Enough," a voice commanded distantly. "Khalil!"

The doors clattered open, and the men receded, revealing the king.

"Remove her from the hall," King Faruq ordered.

Aching, crying, she hunched to protect herself even as she heard the quick steps approach. Her temporary guard grabbed her arm and pulled hard. Pain pinched her shoulder as she scrambled to get upright before he ripped it out of the socket. He thrust her through the doors.

Sniffling, she trembled and stumbled. Fought the tears, her

cheek throbbing from Maaz's hit. It felt stiff, probably from swelling.

"You idiot," Khalil hissed as he marched her through the hall, his grip unrelenting and agonizing. "I told you—" He tensed, then abruptly stopped, giving a sharp nod to the side. "Highness."

Struggling to see past the tears to see what diverted him, Leighton noted Prince Rayan striding into view. Had he come to give her a private beating? She cowered, anticipating more cruelty.

"You should remember, Khalil," Rayan said calmy, blandly, "that even though she earned the ire of our king, she still belongs to him." His gaze pointedly went to the grip that would no doubt leave a bruise.

The vise slackened, and she shuddered around another shaky breath.

Prince Rayan considered her for a second. There was something in his expression she could not decipher. Disappointment?

"If you will excuse us, Highness, I must return her to her room." Khalil gave a curt bow of his head, then started walking again, yanking her onward.

Leighton stumbled through the grand foyer, shooting one last look to Prince Rayan, who stood there, arms folded as he watched her being dragged away. Why did he look regretful?

The ten-minute hike back to her chambers was made in virtual silence, which suited her fine. She did not even care when he all but threw her across the threshold, then slammed and locked the door. At least here, she was alone, safe. Though "safe" was relative. Itching to wash off their spittle, she hurried into the bathroom. Pulled out clean clothes, stripped, and showered.

That night, she curled up on the bed and sobbed into the pillow. When she awoke hours later, she found the room dark. Aches in her side and arm made her groan as she rolled onto her back. Recalled the mob. The hits. All blaming her for this fiasco.

Her thoughts traveled back to Paris and what happened. As

she'd told the royals, she had no idea why the man had attacked or where he'd even come from. Arm over her eyes, she couldn't figure out how she'd missed the burly man or why he'd targeted her. Anyone paying attention would've known she was the least of the four Arabic women on that street.

It hurt—she had done everything right. Played the subservient girl. Obeyed the rules. Then some man tries to rob her and *she* gets blamed!

Though her eyes watered again, she fought it off. Gritted her teeth. This was her choice. She sat up in the bed, hugging a pillow to her chest. Wiped her eyes. *I choose to be here. To save Ummi.*

In her mind, she heard the men hawking up loogies to spit at her. Felt the slimy impacts on her cheek and eyes.

God, please, give me the strength to endure this.

The lock on the door rattled, yanking her attention to it. A moment later, Khalil stormed into her dark solitude, hesitated, then hit the switch.

Light exploded through the room, making her eyes ache after crying.

"Get up. Cover your head."

Confused but moving in compliance with the command, Leighton scooted to the edge of the bed.

"Hurry! The king is waiting."

Oh no.

<hr>

Hood smothering him, Owen worked to cooperate with the thugs hauling him through the air-conditioned structure. The pace slowed, doors opening as he huffed beneath the thick fabric. He had no concept of time before he was pushed to his knees and the hood—along with more than a few strands of hair—was ripped off.

Blinking, he looked around the room. Gaped at the luxurious setting. Unbelievable—it'd worked. It'd really worked. This had to be Omnia Palace. A half dozen seating groups lined the length of the room. Straight ahead, against the wall in front of him, squared-off columns stood tall, curtains draping the corners and marking off a sort of room that remained open to the rest of the hall. Beneath the cornices sat a man. On . . . a throne. His gut cinched as the man rose from a tan high-backed leather chair.

None other than King Faruq.

Owen tried to stand, but a firm hand clamped his shoulder in a viselike grip, forcing him back down. His knee crashed into the veined marble floor, making him grunt.

Faruq came forward another step but stayed a conservative ten feet away. "As you can imagine, my guards are zealous in protecting me." Wearing a white thobe and ghutra, he had a graying beard and more than a few age lines. "What is your name?"

Sniffing, Owen knew they needed to see strength. "You come into my hotel room—I'd like to know how you got past the security lock, by the way—put a hood over my head, fly me here, but you don't know my name?"

A fist slammed toward Owen, who caught it, drove it down and came up, effectively hooking the man's neck and pinning him to the ground, the arm strained painfully backwards, making the guy cry out. He put a knee in his spine. Clearly, King Faruq was not used to being talked to that way, but Owen wasn't here to play nice.

"Enough!" the king barked.

Guns came to bear via the half dozen men in white thobes, who'd been sitting in the tufted leather couches on either side of the "throne room."

Owen hopped back and away, hands in the air. "Sorry." He gave a light shrug. "I *really* don't like people coming at me."

Three men surrounded King Faruq, and he signaled them to lower their weapons. "Omar, you are well?"

The guard cradled his arm and gave a humiliated nod.

Faruq's gaze never left Owen's. "You seem . . . hotheaded, Mr. Apollo."

Another sniff. "Nah, just . . ." He deliberately scanned the room, noting the men who watched him with unabashed interest. "No offense, sir—"

"*Your Majesty*," someone hissed in correction.

Owen lifted his eyebrows, feigning surprise. "Maj—" Drawing his head back, he widened his eyes. "You're what, a prince or something?"

"You want me to believe you do not know who I am, yet you saved my daughter?"

His pulse skipped a beat. "I . . ." *Not too dumb*, he warned himself, or they'd call it and plug him with lead. "Daughter?" He let himself pause, as if thinking. "Wait—the chick on the street? *Paris*—is that what this is about?" Slowly, he let a frown into his expression as he scanned the onlookers again. "Maybe I'm confused—I thought you said I saved her, yet . . . you treat me like some criminal. Gun to my head at the hotel. Bag over my head."

"You speak very freely."

"Call it nerves." It wasn't. He had to show himself strong. Willing to do what most men wouldn't.

The king chuckled. "Why were you in France?"

Owen stretched his jaw. "There's a cool tower there, not sure if you've heard of it." He saw the incoming side-strike too late. Pain exploded across his jaw.

"Watch how you talk to the king!" a guard growled.

Feeling a slick warmth sliding down his jaw, he steadied himself. Tried to shake the ringing in his ear. He held out placating hands. Looked at the king. "Sorry."

The king inclined his head in slow acknowledgment. "Why were you in Paris, Mr. Apollo?"

Owen hesitated at the repeated question. "A job." It was true in more ways than one.

The king paused as he considered him, but seemed annoyed. "What kind of job?"

"Security. I was supposed to meet the guy at a café, but he never showed."

"The café you were at when you saw my daughter get attacked."

"Yeah."

"Let me get this straight," the king said, cocking his head to the side. "You just happened to be there, drinking a cappuccino, eating a pastry, and you just happened to see someone coming at her *from across the street.*"

The fear Owen showed now was legit. "I never said where the café was." He ran a hand over the back of his neck. "Or what I had to eat or drink." Now time to play it off. He gave them an uncertain look, then laughed. "Did you happen to find the guy I was supposed to meet too?"

The king smirked as he considered him. "Clever, Mr. Apollo."

One of the men—princes?—next to him leaned in and whispered something.

Listening, King Faruq studied Owen for a long minute and stroked his beard, then nodded. A second later, the prince strode over and spoke to a guard, who then left as the prince returned to his seat.

"Mahid, help him to his feet." King Faruq motioned two fingers toward Owen. "Would you like a job, Mr. Apollo?"

Owen braced under the guard's rough handling. Halfway up, he faltered. A job had been the intent of the op, but that it'd worked so quickly caught him off guard. "Uh . . ." He wiped his mouth. "I mean—yeah, I need work. Guy ghosted me, and I spent a fortune to get to Paris." He exhaled heavily and shook his head. "Look, man—King . . ." Gaze tracking across the room, he shrugged. "I get it—you're loaded. Could probably compensate me well for . . .

whatever. But considering the gun to my head and hood over my face . . ."

"A man in my position must give great consideration to whom he invites into his home."

Invites. *Yeah, aggressively.*

"Please. Come talk with me." The king indicated to a nearby couch. "Have you interest in working for House al-Zahrani?"

Owen casually moved to the spot and perched on its edge. "It would depend on what that job entails."

King Faruq tilted his head to the side. "If I offered you"—lips pursed, he waved a hand in a circle—"a million dollars, would the *entailment* matter?"

He held the king's dark gaze. "It always matters."

"So, you have a code."

"I do."

"Does that come from your time in the American Army?"

Man, it was whack that this guy knew so much already. "Yeah . . ."

Faruq laughed and considered him. "You do not like that I am so well-informed on your history, eh?"

"It's . . . unsettling."

"I would expect so." The king gave another chuckle, then sobered, rubbing his hands together. "We've vetted your history, you're American, and—quite simply, you are skilled"—he indicated to Omar—"as his arm can attest."

Owen gave a nervous smile.

The king again stroked his beard. "I would have you provide protection for my daughter."

Perfect. But Owen couldn't act too eager and assume the wrong princess, since Leighton's true identity was not public knowledge. "I . . . um, why? She had a dozen guards—"

"*Not* Princess Daria," the king corrected. "I was referring to another daughter. She needs . . . protection." That hand waved again with a flourish.

"Okay . . ." Owen drew out the word. "But you have fifteen men in this room with guns ready to—"

"But only one man who is fleeing the law and in debt to the tune of fifty thousand dollars."

Owen stilled. Man, Omen sure had built up his need for a job well. He just hoped they hadn't made things too obvious. "How do you know that?"

"What *is* important," King Faruq said, "is that I have a daughter who needs protection, and you need the money I can pay you to serve this purpose."

"I don't know, man. This sounds sketch . . ." The warnings from Pike to make sure he didn't sound eager-beaver rang in his head. He heard a door open and noticed the king's gaze shift past him, so Owen checked over his shoulder. His gut cinched at what he saw.

In brown garb that wasn't a far cry from a paper bag, Leighton stood, arm trapped in the vise-grip of a surly man. She winced, drawing attention to the dark bruise on her right cheekbone. Her swollen lip. Someone had struck her. Beat her.

A dark storm rolled through Owen, bringing him to his feet as he pointed to her and met the king's eyes. "She was not battered when I helped her into that limo."

"If I remember the report correctly," the king challenged, "you ran off to chase her attacker. Who is to say what happened to her after that? Nouri, is this"—he swung a hand toward Owen—"the man who intervened on the streets of Paris?"

Owen had no hat to hide his face this time, so he prayed she had zero recollection of him at Soph's party two years ago and that the reassurances he'd given Pike would hold true. They'd had him bleach his hair to alter his appearance, but he hadn't been convinced it'd be enough.

Staring at the floor, she barely skated a glance in his direction to check. "I . . . I believe so." She swallowed. "It happened so fast."

King Faruq appraised Owen for a ten-count. "And . . . what do you think about the look of him?"

What kind of question was that? Owen had no problem letting a scowl into his expression. "How does that matter?"

"I don't understand, Your Majesty," she said quietly, hunching in on herself like a frightened, cornered cat.

"Do you like him? It is not so difficult a question."

Her fingers curled into fists as a long pause lingered. "Why would I? He's American."

Oh cr—

"How do you know he's American?" the king asked, his expression darkening.

Owen fought the urge to interdict for her, but clearly she'd remembered him. If he stepped in now, he'd look guilty too. Instead, he cocked his head and frowned. Praying she came up with a legitimate explanation. One that at least *sounded* legitimate.

"During the attack," she said, no hint of nerves in her voice, "he spoke to me. In clear English. Not French."

Nice save. Impressed since he barely recalled talking to her, Owen watched, anxious for the king's decision. Let his gaze drift to her and felt the blow at his core when their eyes connected. He saw in those caramel eyes the truth mirrored in his soul—their lives were on the line, caught up in a very dangerous game. Had her hiccup there tanked it?

"Take her back," the king said, returning to the curtained throne room.

So, were they good?

King Faruq walked past him, then paused and looked at Owen with muddy but sharp brown eyes. Still uncertain, unconvinced.

Half expecting him to accuse, Owen readied for the challenge. Or could it be the king had decided he liked him? That he'd hire him and—

"Take him to the cellars," King Faruq pronounced and walked out of the room.

SIX

Jeddah, Saudi Arabia

COLD, STINGING WATER PEPPERED HIS BODY.
"Augh!" Owen flinched away from the thin, piercing stream of the hose, then drove around, fists balled. "Hey—"

A guard slammed a right hook into his gut.

Air exploding from his lungs, Owen wheezed. Recovered and responded with an uppercut. Caught the guy in the chin. Drove forward with a hard right.

A blow from behind—another guard—impacted him. Pitched him forward. On the wet concrete, Owen slipped. Went down. Knee cracked against the hard surface.

The needling water became the blast of a fire hydrant, forcing him to stay down. Curl in to protect himself from the pounding onslaught.

While niceties and propriety had been par for the course in the private throne room, let there be no doubt—they were insanely well-versed in subtle and not-so-subtle forms of torture. Like stripping a guy to his skivvies and hosing him down with ice-cold water. All in the name of cleanliness and humiliation. When the water stopped, he heard boots retreat.

"You are nothing here, American. Nothing!" Mahid barked. "Get dressed!"

Knowing better than to trust that the guards' playtime was over, Owen hesitated. Glanced over his shoulder and found the cell door closing. A shiver lanced his composure as he searched for a towel to dry off. Spotted a crumpled pile near the door the guards had exited. He rifled through them. Tunic . . . pants . . . no towel. "Figures." But the chill in the air warned him not to stay stripped, so he fought his way into the provided clothes.

The mission required he endured whatever these people dished out—all to earn his way into becoming her guard, a position vacant after the handiwork of Omen. The whole gig was one massive long shot—and hours into this palace, him being stuffed into a cold, concrete ten-by-ten with no window or bed, a lone drain in the center for a toilet, proved his warning to Pike.

Sitting against the wall, forearms on his upraised knees, Owen tilted his head back and tried to ignore the dull throb in his side. The guard might've bruised a rib. One small step for Owenkind, especially if it got him assigned to Leighton. He closed his eyes. Hoped this was a time of testing while they checked and double-checked his legend and history. He completely trusted Omen to backfill it, since they were doing so with the help of high-level government assets who had experience in prepping legends for operatives in three-letter organizations.

His mind flicked back to those bruises on Leighton. The way she'd cowered in subservience. No doubt *beaten* into her. Nine months had done a number on the girl he'd first encountered two years ago. Back then, she was guarded, wary. Now, she was downright oppressed.

Please let this work, God . . . Help me get her out of here.

Those caramel eyes had telegraphed her worry. It wasn't so much in her expression or the furrowing of the brows. It was something deeper, something . . . soul-born.

You are out of your skull.

No idea how long the king would hold him in the dungeon, but since he didn't have an extra hole in his head, he'd count that as a win and a sign they wouldn't kill him.

Unless they unearthed a different hole—one in his legend as Owen Apollo. Lame concoction, but Pike swore keeping his original name would make it easier for him to avoid mistakes.

Owen sat for what felt like hours. Never knew a monochromatic environment could make time seem like a decrepit old man with a walker, taking slow, agonizing steps. Gradually, time lost its power and meaning. It could've been hours or a whole day.

A low tone sounded in his right ear, and Owen's eyes flew open. He stilled, despite the instinct to lift his head off the wall as the internal comms activated.

"OTG to Apollo," Pike spoke quietly. "You read me?"

"Mm-hmm."

"We have a thirty-second clock. Are you being monitored?"

Owen eyed the bars' metal door and once again visually traced the room for surveillance devices. Using his fist, he covered his mouth. "Unknown."

"Play it safe. Reception's bad. Where are you?"

"Dungeon."

Silence gaped for a long second. "You in trouble? Wounded?"

Knees up, elbows atop them, he steepled his fingers. "Alive. Bruised rib."

"The history we built is getting pinged hard."

He grunted.

"What're you feeling? Want us to pull you?"

Wide caramel eyes ignited in his thoughts. He felt that jolt again. Recalled her desperation, fear. "No."

"If they suspect you, they'll kill you."

Rubbing the bridge of his nose, he quickly replied, "They beat her. Often. She needs to get out. I'm here. I can do this." Desperation coiled through his veins. Did not want another half-cocked effort preventing mission success. "Hitting my history means they're going to let me take the job."

"Or trying to decide if they can get away with killing you."

He stretched his shoulders, covering his words with his arm. "You need to work on your pep talks." The groan of metal on metal in the passage stilled him. "Incoming."

"Omen out."

Climbing to his feet, Owen braced his side and let out a small grunt. He moved to the center of the room, lowering his hands to his sides as the door swung open. He shifted his right foot back, ready for a fight.

The guard jabbed his M4 at him. "Back! Make room for the prince!"

Steeling his spine, Owen remained in place. Prince, huh?

"It is okay, Jamil." A second man stepped into view. Tall and dressed in tan slacks with a black shirt, he wasn't wearing the standard ghutra and thobe like everyone else in this place. He splayed his hand over his chest. "My name is Rayan." His eyes smiled as he considered him. "Come, I will take you to your charge." He stepped back and indicated to the right.

A *prince* escorting him to Leighton? Yeah, not buying it. Hesitant, half expecting an ambush so they could torture him more, Owen knew there was nothing for it. He walked forward, letting his gaze roll to the guard. Daring him to sucker punch him again.

Rayan caught his shoulder, and it wasn't a move designed to control, but one that seemed to tell the guards that Owen was under his protection. "I do apologize that you were forced to spend the night in there. Due to Princess Daria's wedding preparations, guest wings are being utilized for her staff and her guests."

With causal confidence, Rayan strode to the end of the passage and accessed a security panel that opened a door. They climbed the stairs on the other side. "Tell me," he said with a small laugh, "did you imagine you would be coming to a palace to protect someone when you left Virginia?"

Was he trying to unsettle him that he knew that tidbit? Pike had been wise to layer in real facts with the fake persona. "No," Owen said in a huffed laugh, feeling that sweet relief that Pike's plan was working. That the royals were tasking him. "Guessing this is about the chick from Paris? The king's daughter?"

"Nouri," the prince affirmed, arching an eyebrow at him. "It is quite the coincidence that you are from Virginia like her. Did you not know her?"

Owen balked. "Dude. It takes five hours to drive from the bottom to the northern tip of Virginia. And the closer to you get to DC, the more heavily populated."

"Of course. And were you close to DC? Did you see the president?" Rayan asked with a chuckle.

"No, not really into politics." Guess it was this guy's job to ask all the questions that had arisen while probing his legend. "What about you—have you always lived here?"

Dark eyes smiled. "My whole life, save a short time in the US for university," he said as he stepped from the stairwell back onto marble floors and opulence.

Owen grunted. "Can't imagine growing up in a place like this."

"Most cannot, and I try to remember that."

They entered an elevator. "King Faruq said you were in the Army," Rayan began as the doors closed. "Did you not like it? Is that why you are not a soldier now?"

Man, that failure-dagger still dug deep, didn't it? "The Army didn't like me," he said as the box rose.

"You are quite curious, Mr. Apollo."

"Not the first time I've been told that."

The prince laughed and the elevator dinged. "A few ground rules about protecting Nouri, and I ask that you bear with us because of their strict nature, but it is for everyone's safety."

This would be interesting.

"First, neither you nor Nouri are to leave her chambers without permission of the king, Crown Prince Maaz, or myself. She is allowed in the south gardens from ten to eleven each morning, and only then. Meals are served at eight, twelve, and eight." Then he seemed chagrined. "I do apologize, but there is no separate room for you."

Owen faltered. "Come again?"

"As I said, with the wedding, all spare apartments are in use."

All 250 rooms? Was he kidding?

"So, you will be confined to her chambers. It will be no different when you are on safari with her—you remain with her at all times."

"Wait." Owen stopped short. "Are you saying I'm to eat and sleep in her room? *With* her in there?"

Rayan angled back and considered him, dark features not missing a single blemish.

Am I being punked? "Are—are there two beds?"

"No," Rayan said, mirth lifting his lips to the side. "You looked distressed."

That's a word for it.

"If you find this is unacceptable, I can return you to the cellars and notify the king."

Holy fluff. "Unacceptable?" Owen balked, quickly understanding this was a no-win situation. Say he found it unacceptable and he was back in the dungeon. If he didn't, though, they'd call his character into question—also put him back in said dungeon, right? He had to find ground that would appeal to those in this House. "It goes against Sharia law. The Central Kingdom follows that, yes? She—*we*—could be stoned. Killed for being alone together . . ." He stretched his jaw, staring at the man. The prince. "Is this girl I saved some kind of trouble or pariah? I mean, this sure sounds like someone is trying to set her up. Does the king want her gone?"

Which made no sense since they had kidnapped her from London.

"Why would he do that and hire you?"

Owen thought hard but came up with nothing. "Got me, but this . . . *this* is wrong a thousand ways from Sunday."

"Would you prefer I return you to—"

"No." He lifted a staying hand. Guessed he'd figure out a workaround. He motioned the prince onward. "Take me to her." When the prince resumed course, Owen had to force himself to follow. They made a couple of rights before they strode to the end of a narrow passage. The doors here came quicker, making him believe the rooms were smaller.

"Any house phone," Rayan said, indicating to a small table along the balcony rail, "will let you reach me. Dial 766."

"766," Owen repeated, committing that to memory.

A guard stood outside a room and affected a curt bow to the prince.

"Khamil, the king relieves you of duty, which he transfers to Mr. Apollo." He held out his hands. "The key to Nouri's room, please?"

Surprise lit through the man as he eyed Owen and produced the key. "Of course, Your Highness." He headed down the hall.

Rayan unlocked the door.

Owen started—what, they gave Leighton no warning of their intrusion into her privacy?

The prince extended the key to Owen and then knocked. "Nouri, we are coming in." With that, he pushed inside, flinging the door wide.

Surprised at how casually the prince entered her room without her clear permission, Owen caught sight of the princess rising from a padded window seat, book in hand. Swallowing, he followed him in and shifted aside to let the door close.

"Nouri," Prince Rayan said, "I believe you met Apollo last night. He's the one who saved you in Paris."

Though she did not look at him, she inclined her head.

"He is your new guard."

At that, her gaze came up. Swung to Owen.

To his disappointment, she did not look at him with hope or even admiration. But with . . . anger.

"Nouri." Rayan's voice held reprimand.

Her gaze bounced to the thick carpet beneath her feet.

Holy fluff, talk about suppression. Oppression. And every other *-ession* he could think of. It ticked him off to see her so browbeaten.

Rayan pointed to a small round table with two chairs. "Ah, I see breakfast has been served." He grinned at Owen. "I'm afraid she did not leave you much, Mr. Apollo." The prince picked up a date from the tray, tossed it into his mouth, and headed for the door. "Enjoy your stay."

* * *

Shock riddled Leighton as she stood alone in the room with Owen Metcalfe. He had lied to the king about his identity, and she might have completely missed that *he* had been the one to rescue her in Paris. Here, however, standing in the awkward silence, she knew him. Well, not *knew* knew, but after Sophia Neeley's party, she had researched him. Learned everything she could about the guy who had made her feel seen and naked. The guy with killer blue eyes that pierced her soul. Even back then, she'd had this terrible, irrational fear that he would unearth her secrets. Destroy a lifetime of careful, meticulous order that kept her and her secret safe. Kept her ummi safe.

His intrusion tilted her world, sending a thrum of panic and . . .

something else through her—hope. Dangerous hope. Cursing herself for even thinking that, she reminded herself he could ruin everything. She was here for a reason. And it would not be undone by pretty blue eyes.

"Hey," he said, coming forward, his expression eager.

She looked away—not out of the same subservience these royals demanded but because she did not want him to look at her. Expose her. "I'm tired."

"It's 0945," he chuckled.

She turned and stalked to the bathroom. Shut the door—not to use it, but to think. What was happening? *Why* was he here? He made it impossible to think with those blue eyes and smirk. She dropped back against the wall and gripped her head in her hands. Why did it have to be him? Oh, she needed Dad and Mom to help her sort this.

"Hey..." A rap came at the door. "Sorry to interrupt, but garden time is happening now. It's only an hour, so . . . wasn't sure if you wanted to go."

Garden time?

"Okay . . ." he said in resignation.

She stomped over and yanked open the door. "What're you talking about?"

Blue eyes blinked. "It's, uh, ten a.m., and Rayan said you were allowed in the garden from ten till eleven."

Surprised at his words, she left the bathroom, hugging herself. "I . . . I have never had outside privileges."

"Privileges?" A scowl dug into his handsome face and smoothed out just as fast. "So, ready to go?"

Leighton nodded, then remembered. "Wait." She rushed into the dressing room and grabbed a scarf. Draping it over her head and around her neck, she returned.

The storm returned to his eyes. Hey, she didn't like wearing it either, but she would take this over another beating. She silently willed the new guy not to make a fuss. When he tightened his jaw and opened the door, she swallowed her irritation. It was weird to have a semblance of freedom, but as soon as she stepped out and saw someone coming, that infusion of fear reminded her "freedom" was an illusion. She lowered her head and stayed close to Owen as the man she did not recognize passed them.

Halfway down, Owen glanced around, then looked at her. "Right or left?"

Leighton started. "How would I know?"

"You've lived here—"

"Yes, in a dungeon until a week ago, then we were in Paris for three days. I've never been to any gardens."

"I thought you were leading us there."

"I thought *you*—" She snapped her mouth closed at the sight of the crown prince emerging from the other side of the atrium that yawned between them. With a gasp, she realized where they were. "Back!"

"What?"

"We have to go back."

Apollo glanced across the atrium. "Who is that? I saw him last night—"

"The crown prince," she said staring at the floor. "You brought us to the royal apartments—we have to leave. Now."

"That sounds bad."

"You have no idea." She pivoted to return to her room, walking faster. Wanted to run. Did not want an encounter with Maaz and end up with another split lip. When she saw Prince Nasir round a corner ahead, she tensed and slammed her gaze down.

Apollo held a hand in front of her, stopping. "Excuse me, Your Highness. Could you help us?"

No no no. Why on earth was he talking to Nasir?

"What?" Nasir bit out.

"First day on the job. Can you tell me how to get to the gardens?" Apollo asked.

Despite the silence that lingered, Leighton knew better than to look up. In fact, she eased behind Apollo, who seemed to read her cue and shifted to block her from the prince.

"Prince Rayan told me to take her out," Apollo persisted, "and since the king has put me in charge of her, I want to carry out my duties efficiently."

With a huff, Prince Nasir shook his head. "Back down the side hall, take the stairs, then turn left. Door is at the end of the hall."

"Thank you," Apollo said as he stepped aside and urged her toward the passage.

Leighton seized the chance to escape unscathed and strode toward the door he'd mentioned.

Owen hustled ahead of her and pushed open the door. They followed Prince Nasir's instructions and found the garden without trouble. Stepping into the sunshine was glorious, and she inhaled deeply.

"So, the crown prince—"

"Not here," she hissed, yanked out of savoring the day. With determination, she paced to the far hedgerow and surreptitiously glanced back. Noticed that while the armed guards watched from the upper terraces, they were not overly concerned. And there did not seem to be anyone else nearby. Using a tall, thin tree to block herself, she whirled on him. "What on earth are you doing here?"

Apollo drew up sharp. "Whoa. Way to whip out Cruella."

She would not be diverted, no matter how much that hurt. "Why're you here? Tell me Paris was a coincidence."

"I could," he said quietly, glancing around, "but I don't make it a habit to lie."

"Don't you?" she challenged. "*Apollo*."

He smirked. "Callsign."

Leighton felt the tendrils of anger wrapping around her heart. "Do you think this is a joke?"

After another quick scan of the gardens, he focused on her. "Your mom and Navas sent me."

Defenses shattering, she gaped. "H-how do you know that name?" Her heart tripped and fell over this complication. She waved him off. "No, I don't believe you." She couldn't. Wouldn't. It'd be too dangerous.

"Your mom said you wouldn't," Apollo said. "She told me to say, '*religieuse* may be your favorite, but it is not the best pastry.'"

Leighton recoiled, sucking in a breath as those words spilled a torrent of grief and shock through her. Her eyes stung. She turned away, hiding the tears. The ache constricting her chest. Relief that Ummi had not been killed or discovered. But she could not afford weakness. Could not let this man come here— "I don't care." She jutted her jaw. "This can't happen. You cannot be here."

"Well, I am."

"I do not want you here," she spat, anger tumbling over every ounce of self-restraint she had left. "You're going to ruin everything!"

Apollo scowled, glanced around, then edged in, his voice dangerously low. "If by 'everything' you mean ruin your getting beaten again, your getting raped or killed—yeah." He seemed to bare his teeth. "I'm going to ruin things."

"Sweet, merciful menaces!" she hissed. "If they suspect we know each other—"

"So you do remember me."

She wanted to claw that smirk off his too-perfect face! Yet she also faltered that he could even question that she didn't remember him. She'd done nothing for weeks after that party but troll him online. There might even be a screenshot or two—or ten—on her phone that she'd captured from Sophia's social media. But that was beside the point. "*This* is *not* about you!"

"Hate to beg to differ, but it really is—at least, you're making it that way. I was sent here to rescue you, so I'm getting you out, one way or—"

"No!" Heat rose into her cheeks at the infuriating man. "You aren't." How had she ever daydreamed about this egotistical jerk? "I'm staying here, I don't want your help, and I most definitely *do not* need to be rescued!"

"Yeah, because that bruise on your cheek and the insidious way you shrink at every man in this palace says this is such a great place to be."

"It's the *only* place I want to be right now."

"What in the Dark Ages is wrong with you?"

"*You*! You are what's wrong with me."

"So, what—you enjoy being treated like a slave?"

"It's better than Ummi being killed because I couldn't hack it, or worse—because I let some guy overstep what *I* know is right and best."

Apollo drew up at that, eyes sparking in the sunlight as understanding washed away all tension. Compassion and empathy rippled into place, and for the love of all that was holy, he looked even more gorgeous.

"Now," she ground out, "I think my hour is up. At least, I hope it is, because this conversation is over." She marched back toward the house.

"Whoa, whoa. Wait." He caught up and slid in front of her, rocks crunching beneath his shoes. "Two minutes. Just give me two minutes for clarification."

Leighton fought the urge to roll her eyes.

"Your room is bugged?"

Her frustration wavered, but she managed a clipped nod—anything to avoid those eyes.

"And out here it's safe to talk."

"No, I just like to sabotage work I have literally put my entire life into."

His eyebrows winged up. "Girl, you have a lethal bite to your words."

Though her conscience quailed at his rebuke, she wasn't backing down. "Any other questions?"

"So, hear me out . . . If I can somehow get it arranged to extract you on the safari, would you go? Or will you fight me the whole way?"

"My mother—"

"Is safe. My team has her. Navas is with her."

She frowned. "What about Gerard?"

"Who?"

"Her . . . driver-who-is-more. If he's not safe, then she's not safe." She shrugged, feeling a little awkward at mentioning him. "I think there's something between them, though they tried to hide it while I was with them in London."

A look of consternation tangled the strong ridge above those blue eyes. "I hope Navas doesn't find out."

She gave him a speculative look and sniffed. "Navas walked out on her before I was even born, so he doesn't get a vote."

Apollo cleared his throat. "And circling back to the question . . ."

"No." Leighton pushed around him and headed to the house.

"Uh, is that no to the first question or the second?"

She didn't slow, didn't answer, because she honestly wasn't sure which question she'd answered. But she could not fathom altering the entire course of her life because one man said Ummi was safe.

If there had ever been a trap, this was it.

SEVEN

Jeddah, Saudi Arabia

THE GIRL HAD SOME SERIOUS ATTITUDE. BUT beneath it lay a tanker of insecurity and fear, screaming and writhing as he sat with her in the bedchamber that night.

"Don't you have something to do?" she asked after dinner.

"I'm doing it," he answered calmly. If he'd been addicted to his phone like a lot of Scions, he might be twitching uncontrollably after hours without any means to doomscroll. But military life had taught him to make the most of silence and solitude. Now he found it grounding.

"Aren't you going to your own room?"

He hesitated, sloughed his hands together. Had nobody explained the situation to her? "I . . ." He exhaled heavily. "They told me to stay here."

She stared at him blankly. "What?"

"I'm staying. In here, this room," he clarified with a cockeyed nod. "They said all rooms are full because of the wedding."

"*Here?*" she balked. "In *my* room?" Her gaze wandered to the lone bed. "There's only one. No way—"

"I wouldn't dream of asking. Relax."

"Relax? You know what they could do to me, to us—"

"I do," he conceded, "and I think that's their hope—to corrupt you so the king will want to get rid of you, or maybe get rid of me. Which would probably make you happy."

Leighton faltered, her expression flickering as if she wasn't sure what to think or say. She rubbed her forehead and wandered to the bay-window seat. "Look, I may not want you here, but I am not coldhearted." She picked up a throw pillow. "I don't want you dead."

"Glad you clarified that."

She grimaced, then huffed. "But you can't sleep in here."

"Don't plan to." Truth be told, he'd already decided to crash in the hall, directly in front of her door. Much as Uriah the Hittite had done after being pulled from battle when King David wanted to hide his sin with Bathsheba. Because Owen had a gut instinct that said staying *in* the room through the night would have dire consequences and play into whatever bizarre intentions the royals had for her. "Don't worry. I've got a plan."

The nod she gave was slight, wary. For a long, uncertain moment, she studied him before turning and looking out the window. As if she wanted to say something, but with the belief of listening devices or hidden cameras, they had to tread carefully.

He wouldn't lie—this was a surprise, her rejecting him and his efforts. Hadn't expected that. Wasn't really sure he understood wanting to *stay* here.

No . . .

Her reaction wasn't about *want*. People holding a line like that didn't do it out of the same conviction as someone choosing a Mustang over a Camaro. This was deeper. Leighton truly believed that staying here kept her biological mother safe. Worse was the thing he guessed she had considered on a surface level—that she herself would die. He wouldn't put it past this royal family to do something so evil. Her resolution was admirable yet faulty. But how did he get her to see that?

Be her friend.

He sniffed, shaking his head. To her, he was only an irritant. A complication.

So convince her otherwise.

Stretching his neck, he leaned forward in the chair and rested his elbows on his knees. "Can . . . you tell me what you know about the royals?"

In the cushioned window seat, legs crisscrossed, she hugged the pillow like a shield. "Besides the fact the king and crown prince are capable of this," she said, indicating her bruised face, "I don't know much."

"The princess took you to Paris."

"That . . . was a shock." She brushed her dark hair from her shoulder. "I have no idea why, but for some reason Princess Daria has picked me . . . to dote on." She motioned around the room. "I'm here because of her."

"Guessing the safari was her doing too."

"Yeah—wait, you mentioned that." She frowned. "I'd been told it was off."

Owen flicked his hands up in a question. "Got me. Prince Rayan said we'd be going, that I was to remain with you at all times, even on safari."

Leighton rose and paced in front of the window. "This doesn't make sense. Even Paris—I don't know why she wanted me there. I was nothing but an *unglorified* bag carrier and coffee courier. Why would she want me on the safari?"

"Is it possible she's just nice? Maybe she feels sorry for the poor American princess?"

"*Never* call me that. I am *not* a princess." Her expression warned it wasn't something she'd compromise on. Why? By birthright, she *was* a princess of the Central Kingdom.

For his own sake, he should keep that reminder at the front of his brain. "Noted." He shifted to the edge of the chair. "So . . . is she nice?"

"That's a relative term," she said, her pacing amping his own nerves as she chewed her thumbnail. "I mean, she has been nice, but there's this . . . darkness behind her words and eyes. Now Aliyah, on the other hand, *is* nice."

"Who's that?"

"Another princess," she said with a wry grin. "I double-dog dare you to memorize all the names of the Saudi princes."

He lifted his eyebrows at the challenge. "Double-dog . . ." Did she really think he hadn't done his research? "You expect me to memorize fifteen hundred names?"

She laughed and slumped onto the window cushion. "It was worth a try." Leaning back against the wall that framed the little alcove, she sighed and twisted up her face. "I will never believe anyone here is truly interested in friendship or welcoming me to the family."

He was relieved to hear that. "What do you think they hope to gain by holding you?"

"Faruq wants my mother."

That was what Yasmina had said as well, but . . . "Why?"

Ire unlocked, she looked ready to level up. "Are you kidding me?"

"Hey." He flashed his palms at her. "Just trying to get a lay of the land. Understand what's happening, so I can better anticipate threats to you." When she didn't immediately rail or argue, he let himself continue. "I'm here to protect you, Nouri."

She huffed. "No, *Apollo*, you're a prisoner just like me now."

Man, he hated that she called him that—she said it in a tone that put him on one side of the line and her on the other. But he couldn't argue the prisoner thing. "Fair, but I don't have to let that rule me."

A frown flickered across her olive skin. "What does that mean? Are you saying I am?"

He gave a weary smile. "It means that we might not—yet—be able to control our situation, but we can control ourselves. For me"—he put a palm to his chest—"maintaining calm not only helps me remain focused but also keeps my mind in check, allowing said mind to work through hot spots with intelligence, with intent, so I can respond appropriately."

Sunlight streaked through the window and glanced off her caramel irises. "Are you always this . . ."

"Strategic?"

"I was going to say arrogant."

"This is not arrogance but mission readiness. Drilled into me after five years in the Army."

"If you're trying to lecture me about how I'm handling this—"

"Whoa." Man, he couldn't win for losing. "Power down, Supergirl. We're on the same team."

"No, we're not. Because there is no team. I was doing just fine before you got here."

"Yeah, that bruise looks real fine." *Not helping, Apollo.* "You don't have to be the sacrificial lamb. She's safe, fine. The team—"

"Enough!" She glowered, reminding him they were likely being listened in on. "I won't let you ruin anything. As far as I'm concerned, you can leave."

"Actually, I can't . . ."

With a roll of her eyes, she stomped into the bathroom and closed the door.

Again? Owen dragged his hands over his face with a groan and slumped back against the seat. *God, You gotta help me out. This . . . is beyond me.*

How was he supposed to help her, save her, if she wouldn't let him?

And if he didn't—bam. Another "close but no cigar" tick on the scoreboard of his life. Would this be *three strikes, you're out?*

When he heard the shower turn on, he realized he did not have any supplies to shower and shave. At 2200, it was unlikely he could disturb Rayan to get some. How was he supposed to take care of things?

Surely this wing had a standalone bathroom. Maybe it'd have soap he could use. Only one way to find out . . .

First, he snagged a pillow from the window seat, then stepped out into the hall. And because he was not going to risk losing his objective on his first official night on the job, he used the key to lock the door. Although, it'd serve these royals right if she escaped. The reality was that she'd likely get caught and either beaten or killed.

He set the pillow next to the door of the inset space for her apartment, then glanced up and down the concourse looking for someone to ask about a bathroom and toiletries. At the rail that ran around the open-to-below atrium, he searched for help. Nobody. Man. How—

"What are you doing?" hissed a woman.

Owen glanced behind him and found a woman in a black abaya standing there with a stern expression. "Hi, I'm the guard for Nouri. But I don't have a shave kit. I need to take care of business."

Wow, that got embarrassing fast.

With a huff, she waved him to follow her . . . right back toward Nouri's door. She reached for a panel and swiped a key, and a hidden panel popped. She flicked it open and indicated him toward it. "Use."

Surprise had him peeking inside—a private bath. Wow. "Thank you," he said, glancing at her. "And toiletries?" But she was already gone. With a shrug, he slipped into the bathroom, eyed another door, wondering if this was a jack-and-jill, and anchored the bolt lock. Beneath the counter, he found extra toiletries and quickly brushed his teeth and cleaned up. Before leaving, he grabbed a washcloth, stepped out, and pulled the panel almost completely shut before stuffing it along the lock to prevent it from catching. This way he could come back later to shower.

Satisfied, he returned to her apartment alcove and retrieved the pillow. He dropped it on the floor, swallowed his pride, and lay on his back, arms folded over his chest. Why hadn't he thought to grab a blanket?

Though carpeted, the hard floor dug into his shoulder blades. At least he didn't have to worry about sleeping too deeply. Not even sure he could fall asleep. He used the sleeplessness to figure out how to get Leighton to soften up, give him a break. Thinking through everything he'd seen, those he'd met, he catalogued it all. Took stock of it. Worked on a plan to get her back to Yasmina.

The safari. If somehow Omen could get in place . . . Yeah . . . Yeah, that could work. Maybe if they happened upon an area with knolls and hills, trees, he could have the team waiting . . . But he'd need to know locations first. He should ask Rayan for an itinerary, so he could be prepared. It would take more than an itinerary to be prepared, though, especially with her unwilling to cooperate.

———— • ————

Leighton awoke with a start. Not because anything was wrong but because her body had trained her to be up, alert, and dressed before that door opened to deliver the breakfast tray. Vigilance kept her from being intruded upon. It always felt slimy for a male guard to see her in a state of undress, despite being beneath the covers.

Even as she dragged herself out of bed, she recalled a hazy dream.

Laughter . . . *his* laughter, Apollo's. They'd been at the Capitol together, beneath the cherry blossom trees along the tidal basin.

Shaking off the dream, she headed into the bathroom and readied herself for the day. She found makeup in a tray and added some concealer to the bruise that was a garish shade of blue and purple now, then got dressed.

Thud! Crack! Thud!

Startled, she hurried back into the room, looking around. Had something fallen? What had the noise—

Shouts carried outside the door, and her pulse raced. *Thud! Thud!* The door bucked.

She drew back, hand to her throat. That sounded like a fight . . .

Where was Apollo? Was he the one fighting? The thought drew her forward.

The door slammed open.

Leighton took a step back, the moment powering down to a slow, surreal event. Nasir and another man had Apollo by the scruff of the shirt and pitched him in her direction. She tried to brace, but his weight crashed into her. Knocked her backwards. Off her feet. She dropped hard to the floor and careened back. Acutely aware of Apollo atop her. She thumped her head against something. Pain exploded.

He found purchase on the bedframe, and with preternatural skill, leapt up and around. Stood ready for the next punch.

"Stay in there!" Nasir snarled, his own lip bloodied. "If we find you sleeping here again, you will be punished. And if you ever forget to lock her door again, we will—"

"It *was* locked!" Leighton stood behind Owen. "You broke the—"

Eyes dark with outrage and violence, Prince Nasir lunged at her.

That's when she realized her mistake. And though she jerked her gaze down, it was too late. A storm named Apollo swept in front of her. Taller by a head, he squared his stance. Shoulders rose and hands readied as he slammed into place.

Prince Nasir pulled up sharp. "Get out of the way."

"*Not* happening," Apollo growled. "She's under my protection. Touch her and it will be the last thing you do."

"How dare you talk to me like that!"

"Oh, I'm not talking," Apollo snarled. "Any man threatened by a woman speaking her mind isn't a man."

"What did you say to me?" Nasir moved forward.

But a large hand clamped the prince's shoulder. The slightly taller, bulkier build of Crown Prince Maaz appeared there, self-possessed and disapproving.

Leighton saw Apollo's raw, feral reflection in the mirror next to where the crown prince stood. The fury.

"What is this?" demanded Maaz.

Nasir flared his nostrils and dabbed his bloody lip. "This infidel was sleeping in the hall in plain view of all women. When I corrected him—"

"You mean kicked me in the ribs."

Maaz looked between his brother and Apollo. "Why were you sleeping in the hall?"

Leighton started—Owen had been sleeping in the hall? On the *floor*? Guilt curled and lodged itself in her lungs, made it hard to breathe.

"Seems assigning me a room was overlooked," Owen noted acidly.

"You were told to stay in here."

"It's inappropriate," he said. "I will not dishonor Nouri or myself. I'd think more respect would be shown to one of your own."

"She is *not* one of our own," Maaz said with an icy calm, his gaze never meeting hers. He gave a slow nod to Apollo. "We have guests visiting and many staying until Daria's wedding. You cannot sleep in the hall like a vagrant."

"Wasn't my idea of fun either, but it was necessary. I won't give anyone cause to question Nouri's purity or character."

Shocked at his straightforward words, Leighton drew in a breath. Looked away even as she noted the words seemed to impact the princes too.

"If you both do not want to find yourselves in a cell again, *stay* in this room, door locked," Maaz instructed.

The rattle of a tray—her breakfast, no doubt—sounded beyond the door.

Maaz all but shoved his brother out. The crown prince made to leave but paused at the door. Traced the broken jamb. His expression tightened, then they were gone.

Apollo sagged into the chair, holding his side and grimacing.

"What were you thinking?" A tangle of emotions assaulted Leighton at the blood on his knuckles and lip. She diverted to the bathroom, where she wet a towel and hurried back to him. Sitting on the small coffee table, she thought to tend his wounds, but suddenly felt awkward and thrust the towel at him.

He caught it. "Thanks." He pressed it to his lip and dabbed. Winced.

Why it hit her then, she didn't know, but—sweet heavens, he was gorgeous. She wasn't a fan of the bleached hair, but his blue eyes created a vortex that drew her in and forbade escape. His aquiline nose, stubble against tanned skin, and stern brow ridge added so much character.

Focus, Leighton! "Did you really sleep on the floor outside my door?"

He stretched his jaw, expression tightening. "I was fine."

Deflating, she cursed herself for making him leave. "This is my fault."

"Negative," he said firmly, using the damp towel to wipe his knuckles and the angry cut.

"I made you leave."

"Already told you, I never intended to sleep in here."

"But now you have to."

His jaw muscle flexed.

"We'll make it work," she said softly, feeling defeated too. "It's not worth"—she motioned to his hands and lip—"this."

Intensity narrowed his eyes. "Protecting you is my job, and that means protecting not just your person but your honor. I'll put my life down to do that, if I must."

"That's absurd." Leighton drew back, not believing he meant that. Surely he hadn't. But that locked-in-place scowl did not abate, so maybe he had. She stood and moved away, then faced him, hugging herself. "You're complicating everything." She touched her forehead, kneading away the threatening headache.

"That's what my mom said about being pregnant with me."

"What?"

Cringing and bracing his side, he continued to the bathroom, where he inspected his lip and tossed the towel in the sink, running water over it. "Long story, but . . . I was conceived out of wedlock."

Leighton stood at the door, watching him. "I'm not connecting the dots . . ."

He rinsed the towel and looked at her in the mirror. "My parents were on a mission to find some drug lord who'd held her captive for nearly a year. Since she was the only one who'd been to his compound, the US government threatened her with colluding with the enemy and jail time if she didn't deliver this drug lord or his location. So, she led Dad's team to the compound to take out the guy. Dad was plugging painkillers from a back injury. A landslide separated them from the team and they holed up at a hotel. One thing led to another, and here I am."

"Um, wow," she said with a disbelieving laugh. Had he made that up? "But what does that have to do with—"

"She said I'd complicated things but I was the best complication." He wrung out the towel, then draped it over the edge. "Guess

I've been complicating life ever since, so don't think it's personal." Smirking, he drew up the edge of his shirt to inspect his side, where a massive bruise bloomed across his ribs.

She gasped, moving closer. "That's huge."

Arm up, he angled to see the blue and purple marring his very toned abs and deltoids. "It feels huge. Pretty sure the rib cracked this time."

"*This* time?" she balked, then recoiled. "I am so sorry."

"Me too." He grunted and lowered his shirt. "Now to get some clean clothes."

"Oh, they put some in the dressing room, along with a shave kit," she said, pointing past him where a door sat ajar.

He headed in there, drawing his shirt up over his head, muscles rippling and taunting.

Yeah, he was *really* in shape. Mouth dry, she made herself go to the small dinette where breakfast waited and sat down. "I'm really sorry they attacked you . . ." *Because you were protecting my honor.* She shook her head. Was this guy real?

He emerged, threading his arms through a white kaftan, which really complemented his tanned skin and blue eyes. "I'll live."

Her mind replayed how he'd shoved himself into Nasir's path. Like a lion protecting his pride. It had been incredible. Inspiring. Nobody had ever done something like that for her.

He eyed the plate and frowned. "What's that?"

"Shakshuka. It's delicious but spicy."

"You afraid I can't handle it?" he teased as he sat in the other chair.

"I only said it to warn you." She tucked her hair behind her ear and took a sip of the orange juice, trying to ignore the warm, fuzzy feeling at sitting close to him.

He lifted a spoon, then paused. "Do you mind me joining you?"

"I think I *owe* you."

Apollo set down his spoon. "I'll pass."

"What?" She drew back and frowned at him. "Why? You can't be serious—you have to eat."

"I never want you to feel like you owe me anything. This is my job. It's what I do." For a man with so much determination and character, he was pretty young. Handsome, but still young.

"You know, you really don't have to make everything a lesson." She scooped a poached egg with the tomato sauce onto her plate and took some bread.

"Wait, are these—" He grimaced, spoon poised over the pan. "Runny eggs?"

"Don't knock it till you try it."

"Runny eggs are like snot."

Laughing, she covered her mouth, nearly spitting out the bite she'd taken. "That is disgusting."

"Exactly."

"You are not allowed to complain until you try it."

"So, not just captivity but torture too."

She wanted to smile, but his words felt . . . too soon. Especially considering the injuries they'd both sustained within this House. And in the seconds that followed, she felt a wave of guilt for relaxing around him. Somehow, it felt wrong. Like . . . failing.

And that could not happen. She could not let this guy slip in with his smirk, muscles, and charm to dismantle a lifetime of work, tearing control from her grasp.

"So . . . safari," he said, grabbing a chunk of bread to dip in the tomato sauce of the shakshuka. "Do you know how long it'll be or where we're going?"

"I only know it is fourteen days."

Owen gaped. "Two *weeks*? That . . . is longer than expected." He seemed to recover with a wan grin. "But . . . safari."

Folding her arms over her chest, she sat back. "I don't even understand why they'd invite me. In Paris, I carried the bags. Guess Daria wants me to be bait for the wildlife while she flees."

"Bait's my job," he said, thumbing toward himself.

Despite his light tone, she didn't like it. What was the point of Daria including her in all this. What was the long game? Would she be responsible for Apollo getting hurt too?

"Hey." His hand landed on her knees. "You okay?"

She bounced her gaze around the table, thinking. Did they want her to have an unfortunate accident? Hope she'd die? Was Apollo right that the royals were working to turn the king against her? Was the king regretting bringing her here? But . . . how would that reconcile with the fact he wanted Ummi back?

"It just doesn't make sense . . ." That's when she felt the tremor in her chest, the rampage of fear. All her certainty that being here meant she could control staying alive and thereby keep Ummi alive suddenly seemed compromised now. She felt backed into a corner.

EIGHT

Jeddah, Saudi Arabia

SOMETHING HAD SHIFTED BETWEEN HER handing him the plate of tomato-y snotty eggs and this instant. He didn't know what, but her entire posture and demeanor shrank from him. It had gotten worse when he'd talked about the safari—the route he'd hoped to take advantage of to effect an escape. But he couldn't tell her that. Not yet. She was too determined that he not do anything on her behalf.

"Look, before you put gray hairs in that head of yours, let me verify the safari is even happening. Rayan told me how to reach him." He grabbed the phone before she could object, because he needed to know too. He dialed 766, then hit speaker.

"*Sabah al-khayr*," spoke the prince.

Owen stared at the phone, dumbfounded. Arabic?

"He said 'good morning,'" Leighton whispered from beside him.

"Good morning, Prince Rayan. This is Apollo."

"Mr. Apollo," the prince said evenly. " I heard about your unfortunate incident."

"Yeah, fun in reverse," Owen said, not really interested in

rehashing all that. "Listen, I wanted to verify something you told me."

"Of course. How can I help?"

This guy was entirely too nice. "Seems there's a bit of confusion about whether the safari is happening or not."

"The flight departs tomorrow morning at six."

"And . . . Nouri is going?"

"You will both be on the jet."

Leighton arched her eyebrow.

"Good to know."

"Please be ready for pickup at five a.m."

"Are we supposed to pack? How long is the—"

"Fourteen days. All will be provided."

"Understood. Thank you."

Leighton turned away and wore a track in the floor as she chewed that thumbnail again, worry plain on her face.

Owen sensed she wanted to talk without extra ears listening. And look at the time . . . "Ready for the garden?"

She whirled. "Yes!"

This time, they didn't get lost on the way down.

By the time they reached the far wall, Leighton looked ready to combust. "I don't get it," she snapped, walking the length of the path that ran parallel to the brick wall. "Why are they taking me? Do they want me to have some terrible accident?"

"But you said they wanted to get your mom here—that can't happen if they off you."

"Wow, don't spare my feelings."

"I only—"

"Yeah, yeah, I know," she growled. "I know they aren't being nice to me—we've both seen that in this family, the kindness gene is missing."

Did she realize that meant she wasn't kind too?

As if she read his thoughts, she glowered at him. "Don't."

Owen huffed a laugh.

"I see the wheels of your brain turning, Apollo," she bit out. "You want me to escape while we are on safari."

Oh, that. "It would be feasible. My team—"

"Listen to me," she snarled, rushing at him. "It is *not* feasible. It will *not* happen."

Surprised by her venom, he held up his hands. "Hey," he said quietly. "Listen to your voice—it's pitched, frantic. That's fear. *Fear* is driving that decision."

"Yes," she railed. "Yes, it is. I am afraid you will get Ummi killed. These people are capable of that."

"Agreed," he said gently, "but they're also capable of killing *you*. A moment ago, you were afraid they wanted you to die out there."

She swallowed hard, uncertainty filling in the gaps between her vehemence. "Do you think that's why they're letting me go? So I'll die?"

What a loaded question. "It's a legitimate concern. And I know you're dead set against me extracting you, but that *is* my mission. My goal. I will not let you die, and I will not leave you here."

With a groan, she buried her face in her hands, then scrubbed them through her hair beneath her head covering as she pivoted away. Walked to the long hedgerow.

"I'm not going to let them make the first move, not against you, Leighton." He cringed at using her real name aloud but knew they were far from snooping ears.

"And if I forbid you from doing anything?"

He considered her for a hot second. Knew if he told her his stance on that, she'd fight him. And things would be infinitely more complicated.

"Unbelievable!" She whimpered and angled in, shaking her head. "What is wrong with you? Why can't you understand that I want to save my ummi?"

A thought struck him then. "Why don't you call her 'Mom'?"

The question made her withdraw. She sighed, this time moving back and forth but not quite pacing. "It's not an easy answer—and it's confusing. I don't want *my* mother—the one who raised me—to think my biological mother is more important. So, using the Arabic term for mother creates distinction." Sagging against the wall, she looked at the sky. "It's probably dumb, but it seemed better than calling her Yasmina, as if she were a friend or some other person I know. And it helps me avoid the 'adoptive mom,' 'biological mom' thing."

"Both moms are important to you."

"Yeah," she said with relief.

"And you knew . . . where you came from?"

She nodded. "It was necessary—vital that I knew. I grew up being told my story, that I was born here in Jeddah and was secreted to America. All my life, it was this *huge* secret. They taught me that I must be good, must be quiet about the past or Ummi would die. My parents always said Ummi was brave, that she loved me and risked her own life to save mine."

Now he was tracking. "So you feel you have to do the same for her."

Wide, brown eyes pooled with unshed tears. "Yes," she breathed, then her expression knotted as she came off the wall. "Yet . . . no. Never have I felt that I *have* to do this for her. It has only ever been that I want to."

"You want to be the hero too."

Leighton looked to the pebbled path. "Wow, that makes me sound so shallow."

"Wanting to be the hero isn't a bad thing."

"I'm not looking for glory or to be hailed a hero," Leighton said as she wandered the gardens. "I just . . . I want her safe. After what she did to ensure I was safe, I need to do that for her. Really, I want all of us safe."

He understood then that what he had taken for granted his

whole life, she had never experienced. "I legit cannot imagine what it must've been like to grow up keeping this dark secret. What an albatross to hang over a kid's head."

She stopped and looked at him, head tilted. "You aren't hearing me—it *wasn't* a burden."

"Actually, it was," he countered, wishing she could see how this had affected her entire life. "A big one. But a burden isn't always bad. It's heavy, for sure."

Leighton absorbed his words, then conceded with a slow nod.

A sharp whistle crackled in his ear. "Augh!" He touched the spot.

"Apollo, you there?"

"You okay?" Leighton asked, drawing closer.

At the sound of Pike's voice via the implant, Owen turned his back to the palace. "Yeah."

"You alone?"

Owen skated a glance in her direction. "I'm with Nouri."

She angled toward him with a very confused look.

"What's your sit-rep?" Pike asked.

"They're a bit hands-on here, but we're holding our own. Tomorrow, we leave for a two-week safari."

"Interesting."

"Maybe an ideal situation for an extraction."

"No!" Leighton snapped, eyes wide. "Who are you talking to? How are you talking to them?" Panic scratched into her pretty face. "I told you—"

He moved away, keeping his head up in case anyone was watching, so they wouldn't figure out he was on comms with the team.

"We'll get into their system. Work something out."

"Sounds good." Only then did he wonder why she wasn't bothering him or interrupting him. When he glanced over his shoulder to her, he found her gone. What? Where ...? He scanned the gardens and spotted her abaya fluttering through the inner garden. Son of a biscuit! "Gotta go."

"*Problem?*"

"Yeah, all five-seven of her." With a loud pop, the comms went inactive as he broke into a jog, which sent shards of fire through his side and lungs from the cracked rib. But if she went inside without him, they'd both get more hands-on hospitality. And by her fuming expression, she knew that and was willing to endure it. All to stop him from talking with the team. He cut across the gardens to reach her quicker. "Nouri!"

Grabbing the door handle, she shot him a seething look.

He crashed into the door, choking the breath from him, but he'd successfully stopped her. "What's going on?"

"I told you," she hissed, "I'm not—"

A ghostlike figure appeared on the other side of the glass door.

Leighton flinched and yelped. Then gave a nervous laugh to Prince Rayan, who stood on the other side watching them. Had he seen their argument? Her rushing away while he was standing there talking to thin air?

Owen drew open the door. "Ah, just the prince I'd hoped to see."

Stepping aside as they entered the narrow passage, Rayan eyed them. "It would seem being American does not automatically make you two friends."

"Not even close," Leighton snarled as she shifted to the other side of Rayan.

Owen stepped in—and a blur came at him, amid a flurry of Arabic. A knifehand strike nailed the side of his neck. He heard a crack even as the air gusted from the blow. Before he could make sense of what'd just happened, he heard shouts. Saw Nasir and Rayan pull off a red-faced Hassan.

Choking, neck throbbing, Owen shifted back, ready to fight if someone came at him again.

"Are you okay?" Leighton's eyes were wide. Filled with panic and fear.

He nodded, but felt the spot the guy had struck. Recalled that crack—had the guy broken the implant? A knot was forming there. "What was that for?"

The crown prince and his brother drew away the enraged Hassan.

"He said you are a dog who should not be here."

Owen blinked. "What . . . ?"

"I fear," Rayan said as the others left, "he saw you blocking the princess's path."

For the love of all that was holy . . . "He hates her," Owen objected.

"Yes, but she belongs to House al-Zahrani. You do not."

"Got it," Owen said around a grunt in his aching throat.

"This way," Rayan said and started walking. "I came to find you and deliver the itinerary for the trip. You will need to be prepared so you can keep Nouri on schedule to meet trains, flights, and vehicles. I trust you are able to do this, even though you could not remember when to come in from the garden." He gave them both a disapproving look as he led them to an elevator, stepped in, and indicated for them to do the same.

When the doors closed, Rayan huffed. "You will both have to be much better behaved, or you, Mr. Apollo, will be removed from her security detail. If that happens, we cannot promise Nouri's safety."

It took everything in Owen not to react to the not-so-subtle threat.

"As it is," the prince continued, "several have already made threats against her, thus the reason King Faruq put you in this position. Get along or get out, Mr. Apollo."

As if timed to his words, the elevator dinged and the doors opened.

Prince Rayan exited, ever moving in authority and confidence.

Jaw tight, Owen motioned for Leighton to go ahead of him. Her gaze met his for the briefest of moments and he saw both an apology and frustration. Maybe exasperation.

He couldn't blame her—he felt all of those and much more right now. Falling in step behind her, he realized they weren't in the same wing. Or the same level for that matter. They were up one. "Where . . . ?"

"You have been relocated to a suite," Rayan said without preamble. "It has two bedchambers, since you made such a spectacle of yourself this morning, Mr. Apollo. Windows and the shared bath are smaller, but I would advise you not to complain. The king was angry when he heard of the incident." He flung open the door and stepped aside. "In."

Leighton slipped in, head down.

Rayan produced the room key. "Remember to keep it locked at all times."

They had armed gunmen on the roof and perimeter walls. How far did they think someone would get?

"Clothes are in the dressing room," he said, then handed Owen a folio. "All the details. Zayna has already packed a trunk for Nouri and for you."

That was a little weird, having someone pack clothes and gear for him . . . clothes and gear that weren't his. "Thanks," he made himself say.

Rayan caught the shoulder fabric of Owen's kaftan and yanked him over. "Keep her in line, or you will not like what happens." He thrust him back, then released a taut breath, dark eyes telegraphing a warning. "Out there . . . *Be. Careful.*"

Dude totally just gave him Silence of the Lambs vibes right there. Half expected him to call him Clarice.

Owen felt the thrumming nerves and anger from Leighton too. "Understood." He deliberately put more room between him and the prince, trying to send the message he could leave. No idea what was going on, but there was too much to unpack with him in the room.

He looked over his shoulder and found Leighton down the hall.

"Get her under control," Rayan warned. "Maaz and Nasir will be on the safari as well, and they are not known for their patience."

Alarm speared Owen. He eyed the prince.

"They will silence her if you do not."

———— • ————

There were not many days when Leighton beat the sunrise. The humiliating command the prince had given Apollo to "get her under control" was infuriating to the point of tears. Unwilling to let either of them see her cry, she had fled to one of the bedrooms in the suite and stayed there for the rest of the day. Hadn't been able to sleep at the thought of fourteen days on a safari, far from anything she knew, far from hope and any semblance of control.

They rode in a Mercedes van to the airstrip where the royal jet waited. The monstrous thing was unlike anything she'd ever seen, complete with a movie theater, lounge with recliners, and cabins. She and Apollo had been ordered into a small, private area at the back that had a couch, table, and chairs.

"Do you know where we're headed?" she asked.

"Nairobi first," he said. As the plane took off, he flipped a black folio toward her on the table. "There's the itinerary. Would've shown it to you last night . . ."

Yeah, nice way to rub in that she'd given him the cold shoulder. Already regretting talking to him, she glanced at the folder and opened it. Definitely did not want to know when he planned to mess up everything. As she thumbed through it, she could not help but gape. "Nairobi, the Serengeti, Masai Mara in Kenya . . ." She breathed a laugh. "Is this even real?"

"It's extravagant. Guessing cost is upward of fifteen or twenty grand," he said, pinching the bridge of his nose. "Per person."

Shocked, Leighton faltered, letting her gaze drift over the royals and their entourage at the front of the jet. "Seriously? But there's like twenty people on this plane!"

"Eighteen." He shrugged. "When money's no object . . ."

"Not how I would spend money for a bachelorette party." She drew her legs up onto the couch and crisscrossed them. Watching as he reclined, slouching and resting his head on the back of the chair, she wondered how he'd slept last night. Had to have been better than the floor he used the previous night. Did he hate her?

She didn't care. Not true. She did care . . . He resented her, no doubt, because of her refusal to let him mess everything up. But she wasn't going to go quietly.

Right, she could just see that—him trying to get her out and she wrecks it. And someone would get hurt or killed.

Of course, there was a great way to avoid that—not trying to escape in the first place. Which was her preference.

No . . . not her preference—her need. *I want to go home.*

But . . . Ummi . . . Was it possible Ummi really was safe? If she believed him and he was wrong or had lied to her . . . the consequences—it'd be her fault. And what if he tried to get them out and failed? They'd get caught and Faruq would be enraged. Feral.

Elbows on her knees, she braced her head in her hands. She had no idea what was the right thing to do. She'd always followed Dad's instructions. He always had good explanations as to why she should do this or that. And always with love. "Did you see my dad before you came?"

Apollo opened his eyes and rolled his head in her direction. "Your dad?" He seemed to be shaking the dregs of sleep off. "You mean Na—"

"No. *He* is not my dad." Leighton recalled the hug Dad had

given her when she'd flown out. "It wasn't until I'd finished my sophomore year at Carnegie Mellon that I decided it was time to meet Ummi in person. My parents made all the arrangements. They were really cool about it, but . . ."

"You feel guilty."

"Maybe a little, especially now. But I'm worried about them." She shook her head. "All my life, I've lived in fear of this bad king"—she bounced her gaze to the royals to be sure nobody was close enough to hear her—"coming after us. Now, he has . . . and I wonder how my parents are doing."

"Sorry, I haven't communicated with them." He shifted, leaning forward in his chair as he threaded his fingers. "Your bio dad brought me and my dad into this."

Though Leighton wanted to ask what Navas was like, she wasn't really sure she wanted to know. Dad once let it slip that Navas was a mercenary. Not much else she needed to know beyond the fact he killed people for money. Yet his blood pumped in her veins, so . . .

"Look, I think our best course of action on this safari is to simply keep our distance from the royals. Heads down, mouths closed. Don't draw attention. Enjoy the trip, but—"

"Don't die doing it."

One side of his mouth quirked up. "*Not dying* is my MO."

She tried to smile. "This plan is because of what Prince Rayan said to you last night . . ."

His expression changed, morphed into something dark. "You heard . . ." He nodded. "It wasn't just about your behavior at Omnia but the threat that exists to your person—though he did not use those words specifically. Easy to read between the scowls."

Though she felt the words as if they'd been struck with a sledgehammer, she remained still.

"So, let's fly under the radar as much as possible, yeah?"

Four hours of a turbulence-free flight delivered them to the thriving metropolis of Kenya, where they climbed into vehicles and made the drive out of the city. The quaint safari lodge that would be their home for the next few days sat on a working farm perfectly situated against the forested slopes in a conservation area.

"Mercy," she murmured as they entered the ultra-modern facility with a coffee shop. "God does love me."

"I could've told you that," Apollo muttered.

"How?"

He shrugged. "He sent me, didn't He?"

It took everything in her not to laugh. "So, ego *and* arrogance."

"Didn't want one to feel left out."

This time she did roll her eyes, then took in the chic and classy area. Way more amenities than she'd expected on a safari, but she would not complain.

When she noticed the party slowing to enter the building, Leighton hung back, Apollo's warning ringing in her ears. She noticed Hassan hovering close to Princess Daria, who had forgone a headscarf, her naturally curly hair frizzing in the humid air.

Though Leighton considered forgoing hers, she guessed it would not be acceptable, despite the princess's example. When Apollo's presence pressed in, she drew up her courage and followed the royals. They snaked inside, and the guide called out names, assigning rooms. Nasir and Rayan would bunk together. Maaz would share a room with Hassan. Daria and Aliyah were splitting a room.

"Not again," Apollo muttered even as the guide turned to them, the last two standing in the hall.

Only then did she understand they were being forced together. "Maybe there's a bunk."

"Don't bet on it," he huffed as they were let into their room.

One bed.

"Called it," he grumbled.

She swallowed and heard the door click behind them. The walls were mostly glass with generous portions of steel. Not as luxurious as the palace but light-years beyond the tents or open ground she'd expected to camp on. Saw their luggage already at the foot of the bed. There was no couch or cushions for him to make his own bed. "I'll sleep on the floor," she offered.

"Over my rotten corpse." He walked the room, checking the closet and bathroom.

"Your rib is cracked," she reminded him.

"Like your head, if you think I'm letting you sleep on the floor while I crash on the bed."

"You do not have to be heroic about this. I—"

"You think I'm heroic?" He swung those blue eyes toward her with a crooked grin.

She sighed loudly. "Let's get an early dinner and fight over where to sleep later. I'm beat."

"Your wish . . ." he said, motioning to the door.

They headed down the hall and banked toward the main foyer. Doors on the left stood open to a high-ceilinged café. They made their way to the counter and ordered. Armed with burgers and fries a few minutes later, they sat at one of the small window tables.

"After that mushy, snotty stuff you forced me to eat," Apollo teased, "I can't wait to dig in."

"You are uncivilized."

"Thank you." He polished off the burger quickly, then munched his fries while she finished hers. He glanced out the window. "Look!"

When Leighton turned, she spotted the source of his excitement—down by the riverbank, three elephants and a baby were splashing into the waters. One trumpeted water over itself, cooling off. "That's so amazing," she said, wiping her mouth with a napkin. "I love elephants. Always have."

"African or Asian?"

"Yes." Then she laughed and shrugged. "I don't know, I think the African is a tad more majestic, but that's absurd. Majestic is majestic. Beautiful is beautiful."

Arms on the table, he watched her for a long minute, his baby blues tracking over her face. "Yeah . . ."

Her stomach squeezed at the way he watched her, making her swallow as he returned his gaze to the herd. And though she did the same, she let her gaze stray back to him. Sure to keep her head still so she wasn't caught. She couldn't help but admire the blond hair beneath the silly bleached strands. Bet with that dye gone, he'd be handsome. Well, he already was, dyed hair or not. And young . . . "How old are you?"

Surprise winged up his eyebrows, but he stayed focused on the wildlife. "How old do you think I am?"

"By your actions, thirtysomething, but that peach fuzz—"

"Peach fuzz?" he balked, sitting straight and ramming those blues into her. "That's rude."

"But true."

He glowered, then again watched the elephants. "I graduated early, got my dad to sign off on me entering the Army at seventeen. Qualified Ranger. Graduated Special Forces school."

She drew in a breath. "Wait, so you're Special Forces?"

Lips pursed, he drew back and folded his arms. "Spent five years chasing that dream but never got selected, so I got out."

"I guess I don't understand how that works, but it seems harsh that you graduated yet weren't picked."

"Tell me about it."

"Nouri."

At the commanding, intruding voice of Prince Rayan from a dozen paces away, she stiffened and looked down at their plates. "Yes?"

He came to their table. "We are going to the national park in the morning. Be in the courtyard at six."

She inclined her head.

Once Rayan moved away, Apollo leaned in. "I *hate* that."

She frowned. "What?"

"How you look down when they're around."

"It's better than getting backhanded," she quipped, cringing as her own words rang against her ears. "But really, Prince Rayan has been kind to me." She winced. "Well, the kind*est* of those here." How this had become her life, being a girl bowing at the feet of men who lorded over women and treated them worse than most people treated their dogs, she did not know.

But for Ummi . . . I do this for Ummi.

Apollo grunted. "I can't wait to get you out of here."

Skewering him with a warning look that said she did not want to fight, she wished he'd give up the idea of escape. "It's too dangerous."

His gaze locked on to hers, and somehow, despite her very obvious words, his blue eyes brightened. What on earth? Did he not understand English?

Oh, he definitely understood. Problem was, this guy took them as a personal challenge. He was going to be the death of her.

NINE

Nairobi, Kenya

WHILE SHE SHOWERED, HE PREPPED HIS own sleeping space on the small two-person couch. He'd have a few kinks in his neck and spine, but a day out on safari tomorrow should right him.

He touched the small scratch where they'd implanted the comms. It'd scabbed over, but he wished he could do like they did in sci-fi movies and tap it to activate the thing. He had a bad feeling the implant had been damaged when Hassan nailed him with that knifehand.

His mind drifted back to Dillon showing up at the hotel. What was going on? Was he okay? There hadn't been a chance to message the Scions. Send notice back to the 'rents that the hotheaded guy had been sighted again. But why there? What was he doing in Paris? Yeah, tracking someone . . . but that was light on intel and long on crazy. Maybe if Owen had been more like Dillon, he'd have earned his black beret.

But then . . . he wouldn't be here, drawing the ire of a beauty.

He smirked, remembering the fire light through her caramel

irises when she got mad. The way her mouth tightened, yet those lips were still full and—

"What are you doing? No!" Leighton appeared behind the couch and yanked the pillow out from under his head. "Nope, you are not going to put me in a position to feel guilty when Nasir or Maaz beat you again." She pitched his pillow at the bed. "Get on the bed."

Standing, he couldn't stop the scoff from escaping. *Nobody* would believe a beautiful princess had just ordered him into her bed. He lifted his palms. "I'm not doing that."

"Why?"

"Do you know what your dad does for a living?"

"He's a politician."

"I meant the biological one—you know, the *hired killer.*"

At that she faltered, but then fire lit her eyes again. She stomped to the couch and grabbed two cushions. "This is absurd. That bed is stupid-large. There is no reason"—with a grunt, she planted the cushions in the center, forming a line—"we can't both sleep on it without any impropriety."

If he did this, he'd either get her killed—by the royals—or himself killed—by her mercenary father. "Thank you, but I like living."

"You're being ridiculous. I'm not letting a man with a cracked rib sleep caddy-corner on a lumpy couch."

"It was actually pretty—"

She threw a pillow at him.

Owen ducked it, then gaped at her. "What—"

Next, a small narrow pillow winged his way.

"Hey!" *Oh no . . . No no no. This was just like . . .* "Stop."

Amusement made her smile as she reached for a shoe.

"Leighton, no." This was not happening. He pivoted and headed to the bathroom. Felt the shoe bean him in the head. Wincing, he stepped inside and locked the door. Set his face in his hands, trying so hard to block out the story Dad told him about the night in Venezuela between him and Mom.

He slumped back against the wall, tired. Weary. He slid down and tilted his head back. It wasn't that he was weak. And it definitely wasn't because she was into him. He wasn't addicted to painkillers like Dad had been, so . . .

The soft rap of her knuckles made him twinge. "Apollo?"

He exhaled heavily.

"Hey, sorry . . ."

He did not want her to apologize. Now he felt like an idiot for letting that hit him so wrong.

"Guess I didn't know you were a lightweight pillow fighter."

Eyebrows winging up at the taunt, he gave a breathy laugh.

"I'll go easier on you . . ."

Owen hopped up and opened the door. "Lightweight, huh?"

Mirth made her eyes glow brightly, and she tried to hide her smile but it bubbled into laughter. In shorts and a T-shirt, she backed up. "C'mon. Please—this shouldn't be a problem. We're adults, and it's not as if you like me."

His heart tripped over that—hadn't he assumed the same thing? Should he read into the fact she didn't say that *she* wasn't into *him*? Was she? More importantly, should he correct her lie? Even as he wondered that, she slipped between the sheets on her side and scooted down, then turned her back to his side.

Was this really happening?

He sat on the edge of the bed. *I am a man of honor and character.*

Yeah, Dad had been too.

With a silent groan, he stretched his neck and turned out the light. Then angled his head onto the pillow, doing his best to stay at the farthest edge of the mattress as possible without falling off. Sleep collided with him, hard and fast.

Owen snapped wide awake. Room still dark, he eyed the clock on the end table. 0430 hours. Wow, had he really slept six hours straight? Must've needed it. Afraid to move and wake Leighton, he stifled a yawn, then braced his side and drew himself off the mattress, careful not to disturb her. He glanced to her side of the bed.

Leighton lay on her back, staring at the ceiling, hair a dark halo around her head. Awake.

"You okay?"

She let out a small sigh. "You snore."

He froze. "Serious?"

"Loud and long," she said dramatically, rubbing her forehead. "I thought it was Mufasa calling the pride."

Covering his mouth, he tried to hide his laugh and failed. "I'm . . . I'm sorry. Why didn't you wake me?"

Leighton stabbed a hand down the line of pillows. "We had an agreement not to cross the line." She shrugged. "I felt bad that you slept on the floor last night and got beat up by Nasir. And the time Hassan jabbed his hand into your throat."

Shamed that he'd been so easily taken off guard by Hassan, Owen stood and tugged the blanket back into place. "Look, I'm wide awake. I'll sit on the couch, and you can grab an hour of uninterrupted sleep before we head out. First, let me get myself cleaned up."

He ducked into the bathroom and brushed his teeth, changed clothes, and put on deodorant. Light off, he opened the door and stepped out. He stopped short at finding the bed empty. A quick scan located her shadowy form in the corner, where she was tugging her dark hair out from under a black T-shirt. Realizing she'd changed, he frowned. "Thought you were going to rest."

"Too awake." She plodded over to the bathroom and slipped inside, closing the door behind her.

Feeling responsible that they were both up before the sun, he sat on the couch. From the packet Rayan gave them, he reviewed the itinerary in detail. If he managed to get word to Omen, they could be extracted while out here in free-rein country.

Leighton emerged and wandered over, sitting beside him. "So, what's today again? I slept since you told me . . ."

"We're first spending three days here on the bank of the Mbagathi River that borders Nairobi National Park."

"So, lions, tigers, and bears?"

He felt the barest hint of a smile again over her attempt at humor. "No bears, but definitely lions."

"Oh my."

That smile pushed past his carefully constructed barriers as he considered her for a long second. Her caramel gaze held his, ensnaring him.

Slowly, a knot formed between her brows.

"What?"

She wet her lips, then eyed the itinerary. "On one hand, I know I shouldn't enjoy this—they're holding me captive. I'm not here of my own volition. And we both agreed they might be trying to . . . get rid of me."

"That's not guaranteed."

"Granted," she conceded softly, "but it's a possibility. Right?"

He couldn't lie. "Yeah."

"So, here I am on a dream-of-a-lifetime trip . . . This should be enjoyed—I love wildlife, but I sit here wondering how they'll try to kill me."

A profound protective instinct shot through him. "I'm not going to let that happen. That's why I'm here."

"You're here because King Faruq hired you."

"*I'm here* because my team manipulated circumstances in Paris to put me on the king's radar."

Leighton started. "What? Are you—wait." She brushed the hair from her face, as if it got in the way of her thinking clearly. "So the robbery . . ."

"A setup."

"So you're *not* a hero . . ."

That dagger landed squarely between his fourth and fifth ribs, nailing his heart. He stood and grabbed his backpack. "We should get going."

"I didn't mean that the way it came out."

Owen shrugged into the pack. "All good." Cocking his head toward the door, he kept moving. "Ready?"

Though Leighton stood, she did so stiffly. Robotically. And Owen had this idea that the way things had shut down between them left her in a position that wasn't unlike the commands barked at her by the royals. Regret dug deep, but he had no idea how to walk that back.

Within the hour, they were in a soft-sided 4x4 safari Land Cruiser with a turret-like pop-top so people could stand to take better pictures. Or hired guns could protect the tourists. The party of eighteen, not including drivers, had packed into three different vehicles. Naturally, he and Leighton were assigned to the third one.

They'd no sooner reached the Cruiser than he noted Hassan glowering at him.

"Get in," Leighton hissed, pushing Owen toward the door. "Before he can hit you again."

Owen huffed. "I'm supposed to be protecting you."

"Well, protect me by protecting yourself. Go. In." With that, she shoved him forward.

To avoid clipping his shins on the footwell, he hiked his leg up and hauled himself past three rows of seats into the upper back.

A woman careened into him, laughing. "Rafi, stop!"

Owen braced to avoid whacking his skull against the window and shifted around. Found the petite princess—Aliyah, he thought they'd called her—laughing as she settled into the seat next to him. "That was not nice," she complained to a man Owen did not recognize. She gave him a coy look, flashing dimples that looked like craters.

Wait. Hold up. That was supposed to be Leighton's spot. Where—

Leighton stood with one foot in the step, staring at him.

"Oh, Nouri, here!" Aliyah patted the seat in front of her. "Sit here so I can talk to you."

Leighton gave Owen a desperate look, but climbed into the insisted-upon seat.

"Rafi, here, here," Aliyah shouted, patting the seat on her left in front of Owen.

"Yes, yes." The newcomer hiked into the seat next to Leighton and smiled at her. The guy had ink-black hair, eyes, brows, and a beard with a whole lot of mischief. "You must be Nouri. I have heard so much about you."

Leighton gave a shy nod and ducked.

"No, no," Aliyah said quietly, leaning toward Leighton and reaching around her to nudge up her chin. "We are going to have so much fun. No hiding, yes?"

Concern lanced Leighton's features as she yielded to the princess, but her gaze invariably found Owen again.

"Look, look." Rafi focused on someone standing near the first vehicle. "Ghalib!" he shouted, cupping his hands around his mouth. "You will miss out—this is the fun Cruiser." He gave a boisterous laugh.

The stocky Arab next to Crown Prince Maaz seemed to have lasers for eyes, which he dragged over Owen, then Leighton.

"Who is he?" Owen asked as Prince Rayan climbed in, indicated Rafi to switch seats.

"Ghalib?" Rafi asked, without missing a beat as he relocated to the seat in front of the one he vacated. "A terrible bore. Takes his duty as the crown prince's"—he considered Owen—"how would you American say it? . . . eh, *kiss-up* very seriously."

"Oh stop," Aliyah said with a laugh. "Ghalib is one of Maaz's principle advisors."

Everyone seemed carefree. Except Owen. He did not like that Rayan had inserted himself next to Leighton. That this Rafi deferred to the prince, which suggested Rafi held a lesser position.

"Ah, and there is the happy couple," Rafi pronounced as Daria and Hassan boarded the second vehicle.

"There is no way Daria would ride with Maaz. He is too much as Ghalib—grumpy."

Princess Aliyah had just given Owen a guidebook on who might make an attempt on Leighton's life. He'd need to monitor this Ghalib. They were soon underway, and it didn't take long to get from the lodge out to the first sighting—a herd of African buffaloes.

It kind of bugged him to be buried back here and not able to see Leighton's expressions or hear her thoughts as she experienced the safari.

"Oh, look!" Aliyah stretched in front of him to point out the zebras moving along at a slow clip.

Now directly in front of Owen, Prince Rayan leaned on the arm of his chair and said something to Leighton, who offered a small smile.

"So, where are you from?" Aliyah asked Owen with animation.

"America," he stated flatly.

"How long do you think you will stay in Jeddah?" Aliyah asked as the Land Cruiser jounced over the Nairobi plains.

"As long as it takes," Owen said, cursing himself since that cryptic answer might just beg more questions.

Leighton twitched in his direction but stopped herself when Rayan eased even further in.

Owen had a good mind to punch the guy in the head. Protecting her was his responsibility, right?

The driver banked off the beaten road and veered toward

an outcropping where he parked in line behind the other two Cruisers. He'd never been so relieved when everyone started exiting the vehicles. It took too long for the others to clear out so he could too. When he finally had boots on ground, he saw the royals moving en masse toward the edge of the outcropping.

"This is where the giraffes come," Aliyah said softly as she came up beside him. As far as Saudi princesses went, she was pretty—except for the craters in her cheeks. Dark hair flittered on the wind, free since Princess Daria had ruled no head coverings—for safety's sake—while on the trip.

"You've been here before?" he asked, eyeballing Rayan, who walked, hands behind his back, next to Leighton. Attentive. *Too* attentive.

"Mm, once a year for the last decade," Aliyah said. "I am used to it, but Daria loves it so much." She jutted her jaw to Leighton. "Nouri seems to like it too."

Yeah, but was it the wildlife she liked, or the prince's attention? How could Owen compete with that?

As if you have a chance with her.

"Do you have a favorite, Apollo?"

Favorite girl? He frowned down at the petite princess. "What?"

With a smile that exposed those pits again, she nodded beyond the group. "Elephants? Giraffes?"

"Oh." He roughed a hand over his face. "I . . . lions, I guess."

"You are not sure?" she teased with a soft laugh.

"I'm sure." Gaze straying to Leighton in her gray kaftan, walking almost shoulder to shoulder with the prince, Owen clenched his jaw. Scanned the rest of the entourage and found that dude—Ghalib—with his cold, flat eyes boring into Leighton. The realization had Owen negotiating his way to her. Keeping his attention focused on the stocky guy, he paced her, hands at his side in readiness. He heard the soft padding of the princess as she trailed him.

"Here they come!" Daria exclaimed, moving to the edge of the outcropping.

"She had an argument with Hassan before coming," Aliyah mused. "She wanted to bring food so the animals would come closer."

"He wisely helped her see it was a bad idea," Prince Rayan said as his gaze rammed into Owen and locked for a second in which he effectively conveyed his taut disapproval at Owen keeping a tight protective perimeter on Leighton.

Minutes later, the giraffes glided over to the royal troop.

As much as he wanted to act tough, the sight of the two adult giraffes keeping their calf between them stilled Owen. He knew his mom would love this.

"Giraffes are the tallest land mammals," Kiango, the safari guide, said in a level voice as Hassan hovered protectively by his princess, who stretched her hand toward the giraffe. "Males grow as tall as five-point-five meters and can weigh as much as 1,900 kilograms. Females grow up to four-point-eight meters and weigh up to 1,180 kilograms."

"They are so elegant," Aliyah whispered.

"Like our fingerprints or DNA," Kiango continued, "their spot patterns are unique to each one. No two are alike."

Leighton hung back, one arm across her middle and the other covering her mouth in amazement. If the royals hadn't been so determined to keep her on the fringes and in subservience, she'd probably go up and touch the giraffe too. But she stayed there, being robbed of the incredible experience.

He started toward her, to urge her to enjoy this moment too, but before he'd taken two steps, Prince Rayan hooked an arm around her shoulder, motioning her forward.

Frustrated with the way the guy kept showering her with attention, Owen had the sudden and angering idea that this prince, with one kind gesture, could change everything for Leighton. If he showed the others she was accepted, the others might let her in too. No more abuse. But what if this guy had other motives?

"Come," Aliyah said, tugging Owen's arm. "Closer." She drew him over and pushed past the others to get her chance. With one more turn, she lost the grip on his sleeve, allowing him to fall back.

Positioned as an outlier, he felt this strange twisting in his chest. A tightening, as Rayan laughed and got to experience the giraffes with Leighton.

Amazement spread through Leighton that, as she offered her hand, the giraffe nudged it. Then its long tongue dragged over her palm, as if rooting for a bite.

Rayan caught her shoulders. "Careful. We don't want him to drag you away."

She must confess—this was the most wonderful place she'd ever been to, though she did wish the prince would remove his hands. She glanced around, only then realizing she was looking for Apollo.

Wait. Where was her would-be protector? Sidestepping, she gave room for the others to pass, still amazed the prince had led her to the front of the group and nobody—like Maaz or one of the other royals—had objected.

"Rayan."

Ah. Right on cue—that stiff voice belonged to the one and only Maaz.

"She needs to wait till Daria and the others have enjoyed the sight."

"There is plenty of time for all, Cousin," Rayan countered, staying near her at the edge.

A yelp erupted from the side, drawing attention to Aliyah

struggling against one of the adult giraffes, which had her abaya between its teeth.

Apollo intervened, finally managing to convince the elegant animal to release it. Laughter billowed out from Aliyah and Rafi as Apollo ensured the princess was okay. She gave him a laugh, but there was definitely a coyness about that smile, wielding those cute dimples. Everything about the princess was cute—her face, her clothes, her laugh . . . Great mercies, how many times would she flash her dimples at Apollo? Was that what he liked?

Princess Daria's close friend, Inas, whom she'd introduced when they first got out of the vehicles, made her way to Apollo. Joined the trio and more laughter trilled at something she said.

Aliyah stumbled and fell right into Apollo's arms.

Oh, groan! That was as cliché as the day was long. Surely Apollo had a better head on his shoulders than to fall for something like that.

Yet he laughed as he righted her.

Just as Ghalib rushed at Owen and shoved him away. "Do not touch her! Never touch her or I will gut you!"

Startled by the outburst, the giraffes loped away.

Hands up, Owen backstepped, but a dark storm rolled into his blue eyes.

Effervescent Rafi moved between the two, holding his arms out to either side. "Whoa, whoa. Come. Back to the vehicles. Kiango says it is time to move on before the day gets too hot, like your tempers." He laughed, but he was the only one.

"Nouri," Rayan said, his voice neutral yet authoritative.

Something about that set Leighton's teeth on edge. Yet, she followed him back to the Land Cruiser. This time, she hurried up into the back, hoping Rayan would wait for the others so Apollo could claim the seat next to her, but nope.

The prince was right behind and took the seat.

She didn't get it—Rayan had to know there was no chance

for anything between them. While King Faruq might keep her at Jeddah, it was only a display of power. Until Ummi was back under his control.

She tried to catch Owen's gaze as he climbed in, but he offered his hand like a gentleman to help Aliyah into the seat before her, then he hiked in next to her.

"I am truly sorry for Ghalib's violence," Aliyah said, her pretty face wrought.

Without responding, Owen peered out the side window as it pulled away.

Leighton probably shouldn't, but she found a perverse delight in the way he ignored the princess the whole half hour that delivered them to a plain with chest-high vegetation. In the distance, a scraggly tree gnarled its branches over the terrain and supported a cheetah that was lazing about. It looked so chill and uninterested in the entourage.

"Look!" Aliyah caught Apollo's arm and pointed to something behind them.

He looked and visibly tensed.

Leighton checked to see what made him startle and spotted a lioness ambling in their direction. A thread of amazement wove through her—along with one of fear. It was so close.

"Do not get out," their driver said in both Arabic and English. "Keep your hands to yourself."

Heart pounding, she watched as a lion emerged from the foliage and loped alongside the female. Ohhhh, he was so beautiful. Regal. But . . . were they safe in the Land Cruiser? Could the lions get inside?

Aliyah and Rafi used their phones to take pictures, and not for the first time did Leighton wish she had hers to capture the breathtaking moment. Unbelievably, the pair ambled past, the human intruders apparently so commonplace that the beasts were unfazed. The driver resumed their slow trek across the plain. It was crazy seeing the wildlife amid the backdrop of the bustling city of Nairobi and its skyscrapers in the distance. Her mind wrestled with the dichotomy of being around wildlife yet feeling safe. They saw more African buffaloes and a herd of wildebeests trudging toward a small watering hole.

Even as a headache threatened, she heard the driver announce it was time to head back to the lodge because the rising temperatures would make wildlife seek shelter and be less likely to interact. Disappointment clung to her as they turned around.

Back at the lodge, she climbed out of the vehicle. Even as her boot hit the ground, she felt . . . off. Out of sorts. She shifted and glanced back, immediately searching for Apollo. Wondering why she so keenly felt the loss of his presence when he was not someone she was used to being around. They'd only known each other a week!

But where was he? Wasn't he supposed to be guarding her? She glanced around and finally located him with Aliyah and Inas. Why was he with the princess? Again! When he finally looked at Leighton, she stepped back at the ferocity in his eyes. The hard edge. What . . . ?

That's when she noticed Ghalib storming in her direction. *What did I do now?* The guard barked at Rayan to come with him and kept moving.

Kindness ever his shield, Rayan inclined his head. "I will see you later." With that, he intercepted Ghalib, and they both joined the crown prince. When the entourage of men spared her a glance, then left in a huddle, she had a bad feeling.

They'd pulled Rayan away . . . Aliyah was distracting Apollo . . . Was this it? Was this when they planned to kill her?

Weary of the tension and cruelty, she couldn't help but look at Apollo, who was even now staring after Aliyah as she hooked arms with Inas and headed into the lodge.

Sadness infiltrated her weariness. It was no big surprise that a gorgeous guy like Owen would be into a beautiful princess with cute dimples and a sweet laugh. But surely he saw through her sweet act? Just like Leighton saw through Rayan's. After all, Ghalib had all but attacked him for saving Aliyah earlier when she "tripped." No way any of them would authorize a relationship between an American and their apparently sacred bloodline.

"Where is your guard?" demanded Prince Maaz from the other side of the stone courtyard.

Turning, she felt an explosion of icy heat hit her with his ferocious scowl. "I . . ."

"Right here," Apollo said, manifesting at her side.

Stiffening, she shot a look between the two alpha males.

"*Stay* together," Maaz ordered, then returned to the other men with him.

"Walk with me." Apollo started toward the open field that hemmed in the lodge, café, and pool.

You know what? She was really tired of being ordered around. "Why? Is Aliyah too busy?" Leighton nearly choked on her jealous words but was relieved when he kept moving. Though she felt catty, it miffed her more than a little that it hadn't earned at least some kind of a reaction from him. As the distance grew between them, she felt the prickly gaze of the royals on her back and made herself follow. Each step, however, pounded her irritation into a roiling ball of anger.

"What is your problem?" she hissed when she got within earshot.

He said nothing but stopped, scanning the wheat-like field, eyes narrowed.

"And what is with ordering me around? I expect that from them, but not you!" Heart pounding, she gritted her teeth that he hadn't looked at her or replied. "What are you doing? I'm talking to you!"

"Quiet," he hissed.

She lifted her brows. "Excuse me?" Fists balled, she shifted around. "Why won't you . . . ?" Awareness stabbed through her, the intensity in his expression. Nerves and fears thrummed. Had he seen a wild animal in the tall grass? She swallowed and stepped back "What is it?"

Recognition hit his gaze and he shifted course, moving to the right.

Resisting the urge to catch his sleeve—half out of protection and half out of the pulsing need to smack him for ignoring her, she stayed at his side. No idea what he was doing. But hey, they were away from the royals, and he needed to understand about the princess. "Don't you think Aliyah is acting weird?"

His shoulder lifted in a shrug. "Not really." Again, he seemed to be searching for something, frowning.

"Really? All that—*I'm falling and need you to catch me*?"

His blue eyes swung to her with a smirk that had more than a little amusement in it. "Hold up—is that jealousy, princess?"

"Do *not* call me that," she growled. "And no! It's not jealousy." Liar. "Something isn't right. They're acting strange."

"So, it's okay for you to flirt and carry on with Prince Rayan, but when I can't seem to ditch Ali, you—"

"*Ali?*"

"—you suddenly say something is wrong."

"That's not—it's not—" Ugh. She hated her tied tongue and inability to make him listen. To think past her own drumming heart. Had to set aside whatever it was that had her making inane comments about the princess and get to the point. "They're being *too* nice, Apollo. Her *and* Rayan."

"I know." He gave a cockeyed nod and returned his attention to the terrain. Tilted his head again, craned his neck as he squinted, then moved in that direction.

"*What* are you doing?" she hissed, exasperated. "Look, I don't have many people that I can talk to, so can you stop ignoring me and get over your jealousy that Rayan actually seems interested in me?" Okay, she had zero idea why she'd said that, because she didn't *want* the prince interested in her. And she especially regretted her words the instant his gaze rounded on her. "Forget I said that. I—"

"Hey." He shifted to her. Set a hand on her arm. His gaze was weighted, blue eyes shifting past her, toward the house. "Just . . . don't scream."

Breath trapped in her throat, she froze. What had he seen? "Is it a lion? Jackal?" Fear strangled her and forbade her from moving.

"The royals are watching." Apollo extended a staying hand to her, then spoke quietly, "Go ahead, Rawlins."

Rawlins? What in the world—

"You sure?" came a preternatural voice from directly *at her feet.*

She tried. Sweet mercies, she tried not to scream, but confusion and shock arrested her good sense when she saw the grass roll . . . and reveal a heavily camouflaged face. She stumbled back with a strangled yelp.

The voice continued. "Sounds like this lover's quarrel isn't done."

"Hey," Owen rasped to her, lifting his eyebrows in meaning. "Easy."

Inhaling a breath at what was happening—someone he knew was here, in the grass—she saw disappointment in Apollo's gaze that she'd reacted when he'd warned her not to. But what really churned so much outrage through her chest was that this was one of his team, which meant he'd completely ignored her wishes.

Air staggered through her lungs, easing the clamp on her chest. "Are you kidding me right now?" she snarled and flung a hand toward the lodge. "They're right there!"

"Nouri—"

"No!" she snapped and drew straight. "No!" She stomped a foot. Turned, then seeing the curious gazes focused on them, whipped back to him. Stabbing a finger at him, knowing the royals would just assume the same thing his buddy had. "You do not get to chide me!" She shoved her palms against her forehead and pushed up till she dug her fingers into her hair. "I told you—*told* you I did not want *this*." She pointed down, too late realizing the mistake. "I can't believe you." Backing up, she shook her head. "I thought better of you."

———— • ————

"Nouri!" Owen thought to go after her, but there was a reason Rawlins had put his sniper skills to use and low-crawled this far in, putting his life at risk. Pivoting back, he threw a fist in the air—half for good measure since he was being watched and half because he was ticked. "Why are you here, Rawlins?" he spoke straight ahead, hoping it would look to the royals like he was ranting to the elements.

"Your comms isn't working."

He stared toward the high-rise in the distance, recalling when Hassan had struck him in the neck. "A throat punch will do that."

"Some guys just have all the fun. Comms device at your feet," Rawlins stated. "Extraction at Masai Mara. Be ready."

Those words thudded against his conscience, blurring with the ones Leighton had just hissed at him. "I don't know that she'll go."

"Chief says to get your head on straight. She's emotionally compromised and doesn't get a vote. You were put here to get her out, not ask her opinion."

"You sorry—"

"Not my words, man. Take it up with the chief."

"I will." Owen lowered himself to a crouch, plucked a stalk of grass with one hand, and found the device with the other. "This whole thing is muffed up."

"Tell me about it. I've got ticks sucking me dry, and you're playing cozy with a princess whose father is a merc." The grass rolled and the camo face vanished in an impressive, stealthy fluid motion. "Not sure if you're lucky like your dad or just plain dumb."

"Just dumb." He had, after all, volunteered for this.

The slow, almost casual roll of the grass easily blended into the soft, teasing fingers of the wind across the plain. "Get it done, Apollo."

He pushed upright, took a breath, and glanced at the lodge—yep, guards were watching and Maaz was heading over. Owen braced for impact, sliding the comms device into his pocket. Nostrils flaring, he prayed nobody caught on to the drop that just took place out here.

"You are not to leave her!" Maaz barked as he closed in on him. "Or you will both be locked in the room until I can have you flown back to Jeddah and secured in the dungeon."

"You'd be doing me a favor," Owen bit back. The anger wasn't a mask this time—it ticked him off that she wanted to stay here. What, had she really developed feelings for Rayan?

The prince stepped into his path.

Owen stopped short to avoid a collision and prayed this wasn't about to get ugly. Instead of meeting the prince's gaze—which he guessed would be taken as an open challenge—he focused on the half dozen guards who peeled away from the building's shadows.

"You forget your place, Mr. Apollo."

Now Owen couldn't help but look into the dark eyes. "With a cracked rib and bruised neck, kind of hard to forget."

Maaz's cheek tightened. "The king hired you to protect Nouri. How can you do that if you cannot even see her?" Malice colored the prince's visage. "What if she is, even now, having the life cut from her lungs as you sit out here and pout instead of taking her in hand?"

The question seemed like more . . . like a threat. No, a promise. Or a warning. Owen's gaze slammed toward the building. He spotted Rayan and Nasir. But no Hassan. No Ghalib.

He flicked his gaze to the prince, who smirked, then brushed past him. Did everything in his power not to break into a sprint. Where was she? He would kill anyone who went after her!

Inside, he swept the area in search of her. His gaze collided with Rayan, and he envisioned punching that straight nose right into the guy's gray matter. He shoved aside the impulse, noting more than a little concern in the guy's expression. "Have you seen her?"

Hesitating for a second, the prince stood in silent challenge.

Owen could not believe Rayan wanted to challenge him. "Where is she?" When no answer came, he surged at the prince. "So help me, if anyone hurts her—"

A voice—*her* voice—in conversation sailed through the open restaurant doors.

Punched the burning air from his lungs. *Thank You, God!* Relief and anger warred that she had left him. That she was sitting in the open, public. Smart girl—that way, he was less likely to rail at her.

That's what she thinks.

Sliding a smug smile at the prince—it was petty, yeah, but it felt good—he pivoted and headed into the restaurant. Easily spotted her at the same table they'd been sitting at yesterday. However, this time, Aliyah was with her.

The princess's wide, wary eyes rose to him. "Mr. Apollo . . ."

He didn't miss the stiffness in her words. Or that she was referring to him as "mister" again.

Leighton shrank in on herself, hugging her arms. Avoiding his gaze.

Thoughts tangled and roiling, he told himself to get it together like Pike had warned. She was safe—that was the point. Acutely aware of the eyes on them, he pulled a chair up next to her and sat. But as soon as he did, he knew he couldn't maintain this façade. "We need to talk."

"I don't want to talk," she growled.

"We *need* to," he repeated, adding emphasis.

"Nouri, is there a problem?" Rayan stood at the

table—again—fingers pressed to the black. "You seem uncomfortable."

Really? The guy was going to play loyal protector now? Where was he when everyone was ignoring her or backhanding her? Either way, Owen wasn't playing this game. He rose. "King Faruq tasked me—"

"Hey." She caught his arm and pulled him back down to the chair, shooting a manufactured smile to the prince. "I'm okay. Really. Thank you."

Sitting, Owen met the guy's gaze and held it. Sick as it might sound, this felt like that time he'd trained his family's Belgian Malinois and knew if he looked away, Echo would assume the alpha role. And while the prince might have everything—money, power, control, the interest of Leighton—Owen would *never* submit to him.

"You two were arguing in the field," Rayan persisted. "What was that about?"

Her hand was still on his arm, and he felt it tighten, then slip away. "I . . ."

Owen shifted his gaze to hers and stilled at what he saw. Not a threat, but something far worse—belief. Belief that if she told the prince what Omen had planned, that there was an operator out in the fields, it would stop Owen from extracting her. He felt sick.

Please . . . please do not do this, he silently begged her, locked in a visual duel with her.

She wet her lips, gaze sliding back to the prince. "He—"

"*Religieuse*," Owen subvocalized for her ears only.

Leighton's eyes shuttered closed. She swallowed. "N-nothing." She gave a nod to the prince. "It was just a long day."

"That argument did not look like nothing."

Enough already, Prince. "It's my job to protect her, Prince Rayan. Even when she doesn't like it." But as the words left his mouth, Owen knew they had too much edge. "Sometimes, when I suggest things for her safety and protection, it's not what she wants to hear."

Why was he explaining anything to this guy?

"And sometimes," Leighton spat back, "*he* thinks too much of himself, as if he is my master."

Aliyah scowled at Owen, and the prince shifted into a more possessive stance.

The impact of that accusation felt nuclear, shifting Owen's gaze to hers. "No." Was that really what she thought? How she felt? Regret tore at him. "*Never.*"

Surprise leapt through her olive complexion, but like him, she was skilled at holding her ground. "It felt that way."

He had a choice—stay mad, maintain his position in the standoff with Rayan, or let it go and make peace with her. He had never been one to back down, but he realized in that silent duel between them that Leighton held a power over him none else had. "I'm sorry," he said, releasing his venom and pride. "That was unintentional. You are prisoner enough in this life, and I would not be a part in that."

Searching caramel eyes glinted in the afternoon sun that pierced the window. A clear yearning to believe what he said seemed to soften her features. The slightest bob of her head hinted that she accepted his apology.

"Nouri?" Rayan prompted.

Sitting back, she touched her temple. "Thank you for your concern, Your Highness. It has been a long, hot day, and I think I need to eat and rest."

"I can get you something," he offered.

Owen resisted the urge to roll his eyes. Well, he'd meant to, but Mom always said the Metcalfe blues had a life of their own.

Aliyah snickered at his lack of restraint.

Stiffening, the prince tightened his jaw then refocused on her.

"There is a dinner tonight at eight with the wedding party," he said as he stepped back. "You can be my guest, Nouri."

Rankled at the way those words were not an invitation or a request—it seemed more an order—Owen huffed. "Why would she need to be a *guest*? She's a member of the wedding party, right?"

"She is—"

"It's okay," she said to Owen, setting her hand on his arm again. Then she looked up at the prince. "Thank you for your kindness. I accept."

Why in black blazes was she agreeing to that?

"You mentioned wanting to rest," Owen suggested, coming to his feet. Anything to get her away from this guy. Something wasn't adding up. Like she'd said—the royals were suddenly being *too* nice.

"Yes, of course," she said as she stood and inclined her head to the prince. "Again, thank you."

"Until later," Rayan said solemnly, then shifted aside. In a blink, he skewered Owen with a menacing look and pushed into his space. "You should do your job better. She could have been injured out there."

Owen moved into the challenge. "Says the man who watched her get punched by another man and did nothing to stop it."

Rayan twitched, myriad expressions flickering through his dark features. "How—"

Leighton spun to Owen and set her hands to his chest, urging him back. "No," she said emphatically. "Please."

Jaw clenched, he indicated toward the doors. Paced her across the lobby and down the hall to their suite. There, he punched in the room code and let them in.

Leighton moved robotically to the sofa, sat down, and dropped her face into her hands. Quiet sobs shattered whatever bravado had buffeted Owen into facing off with a prince whose uncle held

both their lives in his hands.
Rawlins had it right—Owen was dumb.

TEN

Nairobi, Kenya

I CAN'T DO IT," SHE SOBBED INTO HER HANDS, shoulders bouncing beneath the torment. "I can't do this, Apollo."

"Do what?"

"Escape—I just can't. I have to stay." She lowered her hands, staring at him. "I can…*feel* it," she said with a particular emphasis, followed closely by another shuddering breath. "In my core, I know it's wrong."

"What's wrong? Getting out of here? Getting away from—"

"No!" she balked, angrily smearing away the tears and more than a little irritated with the challenge in his tone. A buzzing tingled beneath her skin, like something trying to get out. It forced her to pace around the back of the couch.

Apollo exhaled heavily. "Okay—so, what *is* wrong?"

The irritation bubbled and simmered at having to explain. Again. Leighton struck a hand in the direction where they'd left the royals. "Him. All of them." She motioned to Apollo. "You." The man who was trying to get her to bail. Abandon and compromise the very purpose she'd served her entire life.

But what if Ummi was okay? What if she could do this? Worse—what if she fed into those beliefs and it turned out she was wrong—then Ummi got hurt or killed?

Leighton pressed the heels of her hands to her eyes and moaned. "It's too much . . . too much."

"Hey . . ."

Breath staggering and feeling miserable, she looked at him, perched on the edge of the table, those blue eyes laced with—sympathy! Ugh! "Don't." She turned away. "Don't look at me as if I'm some weak, broken creature in need of rescuing."

"I . . . never said that," he muttered. "But look at the situation—they're not your friends."

Massaging her forehead, she knew he was right, but she so badly needed this to work out. So she could protect Ummi. Though guilt harangued her, she fixated on the guy hidden in the grass. "He was someone from your team, right?"

Apollo blinked. "Wha—oh." He sighed. "Yeah."

Anger again bubbled to the fore. "I can't believe you *completely* disregarded my wishes in that regard." Arms crossed, she resumed her trek. "But it doesn't matter—I won't go with you. Ummi—"

"*Is safe*," he ground out, frustration turning his tone into pleading. "How many times do I have to say that? What will it take to convince you—"

"It doesn't matter how many times you say it!" she railed, the edges of panic sawing at the thin threads of control she held. "*I* was safe. For twenty-five years, I survived, did everything exactly right. Obeyed the rules. Kept the secret. Lived the secret. Became the secret!"

She threw up her hands, tears pricking, and resumed pacing. Anything to deal with the volatility thrumming in her veins. "As a college graduation gift to myself, I visit London and Ummi for the first time—a lifetime-dream-come-true. It's great! Everything I ever dreamed of—and trust me, I *dreamed*. Every night. Every holiday. Every Parents' Day at school that she would be there. That I would know her. Know what she was like. What parts of me were from her. So, there I am relaxing, feeling like I can breathe for the first time in . . . ever!" Tears slipped down her cheeks, releasing the pent-up frustration. "Shopping, pastries, laughter. Me and Ummi as I'd always hoped. Then we visit a London shopping center where I try on a cute top. When I come out, I sense . . . something behind me. Next thing I know, I'm being beaten awake in a dungeon on the other side of the world!"

"I'm truly sorry this has happened to you." A storm rolled into his expression as he came to his feet. "But if that isn't a reason to escape—them kidnapping and beating you—then I don't know what is. My team—"

"Don't you get it? You *can't* protect me from them! They have *everything*—the money, the power, the control!"

"No, they don't," he said, stepping closer. "They don't have—"

"They *do*!" she shouted, winging away from him, too angry with his distorted view of *her* life and problem—and his arrogant belief that he could accomplish what no one had yet been able to do: free her of a lifetime imprisonment with the secret. "They're planning something—that's why Rayan and Aliyah are being nice. Even you said it." Just saying it fed the panic but also gave voice to the nagging at the back of her brain. "I just . . . I can *see* it in his eyes. Feel it in the way they look at me. There's . . . it's just . . . augh!!"

Never had she felt so unhinged. What on earth was wrong with her?

"Hey, hey." Somehow he'd erased the gap between them and took hold of her shoulders, pulling her close.

"No, no . . ." Though Leighton wanted to flee, she welcomed the ripple of strength coming from Apollo.

"Fear is having a rave in your mind, Nouri."

She resisted, mentally argued—but for some strange reason, she didn't back away this time. Didn't refuse his touch when it landed on her upper arms. "Call me Leighton." Why was she telling him to do that?

Because I'm tired of all the lies and subterfuge.

"No matter what happens, Leighton," he said with particular emphasis, "I want to see you freed from this mental terror that has held you hostage."

Tired of fighting, tired of being on the defensive *every* second of *every* day, she wilted at those words. At hearing someone see her, see the agony in her chest. She yielded to his gentle urging into his embrace. As his arms wrapped around her, she savored the warmth chasing off the chill that had consumed her, and unlocked the fortress walls around her heart, behind which she'd hidden for two decades.

A torrent of grief erupted. Feeling his hand slide around her back and draw her even closer, she surrendered. Dropped her forehead against his chest, weeping. No more . . . She couldn't do this anymore. "I'm so tired . . . of everything."

His other hand cradled her head. "What you've gone through is unfair."

The words rumbling through his chest beneath her ear were strangely comforting. "I've tried," she sniffled into his shoulder, wanting to hide there. No, not *hide—shelter* from the ravenous world eating away at her soul. "I've tried to be what they wanted me to be. Tried not to upset or anger them. I even let Rayan think I like him, but it"—she shuddered—"it terrifies me."

"What does?"

"Where it could lead."

Apollo stiffened. "You mean marriage?"

Leighton jerked up to look into his eyes. "What? No!" Their faces were a whisper apart, ramping up her heart, so she eased out of his embrace. "They're trying to kill me! His interest—Aliyah's kindness, his—it's all a trap. A ruse to get me to relax and . . . and . . ." She moaned. "I don't know what. Or why." Holding her throbbing head, she walked the room again. "I thought he was nice—he'd been kind to me."

"Correction, the kindest of these royals. But that's not true kindness."

She gave a conceding bob of her head. "My point is that I trusted him. And I don't want to believe he's trying to lure me into complacency." She rubbed her forehead where a tension headache was brewing. "I should be ashamed, because what other explanation is there for his sudden attention?"

Apollo sniffed. "That you're beautiful? Intelligent—"

Though his words made her pulse race, she scoffed and pivoted. "The men of the Central Kingdom do not know how to appreciate a woman with a brain." She wilted again and dropped onto the couch again. "I thought, *just play along, Leighton—it doesn't matter as long as Ummi stays alive.*" Letting out a long groan, she tilted her head against the back of the couch and stared up at the gold light fixture. "But my conscience won't let me lie to him." She harrumphed and straightened, folding her arms. "I'm sure it's all over my face that I don't like him, at least not in that way, so lying to him will only make matters worse. No matter how I try to shield my indifference"—she huffed and held both splayed hands in front of her face—"it's right there."

Apollo came around and sat on the chair opposite her, his expression inscrutable. He studied her for a second. "You're not as masterful with that indifference as you might believe."

"What . . . ?"

"I am fairly sure everyone, me included, bought that you were . . . into him. That the flirting today was real."

"*Flirting?*" she balked, widening her eyes. "I was not flirting with him!"

"Then you're an expert-level faker, because I seriously considered punching the guy into next year more than once." He gave a lopsided nod. "The fact that his uncle could have me executed kept me in check."

Though an incredulous laugh escaped her, Leighton stared at him for a long minute. Was he serious? She took in his blue eyes, that squared jaw. Recalled how he'd intercepted Nasir when he'd tried to assault her. "You were . . . *jealous*?" Why did that make her heart skip a beat? But— "You were flirting with Aliyah."

He chortled. "Not in this or *any* lifetime. Every time I turned around—*bam*, she was right there. Couldn't get away from her. Though, God knows I tried."

Was he serious that he didn't like the princess? "But why? She's cute, bubbly. And she likes you—she told me."

"She's *not* cute," he countered, forcefully slicing a hand toward the ground, "and I don't care what she thinks of me. It's not a requisite to getting my job done."

Leighton found it hard to believe. "Everything about her is perfect—her eyes, her smile, those dimples—"

"You mean the *craters*."

Laughing at that word, she stilled. It wasn't funny. Not really. Her mind churned over his emphatic use of that word and how his curled lip confirmed it. His sky-blue eyes were laden with conviction and mortification.

A tremor of relief trickled through her. "You really don't find her attractive?" No idea why she asked again except that she wanted—*needed*—to hear him say it again.

"No."

"Not even a little?" *Don't be desperate, Leighton.*

Apollo hesitated, mouth opening to say something . . . but he didn't. His gaze trekked over her face.

Ah, right. A swift twinge of sadness and disappointment rushed through her. "Ah"—wow, that hurt—"so you do like—"

"No," he snapped. "I *don't*."

"Then why did you hesitate?"

"Because," he said with a half laugh, "I can't believe we're having this conversation."

"Why not? I had to talk about Rayan."

Head cocked to the side, he sniffed and looked away. "You didn't *have* to . . ." That edge had returned to his voice. He *was* jealous.

Her heart pitter-pattered all over that little revelation. It wasn't exactly him saying he found her attractive. And while she might've teased him about jealousy before, she hadn't been serious. In no way considered it could be true. This guy—this *gorgeous* guy she'd seen two years ago, then committed his face and smile to memory—*liked* her?

Could he be jealous but not like her? She did notice how he'd met her eyes across the barn several times at the graduation party. Why had he been there? Even then, he'd been impressive and attention-commanding. "What's your relationship with Sophia?"

He blinked and shook his head. "That came out of left field."

"Avoiding the question?"

"No, you're giving me whiplash with the change of direction."

Still hadn't answered. Disappointment tugged at Leighton, making her way to move away. "Got it." Was Sophia the reason he didn't like Aliyah? Chewing her thumbnail, she headed to the bed and hiked onto the mattress. That he didn't answer hurt more than all his earlier denials.

"Leighton." With a sigh, Apollo crossed the room and stood in front of her, angling his head a bit to look her in the eyes. "I've known Sophia since she was born. Our dads worked together." He slumped back against the mattress next to her. "There's a dozen of us—we call ourselves the Scions and watch out for each other. Soph and I are close—but more like siblings. For some reason, despite our age difference, Soph and I connected."

"She's pretty too." Why did she feel so pathetic pointing that out? "At the party, you hung out with her. Exclusively."

Apollo side-eyed her. "Because I didn't know anyone besides her and her twin brother. For parties and events, Soph always orders me to be her date so she doesn't have to deal with guys hitting on her." He elbowed her. "Speaking of that party, you sure bugged out fast."

Leighton tried to hide the flush rising through her cheeks. He knew about her big secret, so she might as well fill in the rest. "I noticed you watching me . . ."

"And you were watching me." He smirked. "Which I wasn't mad about, in case you were wondering."

Fluttering swarmed her belly, spilling warmth over her shoulders. What would it have been like back then, if she'd felt free to have a boyfriend? To talk to him? "At that point in my life, someone like you was too much to risk."

"Someone like me."

This time, she bumped his shoulder. "Don't be offended. I just had to keep a secret. Letting anyone into my life was dangerous. My parents and I kept my life very ordered, strictly so. Because if we weren't careful enough . . ." She sighed and chewed the side of her cheek. "It happened once. Middle school. You know how it is—you're besties and there are *zero* secrets or you're not real friends." It had been so absurd, so . . . awful. "Kezra knew I had a secret, and she was *relentless* in begging me to tell her. She did this whole ridiculous blood-oath circle thing, but it felt real, ya know?" Even now, remembering . . .

"You told her."

Leighton nodded, still disappointed in herself. "I knew I shouldn't, but she had been so nice. And she was popular, brought me into that circle, so I figured—why not?"

"And it backfired."

"Hugely. She told the entire seventh grade. My parents transferred me to a private school at that point, even considered moving out of state, but that school . . . they were convinced it'd be safe."

"Liberty?" he asked.

She managed a half smile and nodded. "Six years later, I was standing in a barn with friends and there was this guy who was . . ."

"Handsome?"

She laughed. "*Intense*. Every time I shifted to get out of your line of sight, two seconds later, there you were, homed in again."

He grunted an acknowledgment.

Would he fess up to why he'd done that? Or was this going to be another stalemate? He was an expert at those. "Then I saw you plowing through the crowd, coming my way, and I knew it was time to leave."

"Ah, so you *did* run away from me."

"It was more . . . *avoiding* an encounter that had no future or good ending."

"Which turned out to be not entirely true," he countered. "Because here we are."

While Apollo already knew her big secret, he was also the one still ignoring her wish *not* to be rescued. She really had no fight left. This—whatever it was they had between them—was unlike anything she'd ever experienced, and she didn't want to lose it. Or his attention.

But her life had been one braced event after another, and anything with Apollo would not end well. *Nothing* ended well for her.

Weariness weighted her heart and soul, taunted her. Yet, what if . . . what if it somehow worked? Could Leighton escape this spine-of-steel life? Was there a chance she and Mr. Blue Eyes . . .

Oh, he's a *snack*, all right. But . . . hope was dangerous. Treacherous.

———— • ————

Did she realize she was staring at him?

Owen could see the inner workings of her heart darting through those caramel eyes. The desperation to be seen, to be loved. The uncertainty about whether he could be trusted or not. Those questions about Soph and Aliyah tapped at her fear that he'd be into someone else instead of her. But had she seen herself? That face so perfectly set she almost looked like a doll with her satiny-smooth skin, features of both the Latino and Arabic cultures . . . Thick, dark hair framing pinked cheeks and pink lips were a nice contrast to her olive complexion.

Kiss her.

Afraid he'd do just that and scare her off, he set his heels on the footrail and bent forward, resting his arms on his knees. Why did everything suddenly feel awkward or weird? Sitting here, next to her . . . *On the bed*!

Yeah, begging for trouble.

A rap on the door drew his attention.

"Probably Rayan," she suggested, "ordering me to sit with him at dinner."

"Noticed that too, huh?"

She sighed. "I don't want to go . . ."

"Then don't." Owen dug the idea of defying the royals.

Her wary gaze hit his again. "What if it angers him that I do not come?"

"That's his problem." He slid off the bed and pointed to it. "Climb in. I'll answer the door and tell him you're not feeling up to it."

Fear and relief warred in her eyes a second before she scrambled beneath the covers.

Owen strode across the room, glanced back toward the curtained bed to be sure she was settled and still, then opened the door.

Prince Rayan stood there, jaw muscle flexing. "It is time for dinner."

"Oh, uh . . ." Owen slyly opened the door more so the prince could see for himself that Leighton was abed, he glanced that way, then back to the lanky prince. "She's not really feeling up to it."

Rayan's dark eyes slid past him to the semidarkened room, then to Owen, studying him hard. Jaw clenched as he bit out, "We leave at six in the morning."

Not gonna lie—Owen liked ticking off this prince and wondered what reaction he'd get. "And"—he pushed concern into his tone and expression as he shot a look at the bed again—"if she's still not well . . . ?"

Oh, the fury in that smug Arab face. "Maaz is already displeased with her," the prince snarled quietly, "so I would not push him. He would be most angry if his sister's excursion is disrupted by poor decisions."

Owen tilted his head. "So, Nouri not feeling well is a poor decision." He locked on to the guy, recalling Leighton's strained words about it all being a plan to hurt her somehow. "Noted. I'll be sure she's aware." He closed the door quickly—and maybe a little harder than needed. With smug satisfaction, he flipped the bolt.

Leighton sat up in the bed. "He sounded annoyed," she whispered.

"He'll get over it."

"And you sounded a little too pleased to annoy him."

Owen hid his smile as he went to the credenza and retrieved the menu. "What do you want for dinner? I'm probably going to go old school with a burger and fries, since I won't get it again for a while."

"Oh, that sounds perfect."

Grinning at her, he lifted the phone and ordered. Forty minutes later, armed with burgers and fries, they sat on the couch, chowing down. "What're your thoughts on safari-ing again tomorrow?"

Leighton chewed, covering her mouth as she finished the bite, then took a swallow of her water. "Okay, don't hate me . . ."

"Why would I hate you?"

"After your very heroic stand against Prince Rayan"—she scrunched her face—"I kinda want to go tomorrow."

"Heroic, huh?" Buying himself time to think before answering, he took a big bite and chewed. Considering Leighton's misgivings and his tactical experience, he knew this was a great spot to have an unfortunate accident. "I just want you safe."

"This trip is once-in-a-lifetime. I doubt I'll ever get a chance to see these animals or have this experience again." Leighton munched a fry. "And to be here, on an all-expenses-paid trip . . ." She shrugged. "I mean, I really don't want to sit in here hiding when there's amazing wildlife out there to be appreciated."

Made sense. But did she realize . . . that thing she said—*once-in-a-lifetime*—showed him where her mind was. So, while she might be a willing sacrificial lamb for her biological mother, there was a part of her—subconsciously—that did not think she'd spend her whole life at Jeddah as a princess. *That*, he could dig. "I hear you."

She lazily ate her fries, ignoring the other half of her burger on the plate. "Besides, I have you watching my back."

And every other part of her. For more reasons than one. "Glad to hear you say that." He wolfed his down.

"I guess you like the burger," she said with a laugh.

"It was one of the best I've tasted in . . . six days," he teased around the last bite.

"Pretty sure it's hyena meat," she said. "I mean, they don't exactly have cows here . . ."

Owen faltered.

Mischievous gleam in her eyes, Leighton started laughing.

"Not funny. I about tossed my cookies."

"It was worth it to see you finally uncertain for two-point-five seconds." Slumped back against the couch, she drew her legs up and sat cross-legged.

He couldn't help the smile, watching as she settled in, relaxing with a soft sigh. Definitely something he could get used to.

Her gaze came to his, and a rosy flush filled her cheeks. "What?"

Aware of the grave mistake it'd be to push too early into that sliver of a space with her smile and teasing, Owen warned himself to go easy. Leighton was still in a crisis, a place where she'd had to fight for every ounce of freedom. Yet . . . a little more trust like this, and maybe she'd agree to leave of her own volition. Pushing too hard too fast would destroy not only any chance to get her away from these psycho royals but any shot he might have at winning her heart.

Holy what? What are you even thinking?

Leighton wiped her mouth and stood. "I'm going to shower now so I don't have to worry about it in the morning."

Watching her cross the room made him realize how short that distance was. How short their time was. As soon as the bathroom door closed, Owen snagged the short-range comms he'd retrieved from Crow and tucked it in his ear. Heard a tone signal its activation. Anticipated the room might be bugged. "Go ahead," he subvocalized, shifting so he had eyes on the doors to the room and the bathroom.

"Welcome back, Apollo," comm'd Dade. "Chief's getting deets sorted on the plan to exfil your girl. We'll update you when there's more info."

Owen gritted his teeth and covered his mouth. "Can't wear the earpiece. Too many eyes. I'll check in each night."

"Good copy. Give the princess a kiss for us, eh?"

He jerked the piece out and tucked it in his jean pocket for tomorrow. Ten minutes later, Leighton emerged, hair in a towel, and wearing pajama shorts and shirt. He nodded once she climbed back in bed. "I'm going to follow suit."

Cleaned up and changed, he made himself bed down as if there were two, not one. As if this was normal. As if he didn't think about kissing her more than once. But luckily, exhaustion was a powerful adversary, yanking him into the abyss of sleep.

They went into the next day with vigilance, determined to remain observant of the royals. Because of an unexpected summer storm, not many animals were out, almost making the day a wash since wildlife seemed unsettled by the change in atmosphere.

Owen had the same problem.

Rayan was an ever-present pest who insisted on being Leighton's escort. Sitting with her at lunch. Then dinner. Each time treating Owen more like a servant who should walk two steps behind rather than someone charged with her protection.

And of course, Aliyah clung to him the same way the humidity plastered his shirt to him. It was both annoying and embarrassing. He felt a bit let down when nothing of note happened and they were suddenly on the plane, headed to the next location for the safari.

Masai Mara.

ELEVEN

Masai Mara National Reserve, Kenya

IT DIDN'T MAKE SENSE. PRINCE RAYAN WAS vigilant about staying with her, guiding her to this site and that outcropping, while fastened to her side. Notably, he'd done everything in his power to ensure Apollo kept his distance. Which she did not like. At all. When they'd boarded the private jet at Wilson Airport to fly to the Masai Mara National Reserve, Prince Rayan had instructed her to sit next to him, while Aliyah continued sequestering Apollo with herself two rows up, her incessant chatter like fingers on a chalkboard.

There was only one reason they were keeping her and Apollo separated—and it wasn't about jealousy. It was about controlling her movement. Or more correctly—controlling *her*.

Unless . . . something had come to the royals' attention. About Apollo. Or maybe her. What other explanation was there for separating and distracting them?

"I have spoken with Maaz," Rayan said, his voice low as he leaned across the leather arm of his seat to edge closer.

Wary, she eyed him. What good could come of a chat with the ever-irritated crown prince? Especially in relation to her.

"Since you are a member of House Zahrani," Rayan continued, "you will be moved to your own suite at the palace—one bigger than the small one you shared with the bodyguard." He smiled as if he'd just handed her the entire world on a silver platter. "It is wonderful, is it not? You will be closer to me—to us, the family."

Family? Was he out of his skull? There was no family here—not any she wanted to be a part of. But those dark eyes held her fast, and around the amber glints lurked a warning. *Act grateful.* It took everything in her to maintain a neutral façade. Prayed hard her expression wasn't writhing in the disgust she felt at her core.

She should act surprised. "Uh . . ."

Brain, exit stage right.

Leighton had no idea what to say. No words to speak. What he suggested—having her own suite in the palace—should be a good thing. Yet it was such a small concession in a palace with hundreds of rooms. Why should it be earned or celebrated? Especially since she would still be a prisoner. Told when to come, when to go. That this even had to be discussed between two princes . . .

Say something before you give away your true feelings. "And you did this?" Hopefully that did not sound as much like an accusation to him as it did to her.

"Of course," Rayan said, seemingly pleased she'd noticed. "I do not like the restricted privileges they have imposed on you. How are you to acclimate to this life if you are not given opportunities to do so? I have made him see this."

Oh, good heavens. Was he serious? *Acclimate?* "You are too kind," she made herself say, sure that's what he'd intended—to do her a kindness—but being housed in the royal apartments would mean she'd be close to the royals, which meant it'd be easier for them to monitor and scrutinize her every move. To have their condemning gazes searing her every moment of the day.

No, thank you!

"Sadly," Rayan said gently, "I could not dissuade him against a constant escort." He exhaled as if it affected him. "Nor the lock and key."

Leighton fought the urge to scoff. What good would it do to have her own room in the royal apartments if she were still locked up like a prisoner every time? This was not better or even more freedom. It was . . . the same prison, different wing. The only good thing that he had told about her future at Omnia Palace was the escort—Apollo. And that made her heart happy.

A burst of laughter from ahead drew their attention to Aliyah, who was leaning into Apollo's personal space.

"Respect yourself, Aliyah!" Crown Prince Maaz snapped, his expression dark and forbidding as he then sneered at Owen. "An honorable man would not allow a woman to humiliate herself."

Breath caught at the accusation against her protector, Leighton watched—as much as possible, considering she could only see his profile between the seats, but Owen merely looked out the portal-shaped window of the plane.

Oh, she hated that his character was being challenged. There was one of the best men—if not *the* best man—she had ever met. The truth of that shuddered through her. If he was the best man . . . why wasn't she trusting him more?

Should she let him get her out of here? Before it was too late and she was sequestered among the royals in their wing back at Omnia?

When more laughter trilled from the princess, Leighton tensed on her behalf, expecting violence from Maaz. Sure enough, the crown prince shoved to his feet, arm drawn back, ready to strike her.

In a flash, Apollo pitched himself into the line of fire between Aliyah and her cousin, holding out his hands to defuse the situation. "She hears you. We're all a bit tired . . ."

The very air from the cabin seemed to evacuate at his intervention.

Lungs constricting as Maaz faced off with Apollo, Leighton tensed. "Oh no," she murmured.

"This is the captain speaking," a deep, distinctly American voice came over the speaker. "We have begun our descent and will be on the ground in twenty minutes. Flight attendants, prepare the cabin for landing."

The announcement gave Apollo and Maaz the needed excuse to back down without losing face. Both men stepped backwards and reclaimed their seats.

Leighton expelled a pent-up breath.

"He should be more careful," Rayan whispered solemnly. "Maaz is not one to anger."

"I am well aware." As was her cheekbone. Yet, she was not really worried, because she had a feeling Apollo was solid competition for the surly prince. While she had not experienced his anger, she had witnessed a modicum of it. Never would she forget how his broad shoulders had swelled into view as he rushed to protect her from Nasir. It'd been such a simple thing, but he had protected her.

Just as he had now protected Aliyah.

So . . . maybe his protective instinct was just about protecting those who could not do it for themselves. Not about attraction to her. It was just how he was wired. Which was a good thing. Admirable. So why was she so disappointed?

The scorching impact of the plane's tires on the runway startled her.

"You are safe," Rayan said, covering her hand with his.

Stomaching churning at his touch, Leighton pushed her gaze to the industrial-grade carpet. Why must he be so—

Finger beneath her chin, Rayan nudged it upward. "With me, you do not have to do that."

Oh, for heaven's sake. This should be good, him assuring her that he didn't want her cowering. It helped Leighton solidify a couple of things. One, she did not want his attention. Second, even if he was kind—kind*er,* as Owen pointed out—and not prone to violence, she definitely did not want him touching her.

But this was not about her. This was about Ummi. So Leighton managed a smile that felt awkward at best, earning a pleased nod from him and the removal of his touch.

A shaky breath staggered through her, and she swallowed again. Sat back as the plane taxied, her gaze finding Apollo's, whose brows and mouth were taut. He looked ready to kill. Apparently he liked the prince touching her as little as she did.

A few minutes later, everyone deboarded, and she made her way toward the waiting SUVs, too aware of the prince's movements. Did her best to navigate away from him because this was too unsettling. Playing the submissive, subservient, invisible nothing to these royals was one thing. But having the attention of one determined prince could only lead one place, and that was not happening. She recalled Owen suggesting Rayan might have marriage on his mind. At first, she'd thought him crazy, but he was right, wasn't he? Where else would Rayan's attention lead?

Please God . . . please. I can't do that.

"Nouri." Apollo circled behind her, touching her spine. "This way."

Grateful for the direction that pulled her away from the royals, she turned to him. Followed him into one of the vehicles, hoping Rayan didn't notice or intervene. "Thank you," she whispered. Felt a twitch to hurry into the vehicle before they could be thwarted.

Seaborn eyes locked on to her. His brow furrowed. "You o—"

"I wondered where you went," another voice intruded.

Leighton flinched and looked to her left, where Rayan climbed in from the other side and took the seat next to her.

Good night! The guy could not take a hint.

He draped his arm over the back of the seat . . . around her shoulders. "My apologies," he said, indicating his arm, "but it is crowded with three in this row."

"Crowded or not, I'm surprised you're willing to risk the crown prince's anger," Apollo said as he sandwiched her on the right.

"Be concerned with yourself, Mr. Apollo."

"Oh, I am—King Faruq charged me with her protection, and I don't appreciate anyone making her a target of the prince's anger."

Because of the prince's close proximity, she felt him tense. And that made her tense. She looked out the right passenger window. The vehicle lurched forward, giving her time to glower at Apollo for getting into a testosterone war with the prince. "Please, stop."

His expression went tight as those blue eyes considered her, looking both concerned and wounded.

She knew—he was only trying to defend her. Protect her. But she had been protecting herself a lot longer and knew how to navigate tricky situations like this.

But she wanted Apollo to know she appreciated his efforts on her behalf, so she gave him a soft nudge with her shoulder and stayed there. Not because of attraction—*liar*—but to put distance between herself and Rayan. That seemed to assuage Apollo's wounded ego, because he gave a clipped nod.

A while later, the vehicles jounced over the dirt road that led to the tent camp, where large canvas structures huddled amid trees. When they pulled to a stop, Apollo hopped out first and Leighton all but threw herself out his door. She stumbled and he steadied her.

"I got you."

Crazy thing of it was . . . "I know."

His blue eyes found hers, and a smile snuck into his handsome face.

"What do you think"—a vise clamped around her wrist—"you're doing?"

Leighton drew up sharp at Prince Rayan's tight grip and pull. "What—"

"Come." Rayan cocked his head toward an enormous brown tent. "A light lunch first."

"I—"

"Hey, careful," Apollo objected. "You're hurting her."

The prince's gaze darkened. "I do not—"

"Rayan!" Maaz barked, darkness filling the scowl he aimed at his cousin. "Come here."

Though Rayan hesitated, clearly did not want to yield. "I will return," he finally said and released her, giving Owen a stiff glower.

"Hey," Apollo said quietly, slipping closer. "Let's get to our tent."

He guided her past four tents before stepping up onto the porch-like area of a fifth and flinging aside a flap to a much smaller one. Small being relative. This was more of what she'd expected for a safari—rustic, roughing it. Well, after a fashion. These were not the two-person pup tents from her high school camping days.

Leighton hurried in, escaping the prying eyes of the royals. It was a silly, flimsy belief that being in here made her safe. But she'd take it. She let out a sigh. "I could not believe he yanked my wrist," she said quietly.

"I wanted to punch his skull through his gray matter when I saw that."

Leighton started, looking at him. "Then for the moment, I am grateful for Maaz's dislike of me."

"Come again?"

"If his anger had not been aroused at seeing Rayan take me in hand, you would have punched him and they would have killed you."

"And you wouldn't want that . . . ?"

She heard the hope in his words and eyed him again. Felt the vibration of that certain something between them. "Well, then who would protect me?" She deliberately turned her attention to the room for a distraction.

The mosquito-netting walls did not offer much to hide behind or afford much privacy. They did, however, have privacy flaps along the side "walls" that had been rolled up and secured above the nets. To her surprise, despite the tented walls and ceiling, the floors were wood. Solid. That's where the rustic-rather-than-rough started. First with a leather chair and ottoman that hugged the corner. Electricity had been strung to the small patio and a fixture hung in the center of the tent.

She ventured beyond an inner tent wall where curtains were open and secured to the sides. Through there waited a bed—again, a single king with more mosquito netting covering it. It almost seemed pretty, romantic.

Not how she should be thinking. "They keep putting us in one-bed rooms, yet they haven't challenged us . . ."

"It'll come," Apollo promised. "Maaz is meticulous and patient. Not a good combo in a guy like that."

"Yeah, I think you're right." Leighton stepped through and found a small en suite . . . a bathroom with a toilet, two sinks, and a shower with a curtain. So, not as much privacy as before but more than she'd expected for being out in the middle of a safari.

In the main room, Apollo stood at the entrance to their tent, feet shoulder-width apart, arms at his side as he stared out at the royals, who were finding their accommodations. "They're serving lunch," he said, nodding to the large open tent. "Not unlike a mess tent in the field. Except here, they're even offering mixed cocktails."

"I'd kill for water." Sweat slid down her spine as she stood next to him, both noticing the moment Rayan emerged from a tent and looked in the direction of theirs. Her gaze bounced to Apollo. "You okay?"

His jaw muscle jounced. "Not in the least."

At the venom lacing his words, she started. "Why?"

His blue eyes swung in her direction. "You have to ask?"

No, no she supposed she did not. "Look, I get that it's your job to protect me, but you can't antagonize Rayan. He's the one ally I have in that family."

"He is not your ally."

She had to concede the point. "Perhaps, but if anyone in that family will make my life a bit less terrifying, it will be him." A breath shuddered through her, recalling the earlier thoughts she had—how she didn't like Rayan's touch. How Apollo had challenged him in the SUV. "I thought you were going to pounce on each other."

"I hate the way he handles you, talks to you, orders you—"

"Hey." She touched his arm and peered up into those blue eyes. "We can't do anything about my situation, so let's just make the most of this." Wondering if that sounded as Pollyanna to him as it did to her, she shrugged. "Come on. Let's eat before it gets too hot."

Apollo pushed open the door, then hesitated and side-eyed her. "Maybe just stay close to me."

"Believe it or not, I try. They just . . ." She sighed.

He nodded, understanding the heaviness she felt. They crossed the small compound with its dirt paths, stone markers, and down to the food tent where delicious smells wafted out to them.

"Come, come eat!" A guide patted his chest. "Here, Chacha help you." And with that he heaped two paper trays with skewers of meat and veggies. "You take moonlight drive later?" he asked with a big smile.

A moonlight ride? "That sounds amazing," Leighton said, her soul weary and mouth watering from the kebabs she held.

"How do we do that?" Apollo asked, picking up napkins and two bottled waters.

"Meet at trucks at nine," Chacha said, adding a grilled pineapple kebab to her plate with a generous scoop of rice. "Extra for pretty princess."

Though she faltered at the title, Leighton chose to smile and keep moving. But when she turned to pick a table near the front, she saw Maaz, Nasir, and Ghalib headed toward them. Oh no.

She had no energy for the men who treated her like a kebab and skewered her with their attitudes and demands. Pivoting, she hurried out the other side and headed up the path back to the shelter of their tent. She ducked inside and felt the squeeze of panic release with the shade and privacy.

Apollo let the door shut behind him. "Want me to close the curtains?"

Leighton settled in one of the leather chairs and considered his offer. From her position, she couldn't see into the other tents and figured she was safe from prying eyes and heated looks. "It's too hot. Let it breathe."

He nodded and took the remaining chair. They ate without conversation this time, which was markedly different from the night with burgers when they'd laughed and enjoyed each other's company.

Though she ate, she wondered why he was so unusually quiet. Very quiet. "Something wrong?"

He polished off the kebabs, then sipped water, squinting out at the Kenyan plains. "He's crossing a line," he finally managed.

She peered through the netting to see who he meant, but saw nobody out there. Her mind scrambled for purchase on his words. "Rayan."

"And if I see him do it again, I can't be responsible for my actions."

Despite the heat sapping her strength and mood, she felt a ping of exhilaration at her core that he was going all alpha on her. Yet, at the same time, she feared that very persona. "Promise me you will not do anything."

"Can't do that," he said, shaking his head and staring out at the others. "The king is paying me to protect you. That includes from his own family, if necessary."

"He—it isn't . . ." She swallowed a deep sigh. Certainty dug roots in her chest, telling her the prince's attention wasn't what it appeared. "I don't think his attention has anything to do with *romance*."

He slid a severe look in her direction. "Considering his treatment of you, pretty sure you're right. But so help me if he touches you again."

"There are lines we cannot cross. Do not hurt him. Swear it."

Apollo gave her a fierce look. "How can you defend him?"

"Defend?" she balked. "I defend myself—if you go after him, the king's nephew, you will be removed if not killed. Then who will protect me?"

That flexing jaw muscle told her he was ticked but could not argue her words.

"I . . . I had thought Rayan was kind." She sighed heavily. "But I see now that does not exist in the Central Kingdom."

The way he'd grabbed her, worked to keep her from Apollo, felt . . . ominous. A warning clanged at the back of her mind. When they'd first brought her to Jeddah, she had expected torture and rape. Anything to punish her for Ummi's betrayal. Yet, by something she could only ascribe as a miracle of God, they had not. Beatings, yes. But those had stopped quick enough once she understood how they expected her to behave. Once she'd figured out their rules, she knew how to play the game.

But it was *exhausting*.

Not until Apollo arrived did any semblance of light bleed into the darkness that had taken her captive. Maybe . . . maybe she *should* let him get her out of this before something nefarious happened.

The throttle of engines startled her out of the morbid thoughts and drew her gaze to vehicles pulling away from the compound. "Where are they going?"

"Spotlight night drive," he said in a hollow voice. "When you marched out of the tent, I heard Maaz telling the others to meet there immediately after they ate."

"Without us?"

He nodded.

"Why didn't you tell me?"

Furrowing his brows, he eyed her. "Didn't think you wanted to be with them."

"I . . . don't." And yet, she felt sad at not going out to see the wildlife. She stared out past the covered porch. "A moonlight drive amid wildlife sounds kind of dreamy though."

"There's one Cruiser left," he said with a smirk. "Just you and me and the guide."

Excitement pushed Leighton out of the tent.

"I guess this is you wanting to go."

———— • ————

It would be one lifetime too soon if Owen had to deal with another royal. Never had he met such self-serving, self-absorbed people. Which felt a bit whack, since he knew the North and South Kingdoms were light-years different—kind, friends of the West. The Central Kingdom's disregard for life and common decency appalled, especially since the royals on this trip were the ones who would rule, be leaders among nations.

Spoiled, rich fools.

Owen had almost believed Rayan had a thread of honor in him, but that had unraveled in the last twenty-four hours as the prince started crossing lines and treating Leighton like a subservient. As if she were a thing to be owned and controlled instead of a valuable ally and partner, an intelligent woman with a killer sense of humor.

Seeing that piece of slime touching her, ordering her around, had nearly made him a murderer.

They made it to the vehicles, and a driver materialized from the shadows of a nearby tent. "You want spot-lit drive with Bakari?"

"Please," Leighton said calmly.

"In, in," he said with a toothy grin as he circled around and climbed in behind the wheel.

They both sat in the second passenger row as the vehicle rumbled to life and pulled away.

"We will drive out long way, then I use spotlight." The guide tapped the open-top roof. "Show you wildlife."

About twenty minutes later, Bakari slowed to a stop, grabbed a large flashlight, and aimed it out the sunroof toward the left of the Cruiser. He angled the beam over a series of three levels that had bricked walls and planters with directional signs pointing to various locations. The large arrangement seemed ornamental— kind of like a centerpiece to welcome guests. And there in the middle—

"See? See it?" Bakari prodded.

"What?" Leighton craned and squinted, shifting to see. "What is it?"

"Cheetah," the guide said, bobbing the light beam, which struck reflective eyes.

Leighton sucked in a breath. "Wow!"

The large cat darted off, clearly annoyed by the intrusion of people and light into its domain.

"Cats like this area," Bakari explained as he tossed aside the flashlight and pulled away from the spot. "It is elevated and the sign is high. Looks out over the plain." He gave a laugh and pointed ahead of them. "Ah, your friends are on the way back."

"Friends," Leighton sniffed quietly beside him as they both looked and spotted headlamps in the distance.

Yeah, his friends might refer to Omen, but never the royals. Which reminded Owen of Rawlins's warning that the extraction would happen here on this reserve. Which was great . . . but where? When? How was he to ready himself and Leighton if he didn't know the logistics?

Bakari went a little further before again easing to the side of the road. This time, he hiked up from his seat and onto the floorboard, where he straightened to his full height and angled a spotlight over the scraggly plain. There he traced an undulating area that almost seemed like an ebony sea where dark forms slowly took shape.

"Wildebeest!" Leighton said, pushing in front of him to look through the window.

Owen shifted back, appreciating a little too much her nearness. "I can't see them."

"Here." Owen shifted, putting a knee in the seat, and drew her next to himself. The open window allowed them to lean out a bit.

"Oh, perfect." Expression alive, she edged forward, tucking loose strands of hair behind her ears as she visually traced the terrain. Her eyes widened. "I see them!"

Owen joined her, bracing and focusing on the teeming herd. Not on her sweet fragrance that was a bit soapy, a bit rose-smelling, or her effervescent excitement.

The guide's bright beam skidded across the darkness and found two giraffes gliding toward a glistening water source.

"This is amazing," Leighton said, her smile bright and wide. "I'm so glad we came out." She gave him a smile. "Thank you."

His heart jammed into his throat. He coughed a laugh. "Why're you thanking me? All I did was say there was another vehicle."

She shrugged, suddenly shy.

The soft crunch of sticks and brush to his left made his nerves buzz. A soft brush against his fingers, which were dangling down out of the Cruiser, made him jerk back. His mind took two seconds too long to awaken. Alert him to the lion stalking dangerously close.

Leighton let out a yelp and jerked back, pulling her hands and arms back inside as she retreated. "Lions!"

"It's good," Bakari reassured. "It's good."

A lioness loped into view and leapt at the Cruiser in threat.

Owen shoved from the window, falling into Leighton. "Sorry!" he apologized even as they felt the vehicle rock beneath the impact.

With a loud laugh, Bakari cut the light. "She is temperamental."

"Sorry," Owen repeated and scrambled off Leighton, turning to help her off the floorboard. "You okay?"

"I'm fantastic," she breathed with more than a little exuberance. Expression alight, she surged back in the seat, brushed her hair from her face, and released another, airier laugh. "Did that really just happen—it touched my hand!"

"Mine too," he said with a chuckle.

"Much excitement," Bakari said as he hustled back into the driver's seat. And with that they were underway. "She gone. All good."

"Will she come after us?"

"No, we go. All good. Just keep moving."

Headlamps glared straight in through the windshield as the other Cruiser came upon them, then passed their vehicle in an unsettling moment that felt as if the entire world had dropped into a painfully slow-mo reel. While Leighton shifted, putting her back to the windows and other vehicles, clearly not wanting to face the royals, literally or figuratively, Owen wasn't going to cower. He saw Aliyah waving happily, Rayan glowering, but the others feigned as much indifference as Leighton offered.

Once clear, it seemed he could breathe. As if the intense humidity in the air had cleared.

Spine rigid, eyes locked straight ahead, Leighton remained unmoving.

"They're gone," he said.

She shifted her gaze to him. "Was I that obvious?"

"No more than I was while shooting daggers at Rayan."

Leighton held his gaze for a long moment, then a slow smile worked into her expression. "I saw you doing that on the plane."

Man, he liked that amusement in her face. The light in her eyes while they were enjoying the wildlife. And while he wasn't sure how to read her expression right now, he knew he'd do whatever it took to get it done. Make sure it happened, free her of the fear that made her rigid and shoved her gaze to the ground.

He watched her leaning on the window again as they bounced along.

Wind whipped her hair and she laughed. "The moon is amazing! If it weren't so bright, we wouldn't see hardly anything."

Please, God. I have to get her out of here. He looked out over the plains to the left. How did he convince her to let him do this? To go with him? Could he ever?

The Cruiser jerked and surged, then gave a death-rattling shudder before falling silent. Dead.

TWELVE

Masai Mara National Reserve, Kenya

APOLLO SAT FORWARD, HOMING IN ON THE driver. "What's wrong?"

Heart in her throat, Leighton peered through the windows, the incredible moment of taking in the herd of wildebeest near the small water source gone. Her heart, which had felt light a second ago, anchored with worry.

Bakari tried starting the truck a few more times and gave a huff. "Old truck," he said with a mirthless laugh. "You go out. See animals. I will fix."

"Out?" Leighton balked, ducking to again search the moonlit terrain. The soft but coarse hair of the lion's thick mane brushing her fingers was still quite fresh in her mind. "Is that safe?"

"Yes, yes," Bakari assured as he tugged out the keys, reached under the dash, and whatever he did unleashed a resounding *clunk*.

Owen glanced at something between the two front seats and pointed to it. "Can you use the radio to call for help?"

"No, it break long time." Bakari lifted the hand receiver, showing it wasn't working. "Go, go. Have fun." He flung open his door and got out, then he went to the front of the Cruiser and hefted up the hood.

"Is he serious?" Leighton asked, uncertainty all but choking her.

"Yeah, I think he is." Apollo motioned to her. "Let me double-check. Don't exactly want us becoming second breakfast." Door open, he hopped out. He stood there, facing her, glancing in both directions, then held up a staying hand. "Hang tight."

Hovering on the edge of the seat he'd occupied a moment ago, she watched him head to the front, where the driver bent over the engine. "Think you can fix it?" came his distant question.

"Yes." Bakari patted Apollo's shoulder and turned him back in her direction. "You go with your girl. See elephants."

Your girl?

Leighton's heart tripped and fell all over that small phrase. It was such a small thing to say but held a world of implications.

Bakari handed over the flashlight, grinning. Said something that earned a perturbed look, then pushed Apollo back to her.

When he didn't climb in, she took that as her signal to join him. She left the safety of the truck, boots crunching on the hard-packed road. A warm wind tossed her hair in her face, so she tucked it back. "Any idea what's wrong . . . ?"

"No, but we should be underway soon."

She hoped so—what a forced-but-great opportunity to walk out here with the wild animals. Well, not exactly *walk*. More like watch from a distance. A very great distance, thankyouverymuch. While the wildlife here was probably used to humans tromping through their territory, they were still wild animals. "And it's . . . safe?"

Uncertainty scratched at Apollo's blue eyes. "We shouldn't go far." His gaze raked the surrounding area before he jutted that stubbled jaw away from the broken-down Cruiser. "There's a small rise over there. We might be able to see something." Though he angled aside and held out a hand for her to go ahead, he glanced at the driver again with a furrowed brow.

Something inside her wanted to ease that tightness around his mouth and eyes. She searched for something cool to draw his focus to. Spotted zebras, the whites of their stripes all but glowing beneath the full moon. "Look," she reached to him, and their hands smacked.

Apollo caught her fingers before she could yank away, and squeezed.

Her heart spasmed. Unintended, unexpected . . . wonderful. Afraid her expression might betray her feelings, she drew her hand back. Hugged herself, as if that might control how his touch made her nerves bounce.

"Zebras . . . ?" he asked, taking in the view.

"Yeah," she said, recovering her ability to breathe and talk.

This trip—never could she have dreamed of it or imagined it'd happen. Being hostage to House al-Zahrani wasn't the ideal way in which to safari, but the splendor and majesty of the up-close wildlife was unparalleled.

Standing with him on the ridge, she held her hands together just beneath her chin, smiling, then a gliding movement caught her attention off to the side. She pointed there. "More giraffes."

"There's three," Owen noted. "I think they're the same ones we saw at the first stop."

"Ah, I think you're right," she said with a tinge of disappointment. "It's still amazing, isn't it?"

"It's *fire*," he agreed. A banging from the driver and the Cruiser drew Owen's stern gaze in that direction as the clanging echoed. He shook his head. "He should've had the radio replaced. Or the Cruiser."

"I might not be a mechanic, but I'm pretty sure assaulting the engine with a tool isn't the way to fix it," she said with a snicker.

"Def not."

Leighton watched the giraffes gliding along the park. "I saw a documentary one time about a giraffe in a wildlife refuge that was pretty sick. The veterinarians were working so hard to save her." She batted her hair aside again. "Silly me, I was so positive they were going to succeed—why else would they be showing it? But the next thing I know, the giraffe's neck just collapses. Like a wet noodle." She shuddered, the memory still painful. "I cried out. It was the most horrific thing I've ever witnessed. Absolutely traumatized me. Never imagined when they died that their necks did that."

Apollo watched the wildlife. "They truly are some of the most elegant beasts on earth. I'm glad those are healthy."

"Sorry." She sniffed a laugh. "A little too macabre for a special night like this, huh?" Her heart jarred at calling the night special—but it was. She felt so at peace, happy with the animals. With Apollo.

Silently, she thanked God for this small reprieve in the chaos.

"It's poignant," he said softly, as he stared out over the plains. "A good reminder that this"—he bobbed his head to the animals—"deserves due respect. Because even though it's amazing and cool, we are trespassing on their domain."

"True," she whispered, then noticing that just over his shoulder, the area beyond the reach of the spotlight, shadows of gray and darkness morphed. Fluttered, swayed. She stilled, only then feeling a rumbling beneath her feet.

"What . . . ?" She looked down and turned a circle. "What is that?"

"Keep still," he rasped as heavy, thunderous vibrations closed in on them.

A concoction of disbelief, dread, and awe paralyzed her as the ground shook with violence. She heard rocks falling—including from beneath her own feet. She flung out her hands. "What—?"

"Back, back, back," he shouted, hand catching her waist as he stumbled backwards.

With a yelp, Leighton slipped, the ground giving way. She caught his sleeve and held on.

Apollo swung around to steady her, their feet sinking on shifting dirt and rocks that carried them down . . . down a dozen feet. The small avalanche steadied, and she looked at him, latched on to his arms, and gave a tremulous, disbelieving laugh.

"You good?" he asked, holding her firmly.

"Yeah. What was that?" When she looked up, expecting to see his blue eyes, she found him looking past her.

"Holy wow . . ."

She glanced over her shoulder and her breath backed into her throat—a baby elephant stood close, considering them with its dark eyes, fluttering its large ears at them.

Leighton drew in a long, stunned breath.

The calf was *adorable*.

"Aww." She started forward, but a hand on her waist held her firm.

"Wait," Apollo murmured near her ear, sending warm shivers down her spine, but also a cold dread at his warning that resonated as vibrations came again. These were somehow bigger. Harder. Jarring.

That thundering coalesced into the calf's mother. Or father. Hard to tell.

And Leighton was not going to try to find out lest she anger the very large elephant. More thudding came as the shadows and night surrendered—as did her heart—to another mammoth form of a tusked elephant. The right tusk was longer than the left, but both were quite capable of running her through if this adult felt threatened or sought to protect its calf.

Strangling a cry that was both excitement and terror, Leighton gripped Apollo's sleeve, amazed they were this close to two elephants. "Hoooooly—"

"No sudden moves," he said.

"Ya think?"

Apparently surprised at her playful-but-mocking tone, he turned his gaze to her and their eyes met. With the glow of the moon and the shadows of night, there was something godlike in the way moonlight glowed on his bleached hair and crystalline eyes. Despite her many denials, he was *gorgeous*. And sharing this moment with him felt like a solidifying force. He looked as much in awe as she was.

A rough nudge to her elbow startled Leighton. She gasped and found the baby probing her with its trunk. A disbelieving laugh coiled through her. "Dead," she breathed as the calf plopped its trunk on her chest. "I. Am. Dead . . ." She drew in a breath and stepped back, her shoulder blades bumping against Owen's chest.

His hands framed her hips. "Easy," he murmured against her ear, making her stomach contract involuntarily as they shuffled a step away. "Nice and easy . . ."

The adult stomped nearer, swinging its mammoth head to lock a considering eye on Leighton as its calf butted in closer. Ears fanning, the adult sent a subtle warning to the humans messing with its baby.

Leighton tentatively reached out. Let her palm touch the rough hide of the calf's head.

"Careful," Apollo warned, shifting in front of her protectively. "Mama's swatting her ears harder."

Flicking her gaze up to the much larger elephant, Leighton noticed the adult lumber closer, a proximity that made her heart stutter.

Mama lifted her trunk to him, nostrils flexing as it dragged over his head and face.

"Just . . . don't . . . sneeze on me," Owen pleaded.

Leighton choked on a laugh, drawing Mama's attention, who repeated the gesture over Leighton's face and head. With thumps of curiosity, the trunk plopped on her arm, up . . . up . . . curled over her shoulder as the baby bumped Leighton's leg. Mama drew Leighton closer.

Giggles wiggled through Leighton, demanding freedom as she ran a hand up the adult's broad shoulder as she gave it a hug. Heart stirred, soul moved by this incredible experience, she felt like it was a kiss from God. So incredible. So beautiful.

"I think she likes you," Owen said.

"I have always loved pachyderms," she said, smiling up at the great animal, feeling tears prick her eyes—and for the first time in many months, they weren't out of sorrow or fear. "They're so majestic. Powerful yet docile."

"Unless you mess with its baby or herd."

"Did you know when there's a threat, the adults will circle up around the calves, then turn to face the threat?" She sighed, a deep ache yawning in her to be protected like that. To not have to be the one protecting. Running her hand along the trunk and face of the mama, she felt as if her world had finally righted.

She grinned at Apollo and thrilled at the smile he returned. It stirred something deep in her. No, *he* stirred something deep. An ache she'd long ignored—to be content. To not have to hide her way through life.

"You look happy," he said.

Leighton held his gaze, realizing that he was much the reason she felt that way. "I am."

"Goo—"

The rumble of the engine came from the other side of the ridge.

Mama released her and moved past her to catch the calf, who circled back to its mama.

"Aw, shoot," she whispered in disappointment as mama and calf started away. She did not want to leave.

"If he got it running, we should get back," Apollo said, holding a hand out.

That . . . that made leaving this magical moment almost worth it. Accepting his proffered help, Leighton gave the retreating elephants one last, longing look, but really—her mind was on her hand in his. How strong and warm it was. "What a dream come true. A core memory," she whispered, not sure whether she meant the pachyderms or holding his hand as they climbed up the tricky terrain that fought them. "I'm glad I shared it with you."

Hold up. Had she said that out loud? She looked to Apollo, but he had a deep scowl on his face as he started toward the Cruiser.

Yeah. Great. She actually had a moment with him but—she slipped, her knee connected with a rock. "Ow!"

"No!" Apollo let go and threw himself up the incline without her.

Confused at what he was doing and why he'd left her, she struggled up the last stretch and wrangled herself onto solid ground. "Thanks a lot for just abandoning me back—"

Leighton stopped, finding neither Apollo nor the Cruiser on the road. "What . . . ?" she breathed, looking around, as if she were directionally challenged and had forgotten where the Cruiser had broken down. Reality clobbered her, forcing her brain to catch up. "They . . . *left* me?!" she shrieked.

But then she heard shouts and followed the sound up the road to where she spotted Apollo sprinting after . . . taillights in the far distance.

Frozen, she gaped. No. No no no. This wasn't happening. Why was Bakari driving away? She hurried forward as the distance between both her and Apollo—and the Cruiser—increased. Panic ignited and she started running too. They couldn't leave her! She did not have any survival skills other than a stubborn streak. "Owen!" she shouted, hating herself for using that name. "Apollo! Wait!"

A second later, he gave another shout and threw a fist in the air. His growl echoed across the lonely reservation as he stopped and gripped his knees.

"I will kill him!" Fisting his hands, Owen knew the sickening truth—this was intentional. A driver didn't accidentally leave two tourists on the reservation at night.

Heaving breaths that seared, he stared after the pluming dust and fading taillights even as he heard Leighton calling and catching up.

All the facts rushed at him—the royals going without him and Leighton. The treatment she had endured—the way Maaz had demanded Rayan leave Leighton at the camp and come with him. Leighton's conviction the royals were acting strange, too nice. The Cruiser suddenly dying . . .

Had it even really broken down? Or had Bakari faked that?

Senses on high alert, Owen felt a conviction burrow into his soul—the royals hadn't been nice because they liked her. They were nice to distract her. So they could bring her out here and leave her to the literal lions?

Frustrated he had no weapons, no way to protect them, he wished he'd thought to snag one off Crow when he'd low-crawled in. Would it be too much to hope that Omen was planning to snatch her *now*? This would be the perfect time—

Comms device!

He dug in his pocket for the earwig, knowing this was his chance to get her away from these royals. All he had to do was radio Omen and they'd be out of here. The royals would be none the wiser. His hand came up empty.

He checked the other pocket. Not there either. He patted himself down as if it might manifest elsewhere. But no—it wasn't here. It was gone! "You have got to be kidding me!" He'd lost it? How? When?

"Why did you leave me?" Leighton demanded with a feral glare as she reached him. "Why would you do that?"

Owen eyed her. "I wasn't—"

"Clear as day—you left."

Man, he had no time for hysterics. "For the love of— I wasn't leaving you," he bit out, raking a hand through his bleached hair, which felt brittle as this night. "When I realized he was leaving us, I sprinted after him, trying to stop him."

"But you *left* me!"

A clatter came from his left, jacking his heart into his throat. Leighton stiffened and whirled, eyes wildly searching the tall grass.

Owen scanned, wishing he had some NODs or even the scope of a rifle. They were in a safari reservation. With deadly beasts. "We need to keep moving."

"You left me!" This time her voice echoed, emphasizing each word. "You didn't say a word—just took off without me. You weren't worried about me."

He eyed her hustling to stay up with him. Something about her words stopped him. He shifted to look at her, hearing past the shrieks. Past the accusations. *I scared her.* That realization made his heart slow and forced him to dump some of his own frustration at their situation.

"Hey." Regretting what he'd caused her, he caught her upper arms. "I hear you—it scared you. *I* scared you. But I swear I would not have left you."

"But *you did*!" she ground out, her words strained. "What if a lion was nearby? You didn't know there wasn't, and you . . . just left me."

His heart twinged at the desperation in her words and expression. He took her in, pushed down the spiraling attraction as he noticed the way her dark hair seemed to both absorb the light of the moon and refuse it at the same time. He had the craziest thought that she seemed carved of starlight, its gravity pulling him in closer . . .

"I'm sorry." Though her right cheek twitched in anger and her gaze bounced from him, he stepped closer. "You're right, and I'm sorry I scared you. Truly sorry."

A shiver rippled through her frame as he held her in place, a move that had been intended to ground her. Help her abandon the panic. That shiver told him it was working, that she was crashing after the adrenaline spike of believing he'd abandoned her.

She looked away again, then back at him. "I . . . panicked." She lifted one shoulder in a shrug. "Maybe I overreacted. I'm sorry too."

"Your reaction was justified." There were not many people who would own their actions like that. It hiked his respect for her another notch, and good night, he loved having her close. But this wasn't the time for romance—not with the wildlife out there. He made himself release her. "It's okay. I get it." He cocked his head down the road. "We should get moving. It's going to take an hour or more on foot to reach camp."

Another twig snapped to the left, and in the near distance behind Leighton, Owen noticed a shadow riffle through the brush. He paused a half step, let Leighton continue, then circled around to her left to put himself between whatever threat lurked in the shadows beyond the reach of his limited sight in the darkness.

She frowned at his repositioning but didn't ask what he was doing. "Why do you think he left us?" Her nerves were talking now.

Knowing very well she knew that answer, he let the question go—it'd only induce panic, scare her. She also hadn't seemed to notice they were being paced, and he was glad—she didn't need any more fear. It did strange things to people, and she'd experienced enough in her life. So for now, he kept their pace smooth and steady—all while keeping his head on a swivel and paying close attention to their surroundings.

"Owen . . . ?" Her voice pitched, insisting on an answer.

"That rise in your voice says you already know . . ." A soft thump in the field made his heart do the same. Slowly, he slid his gaze alone in that direction and searched the shadows. For a split-second, he thought he saw a rustle of amber—a mane.

God, help us.

Leighton skipped a step to keep up. "Hey, I know you're used to marches with that big backpack on—"

"Ruck."

"—but I'm not," she said pointedly. "Maybe we could slow down before I collapse."

And here he'd thought he'd been doing that, taking a steady pace so he didn't make them look like prey running for their lives to the predators. He just really did not want to be so slow the entire pride caught up with Mufasa, who seemed to be pacing them, in order to take on the two interlopers on their road. He cursed himself for not nabbing a gun or knife off someone. But he'd had nowhere to stow it, and the last thing they needed was for him to get caught with a weapon.

Crack.

Owen flinched, his heart kick-starting. Was it his imagination, or was the big cat closer? Training his ears on the fields, he scanned for a stick. Rock. *Anything* was better than bare hands. He was no Samson or David. Had no experience killing lions. No donkey jawbones. As he surreptitiously scouted for a makeshift weapon, he spotted the multi-level stone sign/monument-style thing.

"You're quiet," Leighton huffed as they moved. "What's wrong?"

Another rustle came from the left.

Definitely closer.

They were too open, too vulnerable out here. Afraid to alarm her and exacerbate the threat by sending fear pheromones into the warm, sticky air, he caught her hand. "We have to get off the road." With that, he diverted toward the monument.

"What are you—"

"Quiet," he rasped, then jutted his jaw toward the multi-tiered monument signs. "Put your spine to that structure."

"What?"

"Do it," he hissed, gaze roving the shadows. Seeing a predator in every blinking shadow and flicker of grass. "Nice and slow." He edged from the last spot he'd heard the lion, maneuvering in front of her. "Hold on to my shirt as you move to guide me."

"You're scaring me," she said as her fingers coiled in his shirt. "W-what is it?"

Owen lifted his arms wide, recalling a long-ago lesson about making oneself look as large as possible to wild cats and to never put your back to them. "Our visitors from earlier." Even as he said it, reflective eyes blinked back at him from the tall grass. His muscles contracted involuntarily, that all-too-powerful fight-or-flight instinct demanding *flight*.

"The *lions*?" Her grip tightened on his shirt.

"Keep your back to the stone and your head down. Slowly but surely climb to the second-highest level," he said in a low voice.

Then, as if their change in behavior drew the big cat, its head slid forward, parting the tall grass. Both relief and alarm speared him—it was the lioness.

But he knew better than to underestimate this predator. The females might be smaller, but they were more agile. Hunters. The lioness stalked into the open, paused and looked down the road, toward camp. Large cats liked to play the nonchalant predator while simultaneously side-eyeing prey.

"First level is right behind you," Leighton muttered, her knee jarring his back. "Sorry."

He shifted onto it. Felt a big rock beneath his hand and closed his fingers around it. Took it with him as he navigated the next two. Having a crude weapon did nothing for the knot in his gut, especially when Mufasa stalked up next to the lioness. Behind those two, the grass was shifting again. He bit back a curse.

"There's another," Leighton whimpered.

"*Two* more." His words birthed a pair without manes.

"Lionesses."

"Or a young lion," he thought aloud, realizing it was a possibility. "Maybe. I'm not a lionologist."

"That's not a word."

"I doubt they'll be offended." Or maybe they would be and would make him dinner. But that'd mean Leighton might be dessert . . .

God, I think we need a miracle or some type of Elijah action here. Feel free to transport us . . . anywhere else.

"The lion!" Leighton rasped from behind, hands on his shoulders. "He's coming!"

Owen blinked, only then seeing the lion stalking forward, straight at them.

Oh no. Not good.

"Guess I offended him." Gut tightening, he gripped the rock he held tighter as the lion lowered its snout. A squall of nerves told Owen he was going to die. Leighton was going to die.

Nope. Not happening. He waved his hands—and the rock— like a maniac, shouting. Then with his best pitcher arm that had gotten him scouted in high school, he threw the rock and nailed the lion.

Who did not even falter—in fact, it seemed to incite him. He came, unyielding. With a roar, he leapt.

God, help me!

In that terrible, terrifying moment as Mufasa sailed across the distance, Owen had the sudden realization that Leighton's gasp had come from over his head. That meant she was in plain view. Targetable.

Even as Mufasa went airborne again, Owen thrust upward, straight into its path.

With a powerful swipe of its paw, the lion clawed him. Nails scored Owen's chest, searing, slicing fire across his chest. "Augh!!"

The lion's momentum sent them careening over the side of the multi-tiered monument.

Twisting to the side, Owen vaulted with everything he had in him away from the lion's forbidding weight and claws. The last thing he wanted was to get trapped beneath the mighty beast. Large cats were known for pinning their prey and using hind claws to disembowel their victims.

He dived into a roll, feeling a razored burn across his left pectoral. Came up and launched himself aside, too late seeing another feral swipe of the paw that was bigger than his head. The claws caught his jaw and neck. Terror seized him, knowing one wrong angle and his carotid would water this safari. Distantly, he grew aware of Leighton's screams. Panic stabbed—was she being attacked by the rest of the pride? Her cries and shouts forced him to look, but even as he did, the lion roared again.

Rocks pelted the big cat, who shook his thick amber mane and gave a roar of objection to Leighton. But then, more annoyed than angered with her puny attempt to thwart his kill, the lion again lowered his head and stalked Owen.

I'm going to die. No way he'd survive. The royals were about to get their wish—him and Leighton gone.

God, please*! Do something!*

A great vibration rattled the ground, the sound drowned by a thunderous trumpeting noise. Before he could sort it out, Owen noticed Mufasa hesitate, swivel his head aside to look behind himself.

The ground shook as if the rocks themselves were going to split in two. Earthquake? Was God answering his desperate prayer by having the ground swallow him or the lion up?

A massive blur stampeded past him.

With a strangled cry, Owen scrambled back as a hind flank the size of a small house barreled past him. An elephant thundered into the fight, coming between Owen and Mufasa.

What . . . ? Body and mind drenched in adrenaline, he watched, shocked and confused as Mufasa challenged the elephant with a more mighty roar, then a smaller one, as if having the last word before deciding the effort wasn't worth it.

That's right—I'd be a terrible last meal. Too chewy.

Mufasa turned and lumbered away, bored.

Wincing at the wounds he'd sustained, Owen dragged himself to his feet, stunned at mama elephant who, along with two other elephants—bulls it seemed—trumpeted their outrage, tusks swinging at the big cats. The lioness turned back with a hissing growl and took a belligerent swat at the elephant, who hustled four pounding steps, warning the cats to yield and slink off, chastised and food-less, into the night.

They saved me . . . Disbelief drowned Owen as he stared at the enormous beasts that had just saved his life.

Correction: *God* saved him through those amazing elephants. The conviction of that truth dug deep even as the sting of his injuries dug past his adrenaline-soaked muscles and mind, the open wounds screaming. Groaning as strength leeched from his limbs, he stumbled, went to a knee to steady himself, hand going over his abdomen, which had taken the worst of the damage.

"Owen!" Distraught, Leighton rushed and knelt beside him, cautiously touching him. "Are you okay? I thought they were going to kill you!"

"Me too."

Her gaze traced his injuries. "What do I do?"

Only then did he notice the elephants behind them. In total, a herd of six surrounded them. Tails twitching and giant wedge-shaped feet stamping, they stood sentry, facing the threat, warning the cats with flashing movement of their large ears not to return. "Holy . . ." Shock held him fast. Had that really happened? He shook his head in awe. Knew he would've been Mufasa's late-night snack if not for these amazing, gentle giants. "Un-freaking-believable."

After considering the pachyderms, Leighton smiled at him. "It's a circle of protection."

He shook his head in awe. "Well, I prayed for a miracle . . ."

Her eyes brightened in the moonlight as she smiled. "So did I." She nodded to the bleeding slices across his chest. "What do I do?"

"Nothing. I need to be stitched and bandaged, and unless you have those supplies on you . . ."

Cool fingers touched his jaw as she angled her head for a better view. "These don't look as bad."

"I was further away," he said, then looked down. "They sting like crazy, but I don't think they're too deep." At least, he hoped not. "The bigger problem is the blood. The wildlife in the reserve will smell it and come hunting the walking meat-stick."

Concern lanced her pretty features. "We have to get back to camp."

"Yeah. Help me up." He braced as she threaded her arm under his, then looped it around his waist. With her help, he rose then hesitated. Looked at the bull, not two feet away.

A wide, blinking eye, glossy beneath the moon, took him in.

Owen reached out his hand and waited in respect.

The great bull flapped his ears, then tossed its trunk to him.

Touching it, Owen couldn't deny the connection he suddenly felt to these amazing beasts and smiled. "Thank you. You saved my life."

Somehow, he believed the bull understood, both that he was thanking them and the great kindness they had done by chasing off the pride. Mama lumbered in, insistent on getting some gratitude as well. Amused, Owen repeated the gesture. To all six.

When he turned to head out, Leighton stood there, hand over her mouth, sniffling.

Alarm speared him. "You okay? Did you get hurt?" He cursed himself for not checking sooner.

"No, I'm fine." She waved him off, wiping her nose. "It's just . . .

beautiful. You—this big, handsome warrior, fierce in your own right—thanking elephants. I didn't think I could like you any more..."

Heady warmth spilled through his gut, pulling Owen to her side. "Is that right?"

Her eyes widened. "I . . . I meant . . ."

When she tried to ease away, he set his hand on her waist. Drew her back to him. "No retreating now, Princess."

A rather forceful thrust to his back—by the bull—shoved Owen into her. He grimaced at the daggers of pain that seared his chest, yet couldn't help but laugh.

Leighton laughed and slipped free. "I think they're telling us to get going."

"Really?" he teased as he started walking, bracing his midsection. "I was pretty sure the bull was telling me to kiss you."

Leighton laughed, but it was a nervous, shy one that had her ducking her head.

It was dark, so he couldn't tell, but Owen thought there was some new color in her cheeks. He let it carry him back up to the road.

She glanced at him. "You're okay to walk . . . ?"

"I'm good." Even as he said that, he heard the steady thump behind them. A check over his shoulder confirmed his suspicions— the herd was following. "Chaperones?"

"Protectors," Leighton corrected as she hooked an arm under his and wrapped it around his waist for support. "Like you."

Surprised at her words, the conviction in them, her sudden belief in him, Owen looked at her, *really* wanting that kiss now. "I'm pretty sure all these cuts earned me a kiss."

Just then, baby elephant shuffled up between them, making Leighton laugh even more, especially when the calf stayed there the entire twenty-minute grueling hike. Owen's chest bled and ached, sucking away his strength.

Relief was thick and heavy when he heard the laughter and firelight of the camp.

Leighton slowed. "Look at them," she whispered with tight words.

On one edge of camp, a large bonfire lit the night with the royals gathered around it.

"Just sitting there, laughing, not caring that we were missing and in danger!"

Indeed, that laughter lent credence to his earlier suspicion that being abandoned was intentional. That someone wanted them gone. "Hey, Leighton. Listen—"

The first shouts came from the guards, who rushed forward with their rifles ready to challenge the elephants, who trumpeted against their rude welcome, then swung away to head back out to the valley.

"No, don't shoot!" Leighton hollered, holding a hand out to stop the guards. "They protected us."

Owen's legs tangled, weakness sapping him from the blood loss.

"Help us," Leighton shouted, her voice trilling. "He's bleeding—badly!"

An older man rushed to Owen, calling to another, who joined them.

Dizziness made Owen's head swim as he stumbled and dropped to his knees. Felt himself fall out of Leighton's grip. He reached for her but was intercepted by the men. Vision blurring, Owen noticed the blur of shapes coming from the campfire. Worry choked him—if he died, she'd be alone. "Leigh—"

"Here. Lift him." Mugo, the safari manager, swam into view and nodded to the side. "Come, come. He needs a doctor."

The world upended, Owen grappling for a grip on reality as the stars swung into view. But that blanket of black morphed into a suffocating void that pulled him into its dark embrace.

THIRTEEN

Outside Masai Mara National Reserve, Kenya

HE LOOKS DEAD.

Leighton hugged herself as Mugo, his son, and the town doctor hurried an unconscious Owen into a small surgical room at the back of the small clinic. Shirt and chest shredded and bloody, he looked so pale. Angry red cuts and welts swelled along his upper neck and jaw.

She and Owen had walked all that way . . . with him in that shape, and she'd never given it a thought. He'd said he was okay . . .

The doctor immediately cut away the shirt, muttering to his nurse, whose spew of medical terminology might as well have been in Swahili for all Leighton could understand as she watched them thread an IV into his arm. The doc *tsk*ed as he assessed the lacerations. Shook his head. His grim expression was stressing her out.

A swirl of nausea threatened what little composure she had left. What if he didn't make it? "Is he going to be okay?" she asked, unable to hold back her concerns.

The doctor scowled in her direction. "You go." He shooed her away.

With a smile that was anything but genuine, the nurse guided Leighton out of the room and to a small foyer at the front of the building that served as a waiting area. The wood was well-worn and the seats rickety. It all made her wonder about the skill of this clinic and its doctor. "Sit. Wait. I will come back soon."

Leighton caught her arm. "Please—is it bad? Will he die?"

The nurse frowned.

"He's all I have." Stunned at her own words, Leighton paused but realized they were entirely true. He *was* all she had. Countries and oceans separated her from her parents, from Ummi. And it sent waves of dread through her. "Tell me he'll live."

"Doctor Abeni will help him." With a nod, the nurse paused. "Some lacerations are deep, bad, but others not so much." Though she managed a pursed-lip-shrug combo, it seemed forced. Then she took Leighton's hands and pressed the palms together. "You pray." Then she left.

Oh sweet mercy—was it that bad?

Morose, Leighton watched the petite nurse vanish back down the hall and slip into the surgical room. Taking in a shuddering breath, she stood there, unwilling to move—an irrational fear that she would put more distance between herself and Owen.

Remembering the nurse's urge to pray, she swallowed. "Please, God," she whispered, but words failed her. She just had a desperate need for Owen to survive. He'd walked all that way . . . never complained. Why hadn't she noticed he wasn't doing well? How had she missed how poorly he was doing? What would happen to her if he died? Nothing good—and it would all be her fault.

"Do not let him die," she finally managed. She wanted to call someone, get some help, but she had nothing—no phone. How could she alert Navas or Owen's friends if he died? They'd been out there, in the grass—why hadn't Omen saved them?

Overwhelmed, she paced to the door, then back to her sentry spot at the juncture of the hall and waiting area. If she had just agreed to escape with him, he wouldn't have gotten hurt. They'd likely already be gone. Safe. Far from this place.

Mugo appeared in the hall, phone pressed to his ear as he stalked toward her with a dark expression. "Yes, yes. He is with the doctor now." He continued past her and sat in the corner, answering more questions.

Realizing he was likely speaking with one of the royals, Leighton eyed him. Couldn't shake the memory of Maaz smirking at Ghalib as the camp workers loaded Owen into the Cruiser. The crown prince's guard said maybe their work was done for them. That little revelation had driven Leighton into the Cruiser, where she hunkered down next to Owen before the engine revved and they headed here to the clinic. It was all true—the royals were trying to have her killed. Get rid of her. But Owen, who had come to protect and rescue—which she'd resented—had paid the price.

"You get me in trouble with the prince," Mugo said.

Surprised at the accusation, Leighton glanced over her shoulder and found him at the door. She could only imagine what Maaz had done when he realized she wasn't still in the camp. "I couldn't leave Apollo alone."

"Prince said you should not be here. He is sending someone to retrieve you."

Oh no. Yes, she feared the possible reprisal she might face, but worse—she feared being separated from Owen. From the only protection she had.

"Wait here, Princess. I will be back." With that, Mugo left the building.

Fingertips to her forehead, Leighton massaged the dull ache forming there. If they came and got her . . .

She swallowed at the thought. Paced down the hall and stood

outside the surgical theater, hugging herself. Praying. Begging God to save him, save her—them!

The front door creaked open, jerking her attention to the waiting area. Retreating into the shadows, she had no idea how long she'd been standing here. Who had come to the clinic this late? Was it Maaz's men?

The question made her slink back further and slip into another medical room. She let the shadows swallow her—did not want to make it easy for them to find her or take her back to that camp. To the royals.

Directly across from her was the surgical bay. Beyond that door, Owen. The sight of him so still, so unconscious . . .

Oh, Owen . . .

She swiveled around. Back to the wall, she let herself slide down, tears swelling. Only now, fearing his death, did she comprehend the hollowness that had consumed her entire existence swarmed once again, reminding her how cold and empty everything had felt before he had come into his life.

She tilted her head back and cried. "Please . . . please don't take him. I need him." Hands steepled over her face, she tried to keep her sniffles quiet. "I'll go with him—please just let him live." Yes, yes, that was good. Right. "Let him live and I'll go. And trust him—You." A sob wracked her. "Please."

"Hello?" someone called from the waiting area.

Dashing away her tears, Leighton rose even as the door to the surgical room opened and the nurse came out. She paused, giving Leighton a scowl, then hurried to the front.

From the surgical bay where the door stood ajar, laughter bubbled out. *His* laughter—Owen's.

Pulled forward by that beautiful sound, Leighton nudged open the door. Saw him on the table—awake. Those blue eyes swung in her direction. *Thank You, God!* She rushed across the hall to him. "Owen!"

"What are you doing here?" Dr. Abeni grunted, but then went back to stitching with a shake of his head.

"Princess," Owen said, lumbering a hand toward her.

She caught it, held it to herself, choking off more tears. "I thought you were dying."

"*I* thought I was dying too," he said, his words slurred, then he angled his head and squinted at her hard. "Were you crying? Over me?"

Heat flushed her cheeks, but she tried to shrug away the embarrassment by rolling her eyes. "Why didn't you tell me you were hurt so bad?"

"Because he's a thickheaded oaf!"

Surprised at the intruding voice, Leighton whirled, her mind amped and expecting Maaz's men, but instead found a large man standing there. A large man stood there. "Who—"

"Dante?" Owen's tone held the very shock Leighton felt. "What're you doing here?"

"Doing what you couldn't, it seems." The tall black man ambled over and let his gaze take in Owen's jagged, raw flesh. "Ouch, guess we can't call you PrettyBoy anymore."

"*Nobody* called me that," Owen ground out, grimacing beneath the doctor's ministrations.

"Bro's got a point," said another black man who stepped in behind Dante. "Def not PrettyBoy anymore." His dark eyes slid to Leighton. "But chicks dig scars, don't they?"

Outrage coursed through Leighton that they were mocking him. "He nearly died!"

"But he's a Scion—knows better than to die on an op." Dante planted a hand on the examination table next to Owen's shoulder and leaned down.

"Dude," Owen said, angling away. "Get off me, man."

When the words slurred into the stale air, Dante sniffed. "He's been doped."

"What's going on?" Leighton asked, frowning at the two men who clearly knew Owen. Were they from the team that wanted to rescue her? "Who are you?"

"You should all not be here," Dr. Abeni complained as he finished the stitching and set down his tools on a metal tray.

"That's the plan—to *not* be here," Dante said, glancing up at Leighton. "I'm Dante, that's Luther." His attention shifted to Apollo. "Time to exfil, Scar."

"I don't need your help, traitor." Looking drunk, Owen strained to sit up and nearly went off the side of the table.

"Whoa, wait!" Leighton caught his arm, bracing him as Dante prevented him from hitting the floor. Why had Owen called him a traitor? Should she be worried?

"No!" the doctor barked, straightening. "He is drugged, still weak."

Luther grabbed a scrub top from the side and edged toward Leighton. "Slide over, Princess." He didn't wait for her to comply and went to work threading the scrub over Owen's head. "What'd you give him, Doc? What's in the IV?"

Dr. Abeni's expression tightened. "I insist you leave. At once."

"That's the plan," Dante said. "I know this seems sus to you, but these two are in a lot of danger, and we need to get them out of here before trouble finds them. Tracking?"

"He's being nice," Luther said, all business. "I'm not—you can be a part of the solution or you can be unconscious."

"Do not threaten me!" Dr. Abeni spat.

This whole situation unsettled Leighton, so she could well imagine how the doctor felt. But these men were Omen. So, she'd trust that because they're the ones who brought Owen to her. "I'm sorry—I know these men must seem quite rude, but we really do need to leave. I think someone is trying to kill us."

Dr. Abeni considered her, then the men, his expression waxing from angry to uncertain. "You are sure you know these men?"

"No, I don't," Leighton admitted, then indicated to Owen. "But he does. He works with them."

"Not quite," Owen slurred and shoved Dante's touch away. "Scions don't like Omen."

"Young and immature," Luther said as he urged Owen to an upright position, bracing him on either side.

"He trusts them, so I do," Leighton focused on the Kenyan doctor. "Can you tell us what drugs you've given him?"

"Saline, antibiotics. Oral ketamine."

Luther muttered an oath.

"Explains the agitation," Dante said, sliding in to assist and steady Owen on the edge of the table.

Feeling powerless, Leighton watched as Owen stood. His knees gave way, but Dante caught and steadied him. Her stomach tightened, imagining how much it must hurt Owen to hook his right arm over Dante's shoulder, what with the raw flesh and stitches.

"At least it'll wear off fast." Luther gathered some supplies, stuffed them into a backpack he had, then moved toward Abeni.

With a heavy breath, Owen darted a look around, reached for Leighton.

She started toward him, but his hand returned to Dante for support. "Are you sure you're up to this? You can't even stand on your own. You nearly died." She looked to the other men, needing them to understand. "He nearly died."

"We saw," Dante said quietly, then adjusted to support Owen better. "I see your fear, but you can trust us."

"I trust Owen," she countered, not liking this rushing Owen from the doctor, but also aware that if Maaz sent people to retrieve her, that front door could open any minute and deliver more trouble.

"And like you said, he trusts us."

"But I don't like you," Owen groused, touching his jaw where the stitches had left the flesh angry.

The nurse hurried to him and held out a bottle of pills. "The cuts are deep. He'll need to stay on antibiotics for a couple of weeks. We don't have that much, but this will get him through until he can see his own doctor."

Owen swiped the bottle, glowering at Dante, then he eyed the pills. He squinted and pinched the bridge of his nose. "Everything is blurry."

"Hey! Hey!" came a shout from the front, then thundering down the hall seconds before Mugo rushed in, skidding to a stop to avoid colliding with Owen and Dante. "The Cruiser—the royals are coming. They are almost here. You must go."

Luther handed the camp manager a stack of bills. "Thanks." Threading his arm into the backpack, he nodded to Dante. "Ready?" He produced a weapon.

Surprise held Leighton fast—not just that he had the gun but also that they'd bribed Mugo to stand watch? It was . . . clever.

Dante angled toward the door with Owen, whose feet seemed to be jelly. He wobbled, making her yelp, expecting him to crash to the wall or floor. Owen met her gaze. Gave a stiff smirk. "No more tears, right, Princess?"

Heat scorched her cheeks, but she straightened, surprised he had noticed her red-rimmed eyes. "You're hallucinating."

"Do you have a back door?" Luther asked the doctor.

"No."

"Front door it is." They shuffled Owen down the hall.

Leighton hurried behind them, not convinced moving him was the right decision but also well aware they had no choice. She watched Dante maneuver Owen to the side as Luther tactically opened the door, cleared it, then motioned them on.

Darkness beyond the door surrendered to string lights, pole lights, and naked bulbs that allowed the local market to descend into nighttime revelry. She eased the door closed behind her as their steps thudded on the hard-packed dirt path. When she turned, Leighton aimed toward the men. Somewhere in that turn, recognition struck. "Wait." She'd seen a familiar pair of eyes that dumped ice down her spine. She drew in a breath, freezing as she searched the street carts and faces of the locals.

"Princess."

"They're here," she breathed, unable to move. "I saw Ghalib!"

Owen faltered. "What—" He whipped around . . . and lost his balance. Staggering, he tried to right himself, but a vendor's display of small wares clipped the back of his legs.

"Owen!" Leighton lunged to catch him.

He caught her hand. Blue eyes widened even as he realized gravity had won the battle—and yanked her down with him.

Pop-pop! Pop!

Her knees cracked against the hard ground. Leighton fought to avoid injuring Owen. "Sorry. Sorry."

He grunted. "What is your problem?"

Shocked at his irritation, she met his blue eyes for a half second. Recalled what Dante had said—the agitation was because of the drugs. But his retort still hurt.

"Princess."

Acutely aware of her position atop of Owen, she shuttled aside and looked at the men from Omen, not sure which had called her.

"Where'd you see the guy?" Dante asked.

"When we came out, he was straight ahead, slightly to the left."

"Like a clock," Dante said. "Eleven or ten?"

Oh, that made sense. "Eleven."

— • —

"Apollo, you good?"

Owen blinked, looking at his Scion brother, who adjusted

positions, aimed out toward the incoming fire. "No thanks to you." Man, it felt like his skin was crawling—and yet also seemed like he didn't know where his feet were. He cursed himself for biting Leighton's head off. The ketamine was wrecking him. "Thought we were exfiling, not sitting around."

A curse seared the air—from Luther, who crouch-ran toward them. "Car's gone—someone took off with it, and enemy reinforcements just pulled up."

"Let's go." But when Owen pushed up, his knees said heck no, sending him back down. Humiliated, he looked around to see what he'd tripped over—but it was only his own two feet.

"He's impaired," Dante said. "No way we can hoof it out of here."

"We have to try," Luther insisted. "Options are that or surrender."

"Not on your life," Owen growled.

Both men glanced down and to the side, listening.

That's when Owen noticed their comms devices. They were listening to Pike, no doubt. And not sharing that info. Which ticked him off. "What's happening?"

Dante exchanged a long look with Luther, then gave a grim nod. "We can do it."

"What?" Leighton asked, as she shifted closer.

Man, why was she all up in his business? Owen rolled his shoulders, telling himself to let it go. Keep his mouth shut. His head was jacked because of the drugs.

"If you don't tell us what's going on," Owen bit out, "then—"

"We came in light with the plan to get you into the car and out of here," Luther snapped. "But now we have no wheels. And overwatch reports five vehicles inbound with armed combatants."

"Badly outnumbered and outgunned," Dante growled.

Owen struggled back to his feet. "C'mon." He'd barely gotten there when he was forced to steady himself by leaning against the table. "We need to move."

"Are you crazy?" Leighton objected. "You can barely walk straight."

"Straight or crooked, it's better than going back to the royals."

"Is it?" she challenged, then looked at Dante and Luther. "I appreciate the chance, but we don't have a prayer. Do we?"

"Talk later." Luther herded them to a bigger vendor cart, crouched there. Positioned himself and popped off a couple rounds.

Leighton glanced at the three of them. "Jeddah—"

"We're in Jeddah?" Owen asked, mind feeling like a thick vat of sludge.

Leighton frowned at him. "What? No—"

"It's the drugs. Causes disorientation and confusion," Dante muttered.

It was? Owen shifted his gaze to the ground. Tried to recall how they'd gotten here.

"I was trying to say Jeddah may be too late for a rescue after this," Leighton said. "We go back to camp, and since you're wounded, we tell the royals you can't go out on safari."

"That's dumb—they don't care about me. They'll still make you go."

"Maybe, but we can play on the king's order for you to protect me. And I can claim exhaustion and weariness after the lion attack. Then you need to insist on me staying behind. You'll demand they comply with the king's orders."

Owen stared at her. "Who made you the boss?" And why hadn't he thought of that?

"Shut up, man," Dante said. "You're not thinking straight."

Crack! Pop!

Dante ducked, then faced the threat, both he and Luther firing back. "We have to move. We're too open."

"The alley," Luther barked. "Go!"

When Leighton reached to help him stand, Owen shoved her

off. Nearly faceplanted. Felt the world shifting and dived for the alley. But relentless little princess was right there, manhandling him. "Get off—"

"Owen, I'm just trying to help."

"Why should I listen? You won't listen and let me get you out of here," he huffed as he slumped against the plastered wall. He tightened his jaw. Knew he was being a jerk. "Sorry." He scratched a hand over his skull. "The drugs . . ."

"I know." Leighton's expression was taut with offense but she let out a shuddering breath. "Seeing you nearly die made me realize what's at stake. The risks are too high." She palmed Dante's spine as he backed into the alley, firing.

Shots pinged off a metal pole. Another cracked a wall nearby, sending them deeper into the alley. "Maybe you should leave and check out the Serengeti—get there early."

"Jeddah is more familiar, easier to recon," Luther said.

"If we survive that long."

"Yo," Dante said with a huff. "That is not cool."

"Let's bake a plan," Owen insisted.

"Not happening. Not discussing this without the chief," Luther said.

"Yeah, don't change any plans. Stick to the itinerary already in play," Dante said. "Just be ready."

"When?" Leighton asked.

"All the time."

Owen knew that'd be the answer but he didn't like it. Couldn't plan accordingly. A constant state of readiness was quickly exhausting. And he was *already* exhausted. Hated that his legs wouldn't cooperate better. He felt drunk and had nothing left after the lion attack and blood loss.

"What do we do?" Leighton asked as they huddled up in the alley.

Dante rubbed his jaw. "Hike out—"

"He cannot do that," Leighton countered. Then she flinched. "I'm sorry. I mean—"

"No, it's good." Owen hated it, but it was the truth, and he needed to face that. Figure out a path to safety and success for Leighton. For both of them. Well, not really him—he wasn't the point here. "She's right—I'm in no shape. If there's no car, I'm just a liability."

"You're *not* a liability," Leighton objected.

"Agree to disagree," he said, then eyed the guys. "Okay, new plan, but first—we have to make this look good."

"Come again?" Luther knelt far enough back to be out of sight but close enough to the opening to provide protective cover.

"They"—Owen bobbed his head toward the fighters—"need to believe you were attacking us, trying to kidnap us."

Dante grinned. "For ransom."

"Yeah, right," Owen said, glad his thoughts were actually making sense this time. "That we weren't trying to escape. Because if we go back and they don't believe that . . ." He gave a cockeyed nod. "Won't matter if we die here in the streets or in a tent—dead is dead."

"If we do this," Leighton said, eyeing the Omen team, "can you two get away safely?"

"Incoming!"

Before Owen could move, he felt more than saw the bullet that seared past. It hit a metal downpipe. Ricocheted.

Leighton yelped, jerking aside and clapping a hand to her cheek.

Pulse jammed, Owen pushed to her. "Leighton!"

"I'm okay," she said, her voice tremoring as she lifted her hand. A trail of red streaked her cheek. She managed a smile. "Will this make it look good?"

He wanted to curse, but a shaky laugh was all he managed. "Yeah." He flinched to the guys. "Go! Go! We'll slow them down, hopefully enough to stop them from coming after you." He took

Leighton's hand and started back toward the street. Prayed the swimming vision would clear.

"I'm scared this won't work," she murmured as they ducked behind a cart to avoid being shot.

"Same." One thing after another had gone wrong, and Owen feared he was failing her already. "My mom always said prayers are better than fear, so—God? We could use a miracle." He ducked around the cart and glanced back, hoping the guys were getting clear of this mess. Two able-bodied and healthy operators had a better chance without an impaired operator and a girl with no training. His balance shifted. He stumbled into Leighton, then tripped over her feet. He went down, and since their hands were clasped, he again pulled her down with him. Heard her yelp in his ear.

Thuds behind him warned the enemy was close. "Scramble with me," he whispered. And they did, as if fleeing for their lives. When he turned, he found two armed men staring down rifles at them.

"Help!" Leighton hadn't missed a beat. She was on all fours, pleading for help from the gunmen sent by the royals. "The men . . ." She looked back down the alley. "They tried to take us."

Impressed with the little actress, Owen did the same. Relief chugged through him that there was no sign of Dante or Luther. But when he looked back up, he found the curled lip of Ghalib and Nasir. "Never thought I'd say this," he said, trying not to laugh at the great irony, "but I'm glad to see you two."

FOURTEEN

Masai Mara National Reserve, Kenya

"GET UP," NASIR SNARLED AS HE CAUGHT Leighton's arm and hauled her upright.

She staggered, reaching for Owen, who groaned when Ghalib and another man grabbed him and jerked him to his feet. "Easy, easy," Leighton pleaded, but her words fell on deaf ears that were hauling Owen to a vehicle.

Stumbling along behind him, she felt every twitch and jerk they levied against him in the pit of her stomach. For a half second, she considered telling them the doctor hadn't finished his ministrations, but she wasn't entirely sure Abeni could be trusted to not betray that the men who'd taken them were actually allies.

Thrust toward the same Cruiser, she climbed in, noticing two more vehicles loaded up and poised to follow. Owen angled into the SUV beside her, wincing as he lowered himself onto a seat with a long moan. When the engine revved and lurched away from the bustling town—earning another groan from Owen—Leighton realized Mugo was their driver. Oh mercy—would he betray them?

No . . . not unless he wanted her to betray that he'd taken a bribe.

Owen leaned his head back and closed his eyes, hand to his right pectoral that the lion had swiped.

"It was very foolish to try to escape," Ghalib growled from the front passenger seat.

"*Escape*?" she balked around a racing heart. "Those men tried to kidnap us!"

"They knew," Owen grunted and braced as the vehicle bounced down the road. "Knew she was a princess. Said a lot of money would be paid for her."

"You expect me to believe that?" Ghalib snapped.

"Up to you, man," Owen said with a moan. "But if you really think I'd try to escape in this condition . . ." He chuckled, then grimaced.

Relieved when silence fell on the vehicle en route back to the reserve, she watched the bustling city vanish beyond the windows. Prayed this story they'd given him would not only be delivered to the crown prince but believed.

She heard another grunt from Owen and glanced at him. "You okay?" Only as she studied him did her mind suddenly, vibrantly return to that terrible attack. She'd never forget watching him throw himself into the fray to protect her. This time—straight at an angry lion. When he'd fallen off the monument and landed beneath the great beast, she just knew he was dead. Or would be soon. But this man, this warrior, was as wild and untamed as the cat he'd fought.

He lolled his head in her direction, winked, then closed his eyes again.

Admiration stirred in her chest. How had she ever deserved to have a man like him in her life? Her stomach rumbled—loudly. The kebabs had been a nice appetizer but not enough to miss their only full meal.

"Me too," Owen murmured.

"We missed dinner."

"Yeah." He swiped a hand over his mouth, then grimaced. He had five stitches along his jaw and six more on his neck. "Hey, uh, Mugo?"

The driver glanced back at them, his eyes likely begging them not to rat him out.

"At camp, is there a way to get something eat?"

"Sure, sure," Mugo said eagerly. "Anything you want, Mugo get."

When they drove up the long road to the tents a half hour later, Leighton spotted Rayan and Maaz walking toward the Cruiser. "Oh no."

Owen's hand covered hers and he squeezed.

It was comforting—but not as much as she needed facing these two. Her heart sank, unplugging the dread that she had managed to bury while with Apollo at the clinic.

"Let me handle it," Apollo said, grim-faced as they climbed out. And he made a really good show of being in pain—or maybe it wasn't a show.

Maaz considered them both. "Apollo, you are well?"

Owen maneuvered to put himself between her and the princes. "Not even hardly. Guide abandons us on the road, I get mauled by a lion, take thirty-something stitches, then have to fight off thugs who wanted to ransom Nouri."

With a sharp intake of breath, Rayan stalked to her. "You are hurt!" He was reaching for the seared path left by the bullet.

"I am okay. Really, your concern should be for O—uh, Apollo." Pulse jackhammering at using his given name—deemed inappropriate here—she worked up a smile. "The doctor did not even get to finish stitching him before the men tried to kidnap me."

"We found them in an alley," Ghalib said. "Running."

Owen gave the guy a glower. "Not sure I like your tone—yeah, we were running—you were shooting at us!"

Maaz snapped a fierce look at the man.

"They were with two other men."

"Kidnappers!" Owen snapped, then drew in a ragged breath and braced himself.

Was he in real pain? Or was he acting to give the story more weight?

"Wasn't like we could get far," Owen continued, leaning against the Cruiser. "Still too weak."

"But you stopped them from taking her," Rayan said in a tone that almost conveyed respect.

"Or was helping them," Ghalib suggested.

Leighton gasped. "No! That is not—"

"Enough." Rayan lifted a hand, his expression tender as he again considered the welt on her cheek. "Perhaps Mr. Apollo should rest. Nouri can come with me—"

"Negative," Owen spoke up, much to her relief. "We're both starved since we missed dinner. Mugo said we could get some food, so that is our pl—"

"This is a lot to believe," Maaz said speculatively. "One would wonder how village men knew Nouri was a princess."

Leave it to Maaz to find a flaw in their story. Leighton held her breath as she eyed Owen.

"Got me," Apollo said. "Wouldn't surprise me, though, if the same man who left the princess and myself on the side of the road to be eaten by lions put word out to locals that they could make some quick cash." He shrugged.

Yes. Yes, that made sense. It even sounded legitimate. She swallowed, silently begging Maaz to believe them.

The crown prince's gaze probed Owen, then Leighton, her heart pounding so loud she was sure all the wildlife in the park would hear it. Finally, he nodded. "Perhaps." He started walking, indicating for them to follow. "Rest. And maybe we should send you both back to Jeddah first thing in the morning. For both safety and health concerns."

"No." Leighton flinched at her quick rejection. Her breath stalled in her throat, the plan for Omen to come for them tomorrow completely upended if they were sent back in the morning. When she saw Maaz's scowl, she stiffened. "I—Dr. Abeni said Mr. Apollo should rest."

"This night has been most regrettable," Prince Maaz said, his expression wrapped in cordiality and . . . something she couldn't quite put her finger on. "What happened out there is inexcusable, and I would understand if you felt it safer to return Nouri to the palace."

Her heart pounded as Owen—she really needed to just stick with Apollo so she remained focused on why he was really here: to get her out—again considered her. To be fair—Omen hadn't agreed to her suggestion. And returning did make sense. But could they risk it? Besides, returning to Jeddah right now somehow felt like a giant step backwards.

"I should rest tomorrow. No travel. My head can't take it. We'll see about the final day later." As he eyed her, Apollo shook his head. "I think Nouri has been enjoying the safari, and I would not want her angry with me if I cost her the Serengeti as well." Hand held to her, he angled toward the tent. "If you'll excuse us . . ."

"The princess can stay with me," Rayan insisted.

"Yeah, I don't think so," Apollo said curtly, pulling her toward himself as he seemed to grow several inches. "Sorry, but after what happened tonight, I'm not taking any chances."

Rayan jerked straight and scowled. "Is that an accusation?"

"Call it what you want. For me, it's a reality check," Apollo countered as he walked backwards toward their tents. "No guide should leave two tourists in the reserve at night to be killed by the wildlife," he noted. "It'll take a lot to convince me that his abandoning us wasn't intentional." He gave them a clipped nod. "Since the king has tasked me with her protection, Nouri stays with me. That includes tomorrow."

When Rayan glowered at Apollo and started forward, the crown prince swung a hand in front of his cousin, stopping him. Leighton wanted to kiss Maaz's feet.

Owen gave a sharp nod. "Night, Your Highnesses." He motioned her onward.

The fifty paces to her tent were the longest ones of her life. Leighton did not breathe easy again until they were inside and Apollo lowered the canvas flap, giving them a modicum of privacy.

"I can't believe that actually worked," Leighton whispered with a giggle as she shoved her hands into her hair. "That look he gave you—I thought for sure he'd punch you or something."

"Half expected him to." Apollo gingerly lowered himself to the couch and hissed a groan.

Guilt harangued her at the obvious pain in his tense posture. She hurried to him. "What can I do?"

"Nothing, I just need to not . . . move." He sagged back and let out a long moan.

"I was so scared Maaz was going to mess up—"

"What?" Owen gave her a stiff look, reminding her that this place wasn't likely secure, that there might be bugs. "Our plans to sleep in?"

Her laugh was hollow, and she couldn't help it as she joined him on the couch, folding her legs up under her.

"Like I told Maaz—food and rest. No change in plans."

Just as Dante had warned them. Which meant if nothing happened tomorrow, then they would fly out the next morning to the final stop on the safari. "Can I confess to a smidgen of relief that I get to see the Serengeti?" Her selfishness screamed across her conscience. "I'm a terrible person—that lion nearly killed you, you were mortally wounded—"

Apollo barked a laugh, then grunted, lightly touching his chest. "I have no mortal wounds."

"Still, it's terrible of me to be excited to see—"

"Nouri, stop," he said, landing a hand on her knee. "I'm glad you have something to look forward to." Some strange thing rippled through his features, tugging his gaze down, away.

"Thanks. I guess I just got scared when Maaz suggested sending us back right away. Not because—" She almost did it again. "Well, you know."

He nodded. "Yeah. Besides, I hope plans don't change because . . ." He swiped a hand over his mouth and winced at the stitches along his jaw.

That mention of plans not changing was about Omen coming. Wasn't it? Thankfully the phraseology kept any spying ears from understanding. But why didn't he want that to happen? Hadn't he been adamant about getting her to safety? "What?"

Turning his gaze to hers seemed to hurt, likely tugging his stitches. There was a concern in those pretty blue eyes. Guilt. A knowing.

"What?" she repeated with a laugh she didn't feel.

"I don't want—"

Two raps on wood startled them both, then a second later, the tent flap adjusted. "Hello? Food for you."

Though Apollo stood as Chacha entered carrying a wood tray piled with meats and vegetables, Leighton found herself paralyzed by the two words he'd spoken before the knock. He didn't want . . . What? What didn't he want?

Me?

It was a silly thought, considering she was just a mission to him. Mercy, after all they'd been through, the truth of that stung.

"You okay?" Apollo returned to the couch, eyeing the meat on the ottoman. "You've got that look again."

Surprise lifted her gaze to his. "What look?"

"The cornered-rabbit look." He gave a weak smile as he chose a kebab and tugged off a cube of cooked meat, then paused. "Look, hey, I know I said some mean things at the clinic. I wasn't myself."

It was easy to wave that off. Not so much that he might not want her. She hated that the thought was in her head now and tried to rebuff it.

Maybe she should ask him about it and get it over with. "Before the food arrived, you'd said you didn't want something, then got interrupted." She eased onto the floor and picked up some cheese from the tray, daring to look up at him.

Guarded, tense, he watched her. Sighed. Pulled the meat from the kebab. "Your suggestion at the clinic . . ."

When he didn't finish again, she eyed him, saw him lift his eyebrows in meaning—a reminder that the room could be bugged.

She nodded that she understood.

"It'll probably happen."

Her heart skipped a beat, locked in his gaze. "That's a good thing."

"Yeah." He focused on the food, chewing. Picking another. "I just . . ." There he went again, not finishing his thought. "I hate not knowing where or when that change will happen. But here is smart."

"Here." Which would mean tomorrow.

He ate a roasted vegetable. "Yeah."

"And you don't want that change to happen tomorrow?" How did that make sense? He'd been all about getting her to agree to an escape.

His expression seemed sheepish. "Yeah," he conceded. "They gave me a way to know"—he tapped his ear and lifted his eyebrows in meaning—"but I think I dropped it. It's gone."

His ear . . . oh, a communication ear piece. Wait— "You lost it?"

Apollo looked chagrined. "Go easy on the wounded hero, okay?"

That made her falter, but questions were zipping through her fried mind. "How will we know . . . if plans change?"

He hesitated, then lowered himself to the floor next to her. "So, you'd go . . . ?"

Yes, she would. But it felt too easy to say that. Too careless.

Leighton leaned back against the couch and wiped her hands. Eyed the raw, stitched flesh of his jaw, a painful reminder of the very real threat to them that existed. "Knowing someone is trying to arrange my death, putting you in danger . . ." she whispered and shifted to face him. "Swear to me Ummi is safe."

"Last I knew . . ." He, too, kept his words very quiet.

"That's not a guarantee."

"I've been with you, so I can't vow that she is still with Omen, but neither can I imagine any scenario where she isn't. But I won't lie—that's speculation on my part."

Leighton shifted her gaze to the food, which now looked terribly blah. "I'd go . . ." When he touched her shoulder, she bounced her gaze to his. Fell into the mesmerizing sea-blue pools.

"Thank you, Leighton. Your trust means a lot to me. And it will make plan changes infinitely more simple."

Wary, she drew a kebab off the tray and stared at it, not sure she had the appetite for it. "Seeing that massive lion knock you to the ground, seeing your chest shredded, I felt . . . *terror*. As if the *one thing* keeping me safe was being ripped away. I knew . . . *knew* if you died, I died." Swallowing around a thick throat, she told herself not to cry. She wasn't weak. She wasn't a helpless maiden. "You stood up to Maaz and Rayan, even Nasir, for me."

"It's my job."

Her heart stuttered a little at that, then she peeked at him. "Is that all I am, your job?"

His hand drifted to her cheek. "No."

Nervous jellies swarmed her belly. "If I'm going to die," she said, tears pricking her eyes—heedless of her command to stay strong, "I don't want to die with *them*, in that palace. I don't want that to be my last memory."

Apollo angled closer and tucked his chin to urge her gaze to his. "I am not going to let you die. It will take a lot more than a lion to bring me down."

"I was *terrified* when the lion knocked you away. When you hit the ground with that awful thud." No idea why, but there was suddenly a torrent of tears. Uncontrollable and all-consuming. It was all so much—Ummi, the royals, the king, the stress of being what everyone wanted her to be, not being what she wanted to be.

His arm hooked her shoulders and pulled her close. She welcomed the comfort, the strength of him as she pressed her face to his shoulder—thankfully the uninjured side—and cried. Furious with herself for doing this again, she tried to stem the tide, but it just made things worse.

He held her close. "I'm going to get you out of here," he whispered against her ear, so soft she almost didn't hear it. "You'll be safe. When this is over, you'll never have to pretend or lie again." His lips teased her temple, making her stomach spasm. "No more secrets."

Which made her cry more. She was a complete, blubbering mess, and he was a lifeline. An anchor in this storm of her life. As the tide overwhelmed her, she clutched his shirt—

Apollo sucked in an audible, tense breath.

The stitches! She jerked up—and cracked her head right against his cheek.

He grunted.

Mortified, she drew back. "I'm killing you!"

He huffed a laugh, and when she tried to pull away, he slid a hand to her nape. "Hey."

Feeling as much as hearing him, Leighton stilled. Didn't want to look up, but also couldn't avoid the lifeline in the chaos that was Owen Metcalfe.

Blue eyes beckoned her into a paradise of hope and protection. Invited her to release the emplacements around her life and heart.

She sank into the warm reassurance of his presence as their foreheads touched. Mercy, he was so close. Smelled so good—even if his scent was tinged with antiseptic from the clinic. It was just a beautiful reminder of what he'd already done for her. That with him, she was safe.

He shifted his face, eyes trained on her mouth.

Oh, yes please! Please, kiss me!

———— • ————

The gentle lift of her chin toward his was the invitation and permission he'd been waiting for. Owen captured her mouth with his, gentle yet firm so she did not doubt the fervency of what he felt. Her lips were supple and sweet against his, yielding, accepting.

He cupped her face, feeling a tremulous, dangerous fire roar through his gut. As if he had unleashed some powerful force that could steal his soul. He wanted her closer, in his arms. To hold her. Reassure her. Claim her as his.

Fueled by that fire, he pulled her closer. And instantly regretted it—her hand at once landing on the stitches of the worst, deepest gouge. Now the fire that erupted had nothing to do with passion or this beauty who had let him into her dark world. He recoiled and choked back a grunt. Broke the moment.

Concern splayed across her features. "I'm sorry—are you okay?"

He hunched as if that might protect his chest. Had this feeling God put those claw marks in exactly the place that would keep him in line. But he couldn't resist flirting with her. "Kiss me and make it better?"

She laughed, her cheeks flushed. "You're incorrigible."

"My mom says that too." He really liked the color he'd put in her face. Liked this casual banter as well.

Leighton laughed. "She sounds like a very smart woman."

Great job ruining the moment, Apollo. But at least she wasn't running off or shoving him away. "My mom is pretty amazing." He visually traced Leighton's face, thought of all she'd been through. All she'd fought and endured, yet came out stronger, tougher. "You're a lot like her." He smoothed the hair around her face. "Right down to your dark hair."

"I can't believe kissing me didn't hurt your jaw," she said.

"If you're really in doubt, we can try again so you're sure." He stole another kiss.

She sniffed and looked down, more color infusing her olive skin. "And here I thought you didn't want me."

He frowned. "Do what?"

"When you said you 'didn't want' and got interrupted—I thought it was me you didn't want."

He sniffed and shook his head. "No . . . I'd planned to say I didn't want to lose you."

Lips parting in surprise, she studied him.

"But then I got gun-shy, wasn't sure I had you to lose." He stroked her cheek. "You are so beautiful."

"Apollo—"

"How about 'Owen' in our kissing moments?"

She arched a rueful eyebrow at him. "Plural?"

"If that means more than one, yes, please."

This time, she gave a full-on belly laugh, then rested her head back on his arm that hooked around behind her, the brush of her hair taunting him. "I'm so glad we've had time together, that we could relax. That I could find out you're so funny." She reached up and tousled his hair, which he felt to his core. "Handsome, despite the bleached hair."

Hold up. "You do know that was only done so you wouldn't recognize me when I walked into the palace, right?" he said quietly, still attentive to the operational security thing.

"What idiot thought bleached hair would do that?"

Owen nearly busted a stitch or two laughing. He had to

remember to tell Pike she'd called him an idiot. But . . . was that a curled lip? Disgust? "You don't like the bleached hair?"

She wrinkled her nose.

The simple gesture seemed as if dark storm clouds had hidden the sun from him. "I'll shave it at first chance."

She gave a disbelieving laugh, then straightened to look him head-on. Considered him. "You're not serious, are you?"

"Anything that gets in the way of you looking at me how you were a minute ago has to go."

Sentimentality coiled through her pretty features. She touched his face. Eyed the stitches on his jaw. "You nearly died today protecting me . . . I did nothing to protect you—"

"Not your job. Besides, remember the elephants—" Owen jerked straight. "Elephant!"

Leighton eyed him as he dug in his pocket. "What—"

"I got you something. Completely forgot about it." He tugged it out and let a necklace of braided black cords with a charm that had an elephant inside a ring dangle before her.

Her eyes went all melty as she reached for it. "The circle of protection," she murmured, her words thick with emotion. She slipped the necklace on and touched the charm at the hollow of her throat. "How does it look?"

"Perfect."

"This is so sweet," she said, fingering the elephant. "Thank you—but how? You didn't have time or money."

"That time I fell into that vendor? I spotted it. Made a bargain the seller couldn't refuse."

"You are . . ." Her lips and chin quavered as she fell silent and studied him. It was as if she wanted to memorize him, his face.

When he spotted her eyes going glossy with unshed tears, he tensed. "Hey, what—"

"My life was so dark before you," she croaked. "I thought the rest of my existence would be spent in that palace, being whatever they wanted me to be." She managed a wan smile. "You have infuriated me and angered me. But you've also made me laugh. Protected me."

"You already said that." Her smiles were getting weaker, and it stressed him. What was going on in that pretty head of hers?

"You *protected* me, even when it meant Maaz or Nasir might kill you for it," she said, a particular emphasis that hauled more tears with it. "*Nobody* has ever done that for me. All my life, I've had to live the lie. Be the lie. To protect Ummi. Protect her secret. Be strong when I didn't have any strength. Lie to friends, hide from friends, avoid having friends. It was so . . . dark. But with you . . ." Tears fell silently, gently.

"I come with the elephant—a circle of protection." As if to emphasize his words, he wrapped his arms around her. "Rest, Leighton. Let me be strong for you. Even if it's just for now." Smoothing a hand along her spine, he stayed there with her, their breaths and hearts mingling.

"I'm so glad you came, Owen."

Food forgotten, they sat on the floor in each other's arms. Resting. Relaxing, existing. Eventually, they settled in and picked at the food, staying close.

When they finally called it a night, Owen felt more awkward than ever climbing into bed next to her. This woman he could see a future with. That thought startled him as he settled in. Sleeping on his side—which ensured he kept to his half of the bed—wasn't an option because of the stitches and still-angry flesh sewn together. So he was forced to lie on his back. More than once in the night, Leighton woke him up, saying he was snoring. He grumbled an apology and fell back asleep. Woke with the sudden realization that Dante had said no change in plans. By staying at base camp, they were breaking plan. He wrestled out of bed, his chest burning and angry as he hurried to the door, only to discover the royals were gone.

"What's wrong?" Leighton asked, coming upright in the bed.

"We . . . he said no change in plans."

She seemed suddenly awake, wary.

"By staying . . ."

She groaned. "We changed plans." She climbed out of bed. "Should we hurry—"

"It's too late. They're gone." He scratched a hand over the back of his thick skull. "We should try to stay in the open, stay visible in case they come here." By dawn, he was a wreck.

They remained at the base camp, wandered out to the mess tent for lunch, watched as the workers prepped for the bonfire. The anticipation that Omen might come hung over them all day, over him. He tried to keep watch. Scanned the terrain for any sign of Rawlins or the others. But night came and the royals returned without incident. They joined the others for the bonfire, not for the camaraderie, but for the visibility.

"Mr. Apollo," Maaz called from the other side. "Will you join us tomorrow? Both of you?"

Was there an insistence to his words? Or was that Owen's imagination? Either way, sitting here wouldn't be good. "Yeah. I think so."

One more day, then the Serengeti.

Which meant tomorrow had to be the day Omen would interdict. The anticipation forbade him from sleeping that night. Nerves buzzed through him the next morning as he checked the stitches for any sign of infection. Cursed when he saw the angry welts around the ones on his jaw. Sweating yesterday hadn't helped. He'd take antibiotics. If he had any. But he'd traded them for the necklace. The one that had seemed to tip the tide between them. He didn't want to lose that. Or her.

God, help me, but I think I'm falling in love with her.

There was this strange symmetry to life when she looked at him, like everything was aligning.

Hours in the heat and sun aggravated his injuries and mood.

Tension radiated through every limb because he expected both to get ambushed and for Omen to interdict. Before he knew it, his jaw and neck were on fire. Maybe from the heat and sweat slipping into the stitched flesh, but the very real possibility existed that it was from the tension of clenching his teeth as he searched for the team.

It's your own stupid fault for losing the comms. For not telling Dante when he had a chance.

A herd of zebras came bolting around them, darting to a water source, he guessed. Or maybe away from a predator.

Huh. Had Mufasa come to finish the job?

Or . . . His gaze snapped in the direction of the zebras. Was Omen out there? He shifted forward in his seat, peering around the side of the doorless vehicle to get a better view. Squinted through the pluming dust blocking his view. Hand fisted, he clenched his jaw, frustrated.

Where were they? What was taking them so long?

A gentle hand on his drew his gaze. Leighton's expression was thick with concern. Then with wariness, silently asking if he saw them. He gave a quick shake of his head.

Her brow furrowed. "Your jaw looks like it's irritated."

"Not the only part of me irritated right now."

"You took the antibiotics?"

"It's fine."

Her gaze darted over his face, tightening, and her intelligence shone again as she tilted her head. "I didn't see the medicine bottle in our tent. Where . . . ?" Her brows lifted, then knotted again. "Please tell me you didn't leave the antibiotics at the clinic." Now she frowned. "No, you had them when we left. I saw them in your hand . . ."

Owen caught her hand. "*Nouri,*" he said, using her Arabic name to remind her there were a lot of ears listening. "I'm fine." Besides, the team was out there. He'd get Dade to give him a shot of something once they were safely away. "It'll be fine."

Hours droned by, his muscles straining with each tick of the proverbial clock. He got out of the Cruiser every chance he had. They hiked for a while to a secluded location where giraffes glided and plucked vegetation from cliff walls.

This . . . surely this was it.

Surreptitiously, he paced the little inlet, a sanctuary from the rest of the preserve, searching high and low for any sign of the team. Watching the grass for Rawlins. His heart climbed into his throat when he noticed a discoloration a dozen paces off. He made his way over and toed the area. "Crow?" he rasped. When no answer came, he tried again. "Crow!" His boot pushed to the ground, and he grunted. Where on earth were th—

"Your stitches do not look well."

The voice of the crown prince whipped Owen around and jammed his heart in his throat. Had Maaz heard him calling for Crow? Belatedly, he recalled the prince's words, which pushed his thoughts to the subtle throb of the stitches. "Yeah, sweat's irritating them."

The six-one crown prince considered him. "Did they not give you medicine?"

That look of concern was almost convincing. "The kidnappers interrupted check-out." Though certain this location was the perfect spot for the extraction, the last thing Owen wanted was for the crown prince to discover the team. Or vice versa.

He tried to go around the prince, but the royal blocked his path with a slight shift to the side. That's when he noticed Maaz's inscrutable expression. "Something wrong?"

"My cousin wants Nouri."

Holy fields of fire and nuclear bombs. "Rayan." There was no way in this world Owen would let that happen. When Maaz nodded an affirmation of the name, Owen did not have a response save for clenched fists. "Why are you telling me? I'm just her bodyguard."

"You are in the way."

A sick sense of satisfaction coursed through Owen. Being in the way was not something he would alter. At least, not willingly. Thank goodness he had a trump card to overrule anything the princes put to him. "The king hired me to protect her. I'm not going anywhere without his command."

"I know," Maaz said quietly, and then . . . there was something in his dark eyes and the twitch of his black beard that gave pause as he edged closer.

Was he threatening him? Owen had pretty solid close-quarters skills, but it wasn't just the crown prince he'd have to face—there would also be the other princes and whatever wildlife got lured in by the chaos.

"The driver," the prince said, glancing to the side, as if making sure they were not being watched or overheard, "I believe he was paid to leave you."

The driver who left them on the side of the road . . .

Was the crown prince confessing? "What makes you think that?"

Narrowing his eyes, Maaz stared at him with near-black irises that were a bottomless pit. "You already suspect that."

"I said as much when we returned to camp, but you didn't answer my question." Owen had nothing to lose. Someone was already trying to kill him and Leighton.

The crown prince never broke eye contact in the seconds that took on the weight of minutes, if not hours, before he finally lifted his palm and showed him something.

Owen glanced down. Horror clawed up his spine at what he saw—the comms piece!

Unable to take a breath, to swallow, or even speak, Owen stared at it. Son of a freak-fried biscuit. Was this the prince's way of calling him out? Trying to see how he'd react? Was this a trap laid for him to careen into?

There was something in the prince's eyes—a knowing. No, not

just a knowing, but a promise of violence. "I found this in camp." Neutrality drenched deceptively calm words. "Do you recognize it?"

Ka-booom! That was the sound of Owen's entire world imploding.

FIFTEEN

Masai Mara National Reserve, Kenya

"TIME TO RETURN TO CAMP."

At the bark of the crown prince, Leighton angled in that direction, secretly grateful for the interruption that afforded her a chance to slip away from the ever-hovering Rayan, who had done everything in his power to keep her apart from Owen. About to duck around to the other side of the vehicle, she spotted Maaz stalking toward them, trailed by Owen.

What was going on? Why did the crown prince look so angry?

"What? We have hours left," complained Daria, turning to her brother. "We still haven't even seen—"

"Do it," Maaz hissed as he stalked back toward the Cruiser trailed by Owen. "Now!"

Leighton moved toward Owen, who said nothing. Face red from the heat and sweat pouring down his face and neck left his shirt drenched. "What—"

"Not now."

Starting at his terse tone, she faltered.

"Sorry." He slowed and touched her arm. "Let's just get back."

They sat in silence the entire forty minutes back to the base camp. When they climbed out, Maaz gathered them up. "Return to your tents. Food will be delivered there."

"Why?" Daria complained again. "This is the last—"

"It seems," Crown Prince Maaz said, "Mr. Apollo is not the only American to learn a hard lesson out here. A ranger has arrested several more on the reserve."

"Poachers?" Aliyah asked.

Several? Several . . . Americans?

Standing rigidly, Apollo balled his fists.

Wait. Leighton's heart tripped over the facts. Over Apollo's reaction. Americans. Arrested. Omen . . . Oh sweet mercies of heaven . . . Had they tried to intercept her and gotten caught?

"So, Mugo must go into the city with his men to make a full report, and we will fly to Tanzania in the morning as planned."

Daria gave a growl. "I cannot believe my adventure is ruined by American poachers!" She stomped off to her tent.

Hassan chased her up the path. "We will make it up to you, my princess."

"C'mon," Apollo rasped to Leighton and headed toward their tent.

Ready to find out what was going on, Leighton started after him. But she was inexplicably yanked backwards, a vise on her wrist.

"Stay," Prince Rayan said. "I insist."

"Too bad," came Apollo's acidic response as he appeared at her side. "She's my charge, and I'm not leaving her alone." When the prince's jaw tightened visibly, Apollo indicated for her to proceed to their tent.

Leighton wasted no time separating herself from the royals.

Once inside their tent, Owen immediately went to work lowering flaps, even though it made it hotter.

"What on earth happened out there?" Leighton whispered, unable to take it any longer. "Was that about your—"

Apollo rushed her, planting a hand to her mouth as he gave a grave shake of his head.

Leighton widened her eyes, heart drumming at the raw intensity and what she saw in his eyes—fear. She'd never seen that in him before.

Apollo pressed his mouth to her ear. "They know," he breathed against her. "Maaz found my lost comms piece."

Panicked, she drew back, looking into his eyes. Searching them. Hoping this was just a really bad joke.

He guided her into the bathroom, shut the door, turned on the water in the sink, then the shower as well. He again huddled close to her. "I played dumb, but—"

"So it *was* Omen they arrested . . ."

Owen tightened his jaw and looked aside. "Maaz wants me to believe that."

"But why would he want that unless he knows about them?"

"I don't think he does—he's assuming. It makes sense if he believes we were escaping in town—he would assume I had friends helping." He touched his jaw and flinched.

Hope shoved its rebellious head past her doubts and terror.

Owen scowled as he thought, then shook his head. "Even if they caught *one* of the team, there's no way they caught all of them. And he never mentioned how many."

Nerves flailing, she studied him. Saw his own uncertainty. "How can you know?"

"Tactics. The MO for extraction," he said. "Those guys are the best, much better than I am."

She wanted to believe him, but that seemed like a lot of guessing. Even if educated ones, they were still guesses.

Owen nodded, as if convincing himself. "I call bull that one reserve ranger took down an elite unit like Omen."

"I see your point, but . . . can you be sure?"

"The only thing I can be sure of is us."

That pushed a smile into her face.

He smiled too, then looked aside, expression weighted. "Just wish I could figure out Maaz's game."

It was then she noticed the yellowish-green pus around his stitches. "It's infected."

Apollo exhaled heavily. "I know."

She grabbed a washcloth and dipped it in the water, then raised it to his face.

"I'm good."

"You're *not*," she countered, catching his stubbled jaw with a firm hand.

"Leigh—"

"*Let* me do this for you." She tried to shoot daggers at him but she was pretty sure it came out wooden. "Keep still."

Surprise widened his eyes a fraction, then a smirk slid into his expression.

"Don't," she warned, knowing him well enough to expect some smart-aleck comment. Gently, she dabbed along his jaw. When he twitched, her stomach squeezed, hating that she'd hurt him. "Sorry."

But she was not going to lie—this was *gross*. "It's a mess." With as much care as she could manage, she wiped it with a little more pressure she knew it needed to cleanse it. "Have you been taking your antibiotic?"

He broke eye contact.

"Apollo . . ."

His hand found her waist, sending a swarm of jellies through her gut. "I said to call me Owen."

She searched his face, moved by the request. Touched that he wanted that . . . intimacy. But she wasn't born yesterday. At the moment, he was using this intimacy as a distraction, and she wasn't falling for it, regardless of his blue eyes. "Nice try. This isn't a kissing moment."

"You sure?" He pushed upward, aiming straight for her mouth.

"No!" She planted her hands on his chest before she realized how much that would hurt.

Breath whooshed out of his lungs, and he dropped back, wincing. Palming his chest.

"Serves you right," she chided, despite the twinge of pain she felt at hurting him. "I'm sorry."

"No," he grunted around a ragged breath. "Deserved that."

"Where are your antibiotics?" she repeated, tossing the washcloth on the edge of the sink. "I'll get them." She reached for the doorknob.

"Gone."

Leighton stopped. "Do what? You had a whole bottle."

Owen shrugged. "Now, I don't."

"Did you take them all?"

He said nothing.

"What, did you lose those too?"

"Can we please let it go?"

"It's not like I'm asking for life secrets here. Why won't you tell me what happened to the antibiotics? Are you embarrassed that you lost them?"

He pinched the bridge of his nose, then sliced his hand up. "I didn't lose them." He grabbed the knob and flung open the door. Stalked out.

"What? Then what is going on here?" she balked, bewildered. "Why are you being so obstinate about telling me the location of something you clearly need to keep your face from rotting off?"

He whirled on her. "I traded them, all right?"

"Traded?" She frowned, recoiling. "Traded with whom? For what?" Even as she asked it, she recalled him saying he'd had made a bargain with the vendor outside the clinic. The necklace … Her hand flew to the elephant charm.

He winced.

"Oh, Owen …"

"I've had stitches before," he muttered. "Never got an infection. When I saw it on the table, I just really wanted you to have that. To remember … us."

Moved beyond belief, she went to him. "You silly fool." This time, before she followed through on the idea to hug him, she remembered the chest stitches. "Trust me," she said, touching the side of his uninjured cheek. "I will *never* forget that night. Being saved by elephants … watching you nearly die … that kiss …"

A mischievous glint hit his blue eyes. "That memorable, huh?"

She was very much in danger of losing her heart to this man. "You're adorable." It was possibly the stupidest thing she could've said, and made her cringe.

He considered for a second, looking as if he might object, but then he shrugged. "I'll take it." And he also took a kiss, which she coiled into, albeit clumsily, afraid to again aggravate his stitches.

When had life been this good, this … full? Happy? It was as if one long, perpetual brooding storm had been her life … until Owen Metcalfe. And yet—was the storm not raging again? Threatening his plan to get her away?

Knocking came from the front porch of the tent.

Owen pivoted toward it, instinctively tucking her behind himself. "I'll get it." He tugged back the tent flap and found Rayan standing there.

The prince held up a tube of ointment. "His Highness said you needed this."

Owen grunted. "Thanks." He did not sound grateful as he took the ointment.

Rayan focused on Leighton. "The plane comes at first light for the airport."

While Leighton did not want to be rude, she was also growing weary of his near-aggressive insistence on inserting himself into her awareness and movements. She eyed Owen, wondering if he'd noticed it too. "Yes—"

"We're aware," Owen bit out, then dropped the flap, which thumped softly against the wood. He sniffed and turned, a smile brightening his eyes.

"You look smug or satisfied with yourself."

He grinned, unrepentant. "Smug works." He thumbed over his shoulder. "All this time, they only wanted you to be humiliated, possibly punished—the whole one-bed thing is ripe."

"*Stoned*," she corrected with an arched brow. "At least, that's what Sharia law would demand as punishment for being alone with a man."

"But that didn't happen. In fact, you've sort of had a biblical Esther moment here where you're the sought-after one."

"Esther had the *king's* favor."

Owen held her gaze. "I'm starting to think you do too. That maybe it's *his* hand staying any retaliation by Maaz or the others."

"But *he* doled it out to me."

"Couldn't look weak . . ." He waved noncommittally. "Anyway, my point is that their motivation was to see you condemned or punished. That hasn't happened, and now Rayan wants you."

"What?"

Another sniff. "That's why I was so ticked out there. Maaz basically told me to stand down, so Rayan could have you." He chuckled. "And the guy was lit just now, seeing the way you looked to me when he spoke to you. He hates that I'm here with you and he's not."

Concern churned through her at his words. "Arousing their anger is not a laughing matter." Didn't he understand that Ummi—

Ummi is safe, she reminded herself.

As she stood there, Leighton grew aware of all these fear

reactions that had become second nature to her, like breathing. She had lived and *breathed* fear. Every response fear-driven. And mercies of heaven, she was so tired of it. But she wasn't really sure how to live any other way.

Serengeti, Tanzania

The relatively short plane ride to Kogatende Airstrip in Tanzania proved uneventful, even the loading and unloading. Then, once again, they piled into Land Cruisers to reach the final safari migration camp, where they'd spend the next few days on Princess Daria's pre-wedding adventure.

"This has to be a joke," complained the princess-bride as they hiked through the brush to the lone tents anchored by a large acacia tree. They explored the first and largest of the tents.

"No more complaining, Daria," Hassan huffed. "I know you are tired of the heat and bugs, but so are we all."

"But it barely has more than a bed," she whined. "Is there even a shower?"

As he neared that tent, Owen noted a shower. He could see it from here. No walls. No curtain. Just a shower head jutting from a panel in the exterior wall.

"You've got to be kidding me," Leighton murmured as she came alongside him. "Do you think our tent will be like that too?"

"Probably worse." They'd gotten the short end of the stick at every camp, and he did not expect that to change, especially with suspicion on him.

A shove came at his back. "Keep moving."

Surprised at the blow that made him stumble a step, Owen glared at the guard behind him. "What the hey, man?"

"Nouri," someone barked—Maaz. He stood to the front with

Rayan and his sister. "You will room with Princess Aliyah at this camp."

Lips parting, Leighton swung her gaze to Owen. "What about—"

The same guard who shoved Owen took it upon himself to do the same to Leighton. "Do not argue with the prince!"

Rage ripped through Owen. He rammed into the guy. Threaded his arm around the guard's chest. Hooked his neck and used his own leg to swipe the guard's out from under him, effectively face-planting him. Knee in the back of the guard's neck, he drove his gaze to the entourage of princes. "Nouri stays with me. I will not let anyone abuse her."

Thick brows drawn tight, Maaz flashed a glower at him.

A blow came from his right. Nailed Owen in the temple. He staggered sideways. Tripped and crashed down.

"You do not tell me the rules," Maaz growled. "We have been too soft on you, American. Nouri is ours. You are a hired gun."

Warmth slid down Owen's temple as he pushed himself straight. Refused to cower to these weak-kneed royals. "Who can't do his job if—"

The guard came at him again.

"No, no!" Leighton rushed in front of him, holding a staying hand to the guard and one to Maaz. "Please—I'll go."

"No!" Owen struggled to his feet. "This isn't—"

She caught his arm and tugged him back. "Please, don't," she whispered . . . Brown eyes pooling with tears pleaded with him to stand down. She pulled herself straight and faced Maaz. "He is badly injured from the lion attack, and it's infected. There is no need for more violence."

"You don't have to do this," Owen hissed to her, shifting closer. He looked to the crown prince. "Don't listen to—"

"I do have to," she said, forlorn eyes coming to him. "I can't let you get hurt anymore."

"I can handle it," he bit out, catching her wrist.

"But I can't," Leighton whispered.

Feeling his world collapse at the thought of not being with her, his chest squeezed. Probably hadn't done his stitches any favors tackling that guy. "I can't protect you if I can't see you." He was certain the royals' interest in having her with pit-cheeked princess was about separating them, isolating him. Preventing him from keeping her safe.

"I knew it was too much to hope for . . ." She bent and retrieved her bag, paused for a breath, then started up the path.

Fists balled, he watched her go. When Rayan reached toward her, Owen lunged, but two men hauled him back.

Ghalib stepped into his path. The broad-chested bodyguard of the crown prince stabbed a hand to Owen's chest.

Fire seared the stitches, and Owen growled through the pain of the intentional, well-placed strike.

"Know when to quit," Ghalib snarled, his curly black hair glistening with sweat. "You would not want her to see you beaten and bloodied right here." By the looks of this guy, he'd do it too.

"The king hired me to protect her," Owen ground out. "I answer to him."

"And when King Faruq is not around, you answer to Prince Maaz." Ghalib's dark eyes sparked, as if begging Owen to fight. "He has spoken." He swiveled to the side and pointed to a long, narrow tent that easily spanned forty to fifty feet. "You will bunk with the other guards."

Owen's gaze slid past the burly royal cousin and found Leighton watching him. Her rigid posture, that look of terror, made him want to raze the camp and flee with her. "If anything happens to her . . . I swear you will regret it."

He'd messed it up. Again. Everything. So close to victory and then the ground got ripped out from under him, dumping him into a quagmire of defeat. He was supposed to have protected her. But *she* had protected him.

"She is a princess and belongs with them." Ghalib let their shoulders collide in a not-so-subtle message. "Not with you. Not with an American."

"Nobody cared that she was a princess when they locked her in a concrete cell away from the world and light."

Ghalib's expression remained neutral for two seconds. And with strength and speed that belied his burliness, the royal coldcocked him, plunging Owen into darkness.

He awoke sometime later, head thundering. Remembering the fist driving at his skull, he tried to sit up. And instantly regretted it. Groaning, he lay there, allowing his body to recover. To get his bearings. He cursed himself for not anticipating that sucker punch.

He'd been right—the guy had it in him. Felt as if he'd hit a brick wall. At least his nose had been left out of the blow this time. But his jaw ached like nobody's business. Probing it, he came to grips with another failed mission.

Just like the Rangers.

Just like the Green Berets.

He'd done his best and through no fault of his own that could be named, failed.

There was only one conclusion: *I suck.*

Would he ever be anything other than the guy who always came up short?

Slowly, he peeled himself off the cot and eased his feet to the ground. Sat there for a long second, pounding head in his hands, trying to sort through what to do. Was there a chance to save this complete trainwreck?

The extraction hadn't happened—yeah, he'd messed up by losing the comms piece—but Dante said not to change things. And pretty much everything had changed. Was Omen even in play now? He didn't believe Maaz's claim that Mugo had arrested them, but that did not necessarily make it a lie.

And forget all that—*Leighton*. The *one* good thing to ever come into his life . . . The one person who truly, deeply needed him to get it right for once—and he'd failed. Failed her.

If ever there was a time to talk to Dad, get advice, this was it. But then, Midas had never met with the incessant failings like his screwup son, so what advice could he share?

"May I make a suggestion?" a man asked quietly.

Owen lifted his head and found Rayan's cousin, Rafi, standing on the threshold of the bunkhouse, holding the door open, daggerlike sunlight piercing the darkness.

It made the back of Owen's eyeballs ache, and he groaned. "As if I could stop you."

"My people respect strength. True strength. But more than that, we respect honor." Rafi eased in a few steps and paused. "I would . . ."

Great. Here we go. A lecture.

But when the guy didn't continue, Owen eyed him.

"Go outside. Be present. Do not back down." Tall and scrawny, Rafi shrugged bony shoulders. "The king . . . It would not bode well if he learns you hid in here when he entrusted his daughter to your skills."

Was he for real? Why was this guy trying to help him? Owen gave him a long look, saw Rafi's hunched posture, the way he shifted his feet. Nervous? Why would he be nervous?

Understanding dawned and drew Owen straight. "What do you know?"

Rafi's expression faltered and he checked over his shoulder, out of the tent.

Owen followed his gaze and spotted the royals gathering around picnic tables. Seeing Leighton standing there in a teal kaftan, one arm over her midsection—as if holding herself together—gutted him.

"I would recommend," Rafi said, "you stay at her side, even if she does not want you there."

Not want him there . . . The guy assumed that because she'd told Owen to stand down. He came to his feet, not liking the warning in the guy's tone. "Why? Is something going to happen?"

"It is considered poor to speak ill of one's family," Rafi said quietly, glancing around, as if making sure nobody was eavesdropping, "but I know two things: they do not like Americans, and all are aware of the circumstances of Nouri's illegitimate birth. As such, to them, she is a blight."

Hot coals burned in Owen's gut.

"Daria will not have her wedding overshadowed by an illegitimacy. She will keep Nouri close, control her, so she ensures she is not outshone. Her fierce protection of family extends to Aliyah," he explained solemnly, the whites of his eyes all but glowing in the dim light of the bunkhouse, "who sought your favor and was rejected."

Cringing at that, Owen wouldn't offer an apology. He hadn't been here for fun times and flirting. "So, feelings were hurt."

"To put it mildly," Rafi said with a sniff. "They are patient—not in a good way. I do not know that they specifically intend to harm her, but I have seen this before. My cousin has a darkness in her whose patience morphs into cruelty, malice." He drew in a long breath, his voice barely a whisper, his expression taut. "I fear the friendship Daria offers Nouri is not one of *friends*—especially after seeing Aliyah snubbed by an American—but of . . . priest to a . . . lamb."

Owen heard the word Rafi left out. The one that would promise pain and heartache. "A *sacrificial* lamb." In other words, they wouldn't hesitate to throw Leighton under the proverbial bus. They'd set it up and shove her into its path. "But why separate us? They could kill two birds with one stone." For lack of better words. "I think they already tried."

Rafi gave a near smile. "Haven't you figured it out? Turning her against you—it would be the ultimate coup, considering your purpose here."

Great balls of fire! They *did* know the comms device had been his.

The preternatural calm Rafi possessed was unsettling. "While Nouri is considered unpure and illegitimate, she still has royal blood. If they can convince her to reject you and you fail to do your job . . ."

Nausea roiled through Owen.

"It would disrupt all your plans, yes? Assuming you—or she—lived that long."

A thought struck Owen. "What would they do if they knew you were warning me?"

Concern flickered through Rafi's eyes, no doubt wondering if Owen intended to betray his confidence. "That would be a very bad day."

The man had sought to help Leighton. And him. He owed the guy. "They won't learn about this from me."

With a gentle incline of his head, Rafi strode to the far end of the bunkhouse, past twenty or more additional cots, and exited through the rear door.

Even as he turned to head out and join Leighton, Owen could not shake the ominous thought that they would not survive this trip. Most people would think the wildlife was the biggest threat here, but they hadn't met the royal spawn of the Central Kingdom.

— • —

Sitting at the folding table, picking at the fruit, Leighton could not forget Ghalib punching Owen the night before last. That horrible crack. The thud of his body hitting the ground . . . The memory made her stomach churn. On top of everything else he'd endured that day—to have been punched so cruelly . . .

A full day of safari and touring, paired with that painful memory, put Leighton's teeth on edge. Why had she fought so hard to stay here? Yes—to protect Ummi, but hadn't he given her many promises that Ummi was okay?

Fear had held her captive long enough.

At the bonfire last night, even the shadows of the night could not hide the large bruise spreading over Owen's face and jaw as he sat off to the side with other workers. It also could not hide the vow of violence in his beautiful eyes.

That scared her more than anything. What if he made good on that promise and started a fight? After all that had happened, surely he understood these people would kill them. And they'd likely do it while in the wild, then leave their bodies for the animals to feast on. Nobody would be the wiser.

"You look a little pale." Rayan edged into her line of sight. "Something from dinner last night not agree with you?"

Yeah, try the brutality leveraged against Owen, the subtle threat to her. But she dared not speak those things. This was her life, this was what she had to do—keep the secret. Play the game. Live the lie. Pray she survived.

She'd survived for twenty-five years. But this last week with Owen had been a sweet reprieve. Showed her what life could be like. Except the lion attacks and the fleeing shooters at the village.

Rayan set a hand on her wrist.

A subtle-but-direct reminder that *she* was not in control, though she doubted Rayan intended it that way. It was the way of things— the al-Zahranis were in control. Always had been. The ominous dark shadow of their power had lingered over every hour of her life.

"Perhaps," Rayan said, his kindness erstwhile yet frustrating as morning light spilled across the savanna behind him, "when we return, try a kebab or some other protein to fortify yourself. I could ask one of the workers to retrieve something if you are faint."

"N-no. All is well." She flashed a smile. "Besides, I'm not sure I could eat right now . . ." It was as good an excuse as any, because the last thing she wanted was him doting over her. "Thank you for the consideration, though."

"Come, come!" Aliyah hooked her arm through Leighton's. "Time to go to the next site." With that, the princess herded Leighton toward the vehicles and all but shoved her up into the second vehicle with Rayan, Daria, and Hassan.

Her gaze found Owen's, and she saw the frustration in his expression. Begged him not to start something. He'd think it was to protect her, defend her, but . . .

Truth be told, she just wasn't worth it. She could never live with herself if he got killed because of her.

"They know . . ." His pained words from a few nights ago, warning her the royals knew he was trying to save her, get her away from them, echoed in her thoughts. Reinforced what she detected from Daria and Aliyah—they were trying to drive a wedge between her and Owen.

It was for the best, being separated from him, even if it angered him. At least his chance of survival increased and he could be mad to his heart's content.

But . . . that wasn't like Owen—he was stronger than bitterness. He was a wolf tracking her.

The Cruiser paused at a wildebeest watering hole.

Leighton watched as a few of the odd-faced beests lumbered over to the vehicles. As the royals took photos with their phones, she slid her gaze to the other Cruiser—and rammed right into Owen. An eruption of warmth rushed through her belly at the impact. Recalled their kiss. The tender moments. His humor.

A rustling to the left drew her attention back to her own vehicle and spotted a beest nibbling Aliyah's sleeve. "Oh, give care," Leighton said.

Aliyah glanced down and shrieked. When she yanked her arm away, a strip of fabric tore away. The princess let out a strangled cry and huffed. "You beast! How dare you!"

As if her upset urged it, the driver pulled away from the watering hole.

Leighton settled in her seat, thoughts and heart spun to the rear—to the Cruiser that held Owen. Were the workers treating him fairly? Or was he the brunt of more ill treatment?

They drove for over an hour without sighting much of anything outside the occasional gazelle and lion—which felt entirely too soon after watching Owen nearly get shredded. A while later, they came upon a large acacia tree whose branches were filled with lions. There had to be a dozen cats lounging up in those branches. So wild! They returned to camp just in time for lunch.

"Nouri."

At Owen's terse call, she felt her insides tighten and slowed to turn to him.

"Keep walking," Daria hissed as she and Aliyah linked arms with her. "Do not stop."

"Do not look at him," Aliyah insisted with a conspiratorial giggle. "He does not deserve you. *You* are an al-Zahrani."

Yet, Owen had *deserved* Aliyah when she sought his attention earlier in the safari? Was it wounded pride that made the princess speak ill of him now?

She allowed the princesses to herd her back toward their tent to freshen up before eating. But she hated this—being rude to him. Guilt plagued her, worried her that he might believe her indifference real. She silently prayed he'd understand it was an act. It crushed her to think that he might believe her cold shoulder. Believe that she had rejected him.

"I cannot wait to get this dust and dirt off me," Daria complained as they made their way back to their shared arrangements. "I thought this safari was supposed to be a luxury venture!"

"Ugh, me too," Aliyah whined as they entered the tent, where servants immediately started toward them. "Every day I wash a pound of grit off me. But at least I don't look like Mr. Apollo with that large black bruise on my face!"

Leighton startled at the way they openly mocked him.

"Hideous," Daria sniffed as the servant stripped her out of the safari clothes and went to work refreshing her appearance. "That's what he gets for overstepping." Her dark, cruel eyes landed on Leighton. "You are far too good and noble for a man like that, Nouri."

Aliyah clucked her tongue. "Yes, indeed." As a servant swathed her down and helped her into clean clothes—why were they even bothering?—she winked at Leighton. "I have it on good authority that my brother is talking to our cousin about a marriage offer for you . . ." Her trilling laugh made Leighton's skin crawl.

As did the threat of marriage. Heart thundering, she put a hand to her throat. Rayan wanted to marry her? No . . . no no no. *I'm going to be sick.*

"Look," Daria said as her servant secured her hair, "poor thing is overcome. She never imagined a prince would want her!"

"Of course she wouldn't. But you do have a *little* royal blood," Aliyah said, giving a pursed-lip nod. "You should not discount yourself so thoroughly, Cousin."

Hearing them draw her into their family with their words—and snobbery—was not as satisfying as Leighton had expected it to be. In fact, it was downright hypocritical of them. She told herself not to react. To let them talk, think she was buying into their absurdities. Their inane comments and existence was definitely not one she had any interest in.

"Oh," Aliyah said excitedly. "Tomorrow we go to the Ngorongoro crater!"

"Forget the crater," Daria sniffed. "I'm looking forward to the spa and a massage afterward." She gave Leighton a long look. "If you would like, I could ask Maaz to put in for you to get one too."

"What a treat that would be," Aliyah said, nodding. "I know you've never had anything like it, but it would do you good to get those knots out of your thick shoulders. It helps, I promise."

Thick shoulders? Was it possible these princesses didn't know they were being insulting? She sincerely doubted it. They talked about blood, that she had their blood, but they didn't have blood in their veins—they had venom.

Regardless, Leighton had to play nice. Bide her time. Bite her tongue. As always.

They were soon back out with the others and went straight to the food table. Stomach rumbling, she was anxious for one of those kebabs. Even as she waited for the princesses to fill their plates first, Leighton swept her gaze around the others. Searching, she realized, for a familiar pair of blue eyes. Where was he?

"Balloons, six p.m." Owen's warm words skated along her neck.

By the time she twitched and turned, he was already moving away. What had he said? Balloons? What was he talking about?

"You are well?"

Leighton yipped and spun to the new voice—Rayan. "Oh. Hi." Embarrassment flooded her at finding him beside her and arching a rueful eyebrow. Had he seen her staring after Owen—or worse, had he heard Owen issue the hushed words?

Rayan's expression softened as he gazed at her, and he clearly believed the color in her cheeks was because of him. Wholly wrong, but she must allow him that misconception. He smiled and ran his knuckles along her jaw. "Even after a safari, you are beautiful."

No, that was too far. She stepped back and ducked. Mentally heard Owen railing about her looking down, which made her smile. Then she cursed herself, because no doubt Rayan would take her smile as being meant for him.

"Rayan," Prince Maaz chided with a warning tone and disapproving look.

Suddenly, Leighton had a deep appreciation for the strict rules of conduct that had driven her crazy before.

The princesses had taken their food to the tables, so Leighton moved forward, picked up a plate and grabbed a kebab, bread, and more fruit. She navigated to a table, her mind ricocheting back to Owen's hushed instructions—*balloons, six p.m.*

Why would he want her to meet him there? More importantly, how was she supposed to get away from Rayan or the princesses?

SIXTEEN

Serengeti, Tanzania

HE WAS LOSING HER. OWEN WAS LOSING Leighton to these infernal royals and couldn't do a thing about it. Sequestered from the royal entourage, he was battling an intense sense of failure. Felt the taunting reins of control slipping from his grip.

Arms folded, he stood on the farthest side of the balloon basket, hoping the royals would not look this way and spot him. But they were all too merry in their drink and laughter to notice him. Would she come? The whole day had been frustrating. She'd only looked at him once, and he'd felt that to his core. A creeping sense of dread swarmed him at what he saw in her eyes. Not attraction or just a simple smile. Not fear as he'd seen the first time he'd encountered her at Soph's party. This time he saw irritation. A flash of it—aimed at him.

That had put him on the knife's edge. *She* was his only reason for being here. And if she was ditching him, siding with the royals, why was he even trying?

Those were the lies filling his head. Owen knew he couldn't let them take root. He had to be strong. Remember that she was up against some pretty slick masters of manipulation who used those around them to get what they wanted.

The entourage had effected a concerted effort to keep him from being anywhere near Leighton. More than once, guards or Ghalib—that man was like a ghoul, manifesting without warning in the strangest places—intervened to prevent Owen from reaching Leighton. He'd nearly given up on putting his plan into place when one glorious moment opened up while she'd been waiting for food.

He hadn't been able to ask if she understood what he'd said. Or get confirmation that she would come. That grating Rayan had been headed her way, so Owen had to veer off to avoid being discovered. What if she hadn't heard him? What if the princesses commandeered her time again? And the question that plagued him, haunted—taunted—him . . . What if she had changed her mind and decided not to let him get her out of their clutches? What if the poison the princesses poured into her ear daily had taken root after all?

"Please, we go?" the balloon driver—or whatever they called him—signaled his impatience.

"Wait . . . Please." Language barriers were no joke, but hopefully hand signals would convince the guy to give him more time. Owen scanned the area, searching the tents. Eyeing the tables, though he kept his head low to avoid being spotted.

Man. Was she not coming?

Surely the royals hadn't turned her already. The kiss he'd shared with her . . . Did it mean the same thing to her as it had to him. She hadn't really seemed like the type to just go around kissing guys . . .

Yet she's not here.

The balloon guy railed at him in his native tongue.

"Please—"

"No, no!" The man started away.

Disappointed, Owen had to concede failure again. It'd been a long shot. But the sting of disappointment bred worry in his chest like maggots on rotten meat. This whole stinkin' thing was rotten. He hadn't—

"Hey!" a voice rasped from behind.

At the tickle-grab at his sides, Owen wheeled around, startled to find Leighton laughing and her eyes bright. "Where'd you come from?" His brain jarred at her presence, his entire being resonating that she was here. That she'd come. "Never mind," he said quietly. "Inside."

Her eyes went round as pancakes and then she grinned—big. "We're going *up*?"

This. *This* was why he was falling in love with her. That glow in her cheeks as he helped her into the basket. Nodded to the guide, who had already freed the balloon anchors. He turned, flaring the gas that drove heat up into the balloon.

Leighton giggled as she shrank, as if to hide. "I can't believe we're doing this."

Owen breathed a little easier as the distance from the ground grew. "I had to see you, talk to you before we headed back to Jeddah."

She gave a nervous yelp. "Have I mentioned I'm scared of heights?"

"Uh, that could be a problem, since we're going high. I'm surprised you came, then."

She hunched away from the sides. "I had to see you. Two days of torture with Daria and Aliyah."

"I was worried they'd turned you to the dark side."

"What?"

"Someone suggested they would turn you against me. I started worrying . . ."

"After two days?" She wrinkled her nose. "You have so little faith in me?"

"Hey, we haven't known each other long."

"Long enough to kiss," she challenged with a whisper. "You think I do that to every guy I've known for all of two weeks?"

"I would hope not, but . . . doubts were large and loud."

"Seriously?" Leighton scoffed. "Give me more credit!" She hugged herself and then covered her mouth, looking a bit pale. "This is beautiful . . . and terrifying!"

He studied her. "You're . . . scared?"

"A little," she conceded.

"I'm sorry."

"No—it's wonderful, and I want to enjoy it. Fully. I don't know how long it will last."

He had no idea how they'd get out of this tangle. "When we go back to Omnia, I don't know what's going to happen."

She sobered. "What do you mean?"

"Maaz knows I'm not who I claimed to be and if he tells Faruq . . ."

"He'll kill you."

"I'm worried more about you."

"Don't." She shivered, the higher altitude chillier. "The princesses . . ." Her caramel eyes came to him, and she shook her head. "I knew they were trying to turn me against you, but . . . I know their friendship and favor is fake. They don't care about me."

He hated that look of disappointment. "Because they're idiots."

She sighed, looking gravely on the billowing plain and wildlife scampering far below. "I just want this to be over." With a groan, she rubbed her forehead. "I was content in my life. Lived with living a lie. Mastered it. I never would've broken that vow to protect Ummi. But then they"—she motioned toward the camp that was steadily shrinking—"rip me out of that life. Why? To kill me?" She groaned, scraping both hands over her face. "I'm so tired of this. I just want to be a normal person."

"Well," he teased, "that will never happen."

Her gaze bounced to his, concerned, then she rolled her eyes. "You are adorkable."

He laughed. "Did you really just say that?"

"Yes." She seemed petulant, but a smile wiggled through her olive complexion. "You have turned my life upside down, Owen Metcalfe."

"To be fair," he said as he settled next to her, forearms resting on the rail of the basket, "*they* did that. I just . . . made it a bit messier."

She reached over and rustled his hair. "Fitting, considering this."

"Okay, okay," he said, leaning back to stop her from mussing his hair again. "I'm shaving it."

Laughing, she shook her head and bumped his shoulder, her expression sobering into something . . . beautiful, sweet. "I'm really glad you came to rescue me, Owen. Even if it didn't work."

RPG to the heart, gutting him. "It's not over yet."

She shifted to face him. "We go back tomorrow. And even still, you know they're going to be furious once we land."

He groaned. "Yeah . . ."

"So why *did* we do this? Why invite me to come up—besides scaring the tar out of me?"

"I had to know . . ." His mouth was full of rocks, his brain sluggish.

"Know what?"

Holy woof, he felt like a twelve-year-old again. "If . . . *we* are okay."

Her eyebrows lifted and her lips parted. "You—"

"Silly fool," he huffed. "Yeah, I know."

She again rustled his hair, but this time, it felt more intimate. Tender. Her hand trailed down the side of his face, lingered on the bruise, and she winced. "I was going to say you had nothing to worry about."

Somehow, she was in his arms. And Owen crushed her there. Held her tight. "I had to know because I don't know what will happen in Jeddah. I needed the anchor of knowing you . . . we . . ." Holy crud, he just couldn't say it. Wasn't even sure what he wanted to say.

Leighton lifted her head and tracked her gaze over his face. "We are, Owen. We are. I can't explain it—we have known each other a very short time, but it has felt like my whole life."

His heart surged into his throat. "Then I can face what's coming. I promise you, no matter what—trust that I'm going to get you out of there."

"You're scaring me."

"I've been begging God to help me figure this out, and . . . I have a plan. Though I doubt you're going to like it."

She faltered for a second, but then gave a slow nod. "I don't have to like it as long as it works. And I won't lie—God hasn't exactly given me a stress-free life."

"Eh," Owen said with a rueful grunt. "Stress-free is boring and teaches us to trust ourselves. It's in the deep darkness that we grow the most. God repeatedly told the Israelites He was giving them the Promised Land, but He didn't just drop it in their laps. They had to fight for it—violently, bloodily." Grim-faced, he held her gaze so she comprehended his resolute determination. "That's what I'm willing to do to get you out of their grip."

She stared at him for a long second, her eyes shining beneath that promise. "Thank you." Then she scrunched that pert nose. "But . . . maybe without the bloodshed."

"I'll shed every drop I have if it means you're free."

<hr>

She had no idea if this would work. As the balloon descended toward the landing area on the south side of the camp, Leighton saw the royals moving en masse toward it. Stomach tight, she told herself not to look to the eastern rise they'd just come up over and mentally rehearsed what Owen had told her to say. While the sun had set long ago, she did not need light to see the scowl digging into Maaz's face as the basket lowered to the ground.

The pilot tossed off a rope to another worker who anchored them, slowly drawing them to settle on the ground. Quickly, he flung open the small gate for her.

Refusing to meet the prince's gaze, she held on to one side and moved to step over the small lip when a hand slid into view. Her heart skidded into her throat as she met Rayan's gaze and forced herself to take the proffered help.

Remember, nothing's wrong. Just out for a ride. "Thank you." As she stepped out, she felt him close in and held her breath.

"Very foolish, Nouri," he whispered at her. "Very foolish. You have angered Maaz."

Old, long-ingrained habits were hard to break. She looked away—and found herself facing Maaz. *God, have mercy!*

"What were you doing?" the crown prince barked.

Look surprised. "I . . . riding in the balloon?" Manufacturing a confused expression, she glanced around. "What . . . ? I thought we were allowed. After everything, I only wanted to clear my head. Seeing the savanna was—"

"Where is he?" Ghalib demanded, his henchmen closing in. "Where's Mr. Apollo?"

"I have no idea," she said, very grateful his escape from the basket as they drifted over a rise meant she truly did not know. "Is he missing?"

"You weren't with him?" Maaz asked, his expression dark. "Someone said they saw you two go up together."

Her heart gave a start at that. Who had seen them? Rather than lie, she indicated back to the balloon basket. "If he did, where is he?"

Ghalib stomped to the pilot, who was prepping the balloon and securing the canopy. "Was this woman alone for the ride?"

Dark eyes found hers. He was young, his expression searching, scared.

Too well she understood that feeling when having the royals breathing down her neck. *Please, God . . . protect us.*

The pilot shrugged. "I tell her it not right to go up alone, but she was crying."

Was he truly helping her? Lying for her? Whoa. They had definitely not asked him to say that.

Maaz's gaze swung to hers. "Why were you crying?"

"Because she was falling in love with the American," Daria crooned from her brother's side. "I guess she understands now how weak Americans are and accepts her place with us."

If you say so.

Weak? Owen Metcalfe was the strongest man she'd ever met. As for accepting her place, it was most definitely *not* among the al-Zahranis. Leighton did the most familiar thing she could summon among these royals—she looked down. Feigned deference.

A shout came from the camp, turning everyone in that direction.

Nasir stomped toward them, hand clamped around Owen's arm. "He is here!"

Maaz stormed in that direction. "Where have you been?"

Once he extricated his arm from the grip, Owen rubbed his shoulder and scowled at the thugs of Jeddah grouping up on him. "Sitting on the rise." He thumbed toward Leighton. "When I saw her get in the balloon, I wanted to keep an eye on her." He was a brilliant actor. "Since it seemed nobody else was watching out for Nouri."

"Your job was to stay with her!" Maaz bit out.

"Kind of hard to do when your enforcers"—Owen nodded to Ghalib—"stop me at every turn. Had to resort to more subtle tactics." He shrugged. "Can't have it both ways—keeping me from her and demanding I protect her."

"He's just trying to get her back," Daria whispered. "He doesn't deserve her."

"Everyone and their dog knows that," Owen snapped. "Nouri is better than every person on this field."

Breath staggered through Leighton at that declaration. Was he *trying* to get killed?

Don't look, don't look.

She looked. Could not help it. Those beautiful crystalline eyes seemed to harness the power of the moon itself. Glorious, intense.

"Do not let him have his job back," Daria said to her brother. "He—"

"Unfortunately," Owen spoke, "that is a decision only King Faruq can make, since my contract is with him."

The crown prince stepped over to him, and it took everything in Leighton to plaster ambivalence and neutrality across her features. But she'd tensed.

"Come," Rayan said softly, turning to her. "You do not—"

"The king trusts my counsel," Maaz said clearly, loudly, since Owen had challenged his authority. "On all threats, especially to our family. Tomorrow, I will drag you before him and make sure he knows how you have lied in order to gain access to his daughter."

Daughter. So in order to set themselves against Owen, they claimed her now? After locking her in a dungeon, beating her, and—

"Dinner, then everyone rest. We have an early start," Maaz barked and strode away from the gathering.

"Can you believe that rancid American?" Aliyah complained as she threaded her arm through Leighton's. "Does he really think we need him?"

I do. I most definitely need him.

Rayan and Aliyah ushered her back across the field, up the path to camp . . . straight toward Owen. It took everything in her not to make eye contact. Instead, she lifted her jaw, not to show indifference but to convince the royals she would not be a problem. To show her strength. That he could trust her to keep their pact.

Yet, even as she moved past him, it crushed something deep in her to act so cold toward him as everyone else was doing. To see him so cruelly isolated and targeted.

The next morning on the plane, Owen was forced to the rear, guarded by Ghalib and Nasir. With the way Rayan and Aliyah stayed near Leighton—Daria had returned her affection to Hassan once more and had little to do with her now—she was even more a prisoner than when they'd shut her in that windowless concrete cell. Practice perfected over the years saved her sanity on that hours-long flight, then the drive from the airport to Omnia Palace.

Her heart raced as they emerged from the armored SUV and she stepped aside. Behind them came a grunt and muttered oath. She glanced back and saw Ghalib and Nasir shove a hood over Owen's head.

Concern lanced her composure. "Why are they doing that?"

"Many guests have already arrived for the wedding," Rayan said solemnly as he urged her in through the side door of the royal residence. "It is for his protection."

"Do not worry," Aliyah said. "They will make sure he is punished for his lies."

"I would not want anyone injured on my account," she said, wishing her thoughts could be heard by the king. Perhaps Owen might have a chance . . . Nerves thrummed and she feared this plan of his might be backfiring.

"Your kindness is one of the things I admire about you," Rayan said softly, touching the small of her back as they moved through the lower corridor.

Belly quailing, she fought every impulse to twitch from his touch. He was nice. Kind even. Handsome. But . . .

He's not Owen. And her story did not end here at this palace.

At least, she hoped not.

SEVENTEEN

Jeddah, Saudi Arabia

TWO DAYS. IT HAD BEEN TWO DAYS SINCE they'd sandbagged his head and rushed him into this dungeon-of-a-cell. Two days and nobody had come. No food, no water. Only light came from the barred window in the steel door. When they'd locked him in, he'd anticipated either being dragged before the king or having the king appear and pronounce sentence—death. But nothing had happened. Nobody visited.

Growling, he paced. How? How was he in the exact same position as every other pivotal moment in his life—enmeshed in failure?

It was like some cosmic joke.

Only, he didn't believe in that. He believed in God, Who wasn't one to play with the affections of His faithful. To torment them, though at times His discipline felt that way. Was that what this was—discipline? But for what?

The kiss he'd shared with Leighton leapt to mind.

With a groan, he ran his hand over his head. Was the kiss wrong?

No. It was the only right thing in his life—*she* was the only right thing.

Please. God. Let me help her.

Distant voices carried down the passage, and the thrum of the air-conditioning rattled high in the wall vent.

Jaw tight, he felt the throb of infection. It had grown into a constant, angry thrum. Much like his raw nerves. How? How was he going to escape? Dad's stiff demand to know if Owen knew how to get out of a foreign country taunted him now.

The distant voices grew closer. There was some discordance, some . . . tension to the way they spoke. The chatter became clearer as two men strode down the darkened passage. It registered then what was odd—they weren't speaking Arabic. Or some other language he didn't know. This was . . . Spanish.

The wedding was tomorrow, if he'd calculated the days right. But he heard the din of celebrations and knew Saudi wedding traditions spanned days, not one day. There were guests from all over the world here to celebrate the marriage of King Faruq's daughter. But what were guests doing down here in the dungeons?

"*¿Encontraste su favorito?*" a deep voice asked.

"*Sí, Tamarind,*" came a nasally reply.

"*Bueno, bueno,*" the first said with a chuckle. "*Demasiado cerca.*"

"*En efecto.*"

From his limited skill with the language, Owen could tell the one in a deeper voice asked about a favorite . . . something. The other said it was "tamarind." Deeper then said it had been too close, and Nasally agreed.

Owen stood, aware he was wholly in shadow, and watched as they moved past his cell, pausing at the far end of a juncture, where Nasally handed something to the other.

"*Gracias.*" Deeper slapped the guy on the shoulder, then turned back the direction he'd come.

Ducking out of sight, Owen felt his heart climb into his throat—Oskar Bruzon! *He's here.* Bruzon was here.

That meant . . . "Leighton!"

Bruzon was here to kill Leighton and get back at Navas, her biological dad.

No. No, no, no! This was bad. Beyond bad!

He balled his fists that the threat to Leighton was walking the halls of the palace and Owen was locked behind a steel door, unable to do a single, stinking thing.

I have to get out of here. But how?

Son of a freak-fried biscuit. What could he do?

Pray.

"God," he muttered, shaking his head as he paced before the door. "I have to get out of here."

How?!

The king . . . the king would want to know of a threat against his daughter. Correction: his believed-to-be daughter. If he could get the king to come down here . . .

Owen angled around. Tiptoed up and strained to see down both directions of the passage. "Guard!" he shouted. "Guard!" With his limited view, he had no idea if anyone was anywhere near close. But he wouldn't miss the chance to get help because he didn't shout loud enough. "*Guard!*"

Silence met his bellow, though the bars rattled in response.

"GUARD! *GUARD!*" The image of Leighton being killed at the festivities demanded he keep raising cane to get the guard here. He kicked the door, ignoring the pain spiking up his foot. Punched it.

"*Askut!*" came a terse voice seconds before a guard in the standard thobe and ghutra appeared. "*Askut!*"

No idea what that meant, but it probably wasn't the guard asking how he could help.

"The king," Owen snapped. "I need to speak to the king!"

"No king!" the guard barked. "No king!"

"Get me the king! His daughter is in danger!"

The guard looked at him, confused. Clearly not understanding. Or choosing not to. With a shrug he started away.

Owen bucked. Shouted, "GET. ME. THE. KING!"

The guard shuffled back and lifted a rifle at the window.

Scrambling back, Owen stumbled and went down even as the report of the rifle clapped through the cell. He felt more than saw the track of the bullet whiz past his ear. Shock ripped through him at how close he'd come to eating lead.

But Leighton.

His vow to give every drop of his blood if it saved her rang in his head. He leapt at the door. "Please! Call the king. I need the king!"

The guard was gone.

Holding the ledge of the small window, he hung his head. Fought the intense frustration that made his chest feel like an elephant sat on it.

Elephant . . . Leighton . . .

Thud. Oof!

Owen stilled at the very distinct sounds. That . . . that sounded like a fist on bone—as in a punch. He lifted his head as a grunt sounded. Peering through the window, he found the guard face-down on the stone floor. What . . . ?

Had Bruzon heard him? Come back?

The guard's body was dragged backward, out of sight. A cell door clanged.

A blur manifested in front of his window.

Owen shoved back, heart vaulting into his throat as he landed in a fighting stance. It took entirely too long for the face beneath the ghutra to register. "*Chief?*"

"You make more noise than Dante's goat."

"Not cool, man," Dante complained from somewhere out of sight.

Panic and adrenaline surrendered amid an intense wave of relief that nearly buckled Owen's knees. "Thank You, God."

"Hey, I've been called a lot of things..." Pike teased, swung his weapon on the sling to his back.

"Get me out of here! Bruzon's on-site!"

———— • ————

Zayna left the room after pronouncing Leighton's attire satisfactory. The abaya far exceeded that dull word. Yesterday, Daria and Hassan had signed the wedding contract in an intimate ceremony to which Leighton had not been invited. Now, however, they were hosting a very public reception and celebrations.

Leighton glanced down at the emerald green abaya, heavily beaded along the wide band that encircled her waist. Beads and crystals formed whorls, and flowers ran down the sleeves, cuffs, and hem. The simple white dress beneath it was a sharp but pretty contrast to the heavily ornamented green. A sheer green headscarf set it off beautifully.

She had tried to wear the elephant necklace, but Zayna forbade it. Thankfully, the double-layered skirt of the abaya had pockets, so she kept it there. It was the only piece of Owen she had left, and upon their return from the safari, she had been abandoned in the new suite Rayan had promised her while on safari. This one had a doorknob, though the royal still kept her locked in. But the tiny treasure had steadied her. The quiet, the solitude was good for her on one hand, but on the other, it became a haunting playground for her terror. Like the daunting fear that had burrowed into her chest that said they'd killed him.

Rubbing the double cords of the necklace between her fingers, she dashed away a lone tear. If she ruined the makeup Zayna had spent forty minutes applying, the stern woman would probably give her a lashing. But Leighton's heart ached. *Where is he?*

Maybe he should've just run away in the Serengeti. Somehow, she felt he would've had a better chance against lions than the al-Zahranis.

"I'll shed every drop I have if it means you're free."

His words lingered in her heart. Had he? Had he ended up giving every drop of blood beneath the fury of King Faruq? Or Maaz?

"Please, God . . ."

A sharp rap came on her door.

Leighton turned from the window and eyed the door. The knob rattled, then she heard the distinct sounds of metal scraping.

Drawing back, putting the furniture between her and the door, she felt her heart drum.

The door opened, delivering a guard into the room. His thobe fluttered as he pivoted, flicked the door closed, and flipped the lock.

What was he doing? She stood, unsettled at being locked with him. *"Madha turid?"* she asked in Arabic as he turned to her.

"It's okay," he said, flashing her his palms. "I'm not here to hurt you."

Her gaze hit the lock. Who locked himself in a room with a woman? And why was he speaking English?

"I locked the door to buy us time in case someone comes."

Her mind scrambled to keep up. "I'm sorry—who are you?"

A smile flashed through his Middle Eastern features. "Tariq. I'm with Ap—"

"No!" Pulse pounding, she realized what he'd been about to say—Apollo. So, Owen. She took a step forward as she pointed to her ear, indicating the room was bugged.

Understanding spread over his face and he nodded.

She drew in a ragged breath and let it out, then bobbed her head toward the bathroom. In there, she turned on the faucet and extractor fan, then flushed the toilet.

"I'm here to get you out," he said. "But we can't while you're up here."

She nodded. Flushed the toilet again.

"I'll escort you to the reception."

Surprised that he knew, she supposed this was her confirmation that he was who he claimed to be. That meant— She took a step forward. "He's okay?"

Tariq held her gaze for a minute. "Bad infection, but he'll live."

She wilted, feeling her knees go weak. "I was so sure they'd killed him."

"Yeah, trouble's not over. The assassin we feared might come for you is here."

Stomach quailing, she felt a wave of nausea that an assassin was here.

"We'll go down. I'll stay close, then—"

Sharp raps came at the door.

The lock rattled.

Leighton caught Tariq's hand and hurried him back to the main room. Indicating for him to move near the door, she went to the table and bent over it, as if she were looking for something.

The door opened. "Nour—" Prince Rayan's eyes darkened as he spotted the new guard. "*Madha tafeal huna?*" he barked, asking what the guard was doing in here.

Realizing Tariq likely did not know this was a prince, she straightened. "Ah—"

"*Sumukam.*" Tariq snapped a bow of his head. "*Laqad qil li 'an 'ahdur al'amirata.*"

Well. She supposed he *did* know whom he addressed if he called him "Your Highness." And quite a good ruse, saying he was instructed to bring her down.

"*Biwasitat min?*"

Tensing as Rayan demanded who sent him to escort her, she resented how he acted like he owned her.

"*Almalaku.*"

"The king" was the only answer Tariq could've given that would stay Rayan's commanding-but-dour mood, and she was glad the Omen guy knew that.

"Is there a problem?" Nouri asked in Arabic, since that seemed to be the flavor of the day.

Rayan's gaze finally fixed on her. His gaze swept her from head to toe in slow, ardent appreciation of what he saw. He closed the gap between them, hands extended to her. "You are radiant!"

A blush filled her cheeks. Not at his compliment, but out of concern that Tariq stood there watching. It was humiliating. "Daria chose well," she said as she forced herself to place her fingers in his hands.

"Indeed!" Rayan laughed. "She has had every detail planned down to the glitter on the banners."

"No doubt." She looked down to lift her long abaya, which dusted the carpet, and when she straightened, Rayan moved in. Planted a kiss on her temple. She drew in a quick breath, feeling a cascade of sickening heat wash down her body at the unwanted gesture. "Rayan." Her gaze slid to Tariq, who jerked his gaze away.

"Forgive me, but I could not resist your beauty."

Uncomfortable, she swallowed. Felt paralyzed.

A *thunk* behind Rayan drew his attention to Tariq, who had knocked over a small figurine that had been on the side table. "Give care with the princess's things!"

Leighton nearly smiled—there was no way that was accidental. The piece had been in the center. On a tray. She appreciated his effort to save her from any more awkwardness. Too, nothing in this room was truly hers. The suite had been fully furnished and decorated when Leighton arrived.

"Come." Rayan moved between her and Tariq, motioning to the door. "Time for the wedding. The Zaffa is done."

She imagined what it must have been like to see the procession by which the groom and his male attendants marched to the bride's quarters to claim her. They left the suite and made their way down the open concourse surrounding the open atrium to the lower level. A hum of conversation roared through the cavernous space. The complexity of the Saudi Arabian wedding left her confused, yet in awe. It was customary for men and women to celebrate separately. The reception, however, had been adjusted on order of the king to accommodate their many international guests, among which were royalty, nobility, and wealthy alike.

Tonight was a type of wedding reception in the vast hall, festooned with flowers and countless rows of tables, all around a tufted sofa and a gorgeous floral backdrop. "You may go," Rayan said to Tariq. "*I* will escort her. Return to your duties."

Alarmed that she would be separated from Owen's buddy, she faltered. Scrambled for a way to keep him close.

"The king—"

"Is waiting. You are not needed." Rayan caught her elbow and pulled her on.

Oh heavens. What was she supposed to do? She glanced back at Tariq, and his expression blazed with anger, but he gave her a grim nod. What did that mean? She could do nothing but keep walking with Rayan.

"I did not like him," Rayan said as he rounded a corner. "Had a look about him."

Swallowing her dread, she descended the stairs. Though she would prefer not to touch him again, she was grateful for his hand so she did not slip on the slick marble in the strappy pumps that matched her dress.

Moments later she entered the reception hall filled with a hundred seats or more. Was this the wedding hall? But Rayan moved down the line, hugging person after person. Introducing her as Princess Nouri. Only about halfway down did she realize everyone in here *was* family.

The crowd parted and she forgot to breathe.

King Faruq stood there in a thobe and bisht with a flowing black overcloak that had a gold band. Sharp, probing eyes razored across her.

This was the first time she had seen him since that day in his hall where he'd asked if Owen was the man who had saved her in Paris. Goodness, that seemed forever ago. She lowered her gaze, not expecting anything from him. Not *wanting* anything from him.

"Nouri," he said in a gentle voice. "You are beautiful. So much like your mother."

Surprise leapt through her that he would mention Ummi. "Th-thank you, Your Majesty." Heat flushing her face, she touched the abaya. "Princess Daria was very gracious."

"As she should be." The king leaned to the side as another man angled in to speak to him. His gaze shifted to the room. "It is time."

Not sure what was happening, she glanced around.

"Stay at my side." Rayan gave her a nod as they fell in behind the king's heirs.

In minutes, they were walking into the hall where guests were already seated and waiting. She was positioned near the front with the other royals, and sandwiched between Rayan and Ghalib. She despised the latter for his treatment of Owen and avoided eye contact. Soon, Daria and Hassan entered as husband and wife, walking to the center where they sat on the tufted sofa. Once the marriage was officially announced by King Faruq, the couple exchanged rings, pictures were taken, and then the festivities began.

Throughout the reception, she scanned the crowd, looking for Tariq. Was he still here? She did not imagine he would leave.

Aliyah sat across from her. "I wish you had come for the Gomrah." She wagged her henna-tattooed hands. "It was great fun! We laughed and ate so much."

The spiced coffee served in abundance, along with juices and sodas—after all, alcohol was considered haram—left her bladder quite full. A perfect excuse to get away from the table. Maybe find Tariq. She leaned toward the princess. "I need to use the restroom."

With a groan, Aliyah sat back. Then harrumphed. "Come. Let us hurry. I do not want to miss dessert."

Once out of the reception hall, she felt as if her ears popped for the silence that clapped them. She laughed. "It was so loud in there."

Aliyah wrinkled her nose. "It's too quiet out here. We are missing the fun!" She hurried down the corridor and around another.

Trailing the princess, Leighton tried hard to remember the route, but lost count of turns. Finally, she ducked into a bathroom stall and relieved herself. When she came out to wash her hands, Aliyah was gone. Was she waiting outside? She stepped into the hall and glanced both ways. *Are you kidding me?* Where was the princess? Had she really left her? How was she supposed to get back to the reception hall?

She turned left, telling herself she could do this. After a few more turns, she felt her confidence growing. Headed down—

Wait. No, this wasn't right. She backed up.

A door swung open, revealing a long prep table with a tray of carafes. Kitchen? Even as she collided with a man exiting the kitchen, she wondered how she had gotten so far off course. The man was moving so fast that a collision could not be avoided.

Embarrassment flooded her at being caught in the wrong part of the palace and ramming into him. "*Oh, 'ana asf,*" she apologized and backed up. At least she tried to, but he'd grabbed her shoulders. Startled at his crushing grip, she drew in a breath. Looked up . . . into malevolent eyes.

Dark, terrible eyes that seemed borne of a storm.

Terror ripped down her spine as she tried to pull away but he held her fast. "*Law samahta. Atrukh.*" The plea to release her went unanswered. "*Law samahta.*"

"*Eres tú,*" he whispered.

Surprised at his words—that wasn't Arabic—she had a reckoning with the man before her. It was *him*. The man who hated Navas. The assassin! "Let go!"

"Release her!" A barked voice sent the large man rushing in the opposite direction. "Princess."

Pulse thundering, legs weak, Leighton stumbled back against the wall and shuddered around a few, heaving breaths.

The man who'd intruded rushed to her in a thobe and ghutra. "Are you okay?"

She waved him off, but only then realized he was speaking English. She glanced up into gray eyes that churned with ferocity. Not like the violence of the Latino man. This man . . . "You're American." Hope leapt through her.

He cast a glance in both directions, then reached under his ghutra and touched his ear. When he withdrew his hand, he held a tiny device. "Put it in your ear."

Warily, she stared at the thing. "Why . . . ?"

He nodded to the earpiece. "Listen to him. We're short on time."

To him? Confused, she reached for it. Tucked it in her ear, listening, her gaze skidding around the narrow passage as a hiss echoed in her ear. "Hello?"

"Leighton."

Oh sweet mercies. Her heart did a jagged dance in her chest. "Owen." She straightened, her legs going to putty at the sound of his voice, and turned from the man. Put her face to the wall, fighting tears.

"I can't be on the floor—they'd recognize me," he said. "Omen's in play. Pike thought you'd benefit from hearing from me. The team is working to get you out of there. Tonight."

Her mind buzzed with his words. But then— "Bruzon's here."

"You saw him?" The question came from both Owen and the man before her, Pike.

"Just now." But she recalled the room, the cups being wiped, and the way Bruzon stared hard at her. "I think he recognized me."

Pike monitored both ends of the passage.

"Be ready," Owen said. "When they bring out the cake—ask to use the bathroom again and be ready."

"For what?"

"Incoming," Pike muttered, wagging his hand at her.

"Have to go," she said, reaching for the piece.

"I love you," Owen said. "Be brave. I'll see you soon."

I love you. Had he really said that?

"Now!" Pike barked.

Leighton removed the piece. In her haste, she dropped it.

EIGHTEEN

Jeddah, Saudi Arabia

PIKE MUTTERED AN OATH IN THE COMMS.

"What's wrong?" Owen demanded. Seconds fell off the clock with the weight of iron. "Pike, what—"

"It's under control."

He couldn't take it anymore, sitting in the van and watching from live feeds. Hearing her voice, the terror in it after encountering Bruzon, Owen made a decision. "I'm going in."

"Stay put," Pike growled. "That infected face of yours and the bruises are enough to scare the most hardened of thugs."

Hand on the door of the van, Owen faltered. *I can't . . . I can't stay out here.*

"Don't worry, Apollo. We got her." Dante's words weren't much reassurance.

Not while Leighton was inside and Bruzon was on the loose. His gaze lit on something in the feed. "Chief, eyes on Bruzon."

"Affirmative," Pike said in his preternatural calm. "OTG, north corner of the reception hall."

"Got him," Tariq reported.

Brick Archer, far too burly and red-bearded to blend in well, sat in the catering van with him. "I don't know how you do it," he muttered. "I'd be all over that like white on rice. No way I'd sit here."

That was all Owen needed. He grabbed the thobe and ghutra from the stack purchased for the insertion.

"Hold up," Brick said, straightening from the feeds. "That was figurative, lover boy."

Owen secured a ghutra on his head. "Sounded literal." With that, he shoved out of the concealed van and made his way through the rear of the building. He picked up a box of supplies. Didn't care what it was. Just had to get it and himself into the palace.

"Chief," Brick said in his distinctive twang, "Apollo incoming."

"Negative," Pike hissed. "Apollo, stand down!"

Owen ignored the chatter and entered through the rear of the kitchen. If he held the ghutra just right, he could conceal the marred mess on his jaw. In the kitchen area, he set aside the box and kept going.

A shout went up, and he forced himself to remain calm. Look to the side where a chef with a very large kitchen knife pointed to the box, misunderstanding Owen's identity. Assuming he was a worker. He said something then indicated to the corner.

Acquiescing, Owen relocated the box. Waited till the cook looked away, and then eyed the door where servers were entering and exiting. He grabbed a tray and moved with purpose toward the door. Ducked through and followed the stream of staff filtering from the kitchens, down the hall that seemed mildly familiar from the times he'd walked Leighton to the garden. Feeling his bearings grind into place, he followed staff into the reception hall that was insanely decorated. Festooned with flowers and pink . . . so much pink. As if a bottle of Pepto vomited here.

Holy what? This was like something from some fantasy movie.

"Okay, Apollo," Brick comm'd, "since you dived in with both feet, she's up front. Your two o'clock. *Don't* mess this up. Unlike you, we have a plan."

"Understood," he subvocalized as he set the tray on a serving table and with a few steaming mugs in hand, worked his way over to her. But there were hundreds of people, women with their heads covered. Where . . . ?

"Green, she's wearing green," Brick muttered. "Good night, do I have to hand her to you?"

"Shut up," Owen muttered even as his gaze struck her. Something in his gut tightened. "I see her. En route."

———— • ————

Settled back in her seat near the head table, where Hassan and Daria were eating and laughing, receiving well wishes from their guests, Leighton . . . felt this prickling dread. Something . . .

Her gaze wandered over the crowd, wondering where Bruzon was. Had he left? Despite the hundreds feasting in honor of Daria and Hassan, she quickly located the man. Navas's enemy—that's who he was, right?

Mercies, she did not like his expression. He seemed . . . predatory. Just as he had in the hall when Pike intercepted her. Intervened, really. She knew it for what it was. And thank goodness. Who knew what the man would've done?

Stop. You're stressing over nothing. She eyed the head table. Saw the king smile at her. She hated deceiving him. He would not appreciate the truth of her birth. And that nauseated her.

King Faruq lifted his mug and swung it at her, as if in toast.

Though she lowered her gaze, something pricked at her mind.

The mug. Was that . . . Her thoughts flicked back to the prep hall. Before the man came out. Someone had wiped the mugs . . .

Her gaze bounced to the cup the king aimed toward his mouth. Jerked her attention to the man.

He was leaning forward. Eager. Anxious.

The cup. *It's the cup.* She started to rise.

A hand landed on her shoulder. She startled and looked up and behind her. Penetrating blue eyes held hers. "Owen!"

"It's time. Let's go."

Already on her way to her feet, she swung her gaze back to the king.

"Come on. Now." Owen tugged her—gently, but firmly.

But . . . the cup. Had they done something to his cup? Her heart hammered as she stalled.

"Nouri."

"No," she said as the moment powered down to an infinitesimal speed. The greedy gleam in Bruzon's eyes. The king's cup—the same one she'd seen someone wiping in the side room. "No!" she cried, wrenching out of Owen's grasp. She stumbled and knocked the table.

The din in the room faltered, gazes swinging to her.

"King Faruq! Don't drink from that cup!" she shouted, but it was still too loud in the hall. Even as she saw his mouth touch the rim, she snatched up a small tart and pitched it at him, desperate to stop him. "Don't drink it!"

The pastry careened into his forehead. He jerked visibly from the impact. Spiced coffee splashed his face, and he shoved upward with a roar.

Weight plowed into her back and slammed her onto the table.

Owen had no idea what she was screaming about, but he went headlong into the table with her, two guards pinning them both there.

"What the Hades just happened?" Brick grumbled.

"Apollo screwed it up," someone muttered in the comms.

Gritting his teeth, Owen found his cheek pressed to a plate that cracked beneath the impact and made his stitches sting.

Leighton was next to him, shouting, "It's poisoned! It's poisoned."

Guards in black attire hauled them up out of the room, barely letting their feet touch the ground. Coming out of the shock of seeing her shout and throw food at the king, he realized what had happened. She'd realized something. Something they'd all missed.

He'd expected to find themselves in a dungeon cell or the executioner's block. Instead, they were delivered to the same hall that Owen had been brought to—the king's reception room—that first day.

Forced into the couches that lined the hall, he dragged off the Arabic attire.

Leighton looked at him, pale and shaken. "They . . . the assassin—"

"Bruzon."

She nodded. "I think he tried to poison the king."

"You *think*?" Owen grimaced. "I hope you're right . . ."

"Me too."

His gaze tracked over her. "You look amazing."

"Shut up!" a guard shouted, staggering toward them as if to strike her, but instead just shook his fist. "How dare you attack our king! He has given you everything!"

They waited in silence for what felt like hours. Finally, the doors opened and the king—in clean clothes—stormed in with Crown Prince Maaz. They strode to the front without looking at anyone, then the king turned to them. Scowled at Leighton. "Explain yourself, Nouri." He pointed to the center, directly in front of himself.

She stood, slowly moved to the middle of the hall. "Earlier, I was returning to the reception hall when I got lost. Made wrong turns. I stumbled upon a door that opened. That's when I saw a tray of mugs and cups. Someone was wiping one with a cloth and gloves. A man then barreled out and crashed into me. Later, I saw him in the reception hall. He seemed eager. Anxious. He was watching Your Majesty. That's when I noticed your mug was the one I'd seen being wiped. I could only guess they were trying to poison you."

Owen waited, watched. Saw the tight expression on the king. The rage in the crown prince's gaze.

"So you threw food at me."

She flinched and drove her gaze to the marble again. "My apologies, Your Majesty. I was too far away, and when I cried out, you could not hear me. I was afraid you would drink from it."

Silence gaped through the hall for several long minutes. A man rushed down the side and hurried to the king, delivering a paper to him with a firm nod.

King Faruq glanced at the paper, then to Leighton. "Would you recognize this man again if you saw him?"

"I would, sire."

The king motioned for the side doors to be opened. A moment later, ten men were ushered into the room.

Oh no. Pike, Dante, Crow, and Tariq stood with Bruzon.

"These men have false IDs," the king said. "Is the man you saw here?"

Leighton scanned the men, then pointed to Bruzon. "That's him."

The king jutted his jaw, and guards set upon him. Pulled him from the room.

"Apollo."

The bark of his callsign jerked Owen to his feet. "Sir—er Majesty."

"How did you get out of your dungeon?"

Owen swallowed. "With help."

The king indicated to the team. "From these men?"

He did not want to rat out Omen, but he also had a feeling the king already knew the answers.

"To save Nouri."

Again, another trap. "To save Leighton."

The king drew up.

"You should know, Your Majesty," Leighton said softly, "that I am grateful for the protection you have afforded me all these months I have been here."

His eyes narrowed.

"You believe me your daughter—"

"Leighton," Owen hissed.

"—but I am not," she said, unyielding. She did not seem to care when Prince Rayan moved to her side.

Owen didn't miss how pale the prince looked now. Or how Omen shifted, their postures screaming readiness to protect her. To act. Respond to any threat presented. It was the same one roiling through him. He adjusted to her left.

King Faruq stepped toward her. "Go on."

"My father is a mercenary whom my mother, Princess Yasmina, met on a vacation with her mother. Despite what you . . . did to her, you did not father me."

His gaze darkened, then he pivoted and returned to the front. He swiped a hand over his beard.

Owen was proud to stand with her. Hated that Rayan was there too, but he'd take what he could get.

Leighton, however, only gave him her eyes. Sorrow cut through them, but also resolve.

"You did the right thing," he whispered.

Though grieved—what she had done, said, would have consequences—she nodded.

"You are right, Nouri," the king pronounced, his gaze finding her again as he raised the paper given to him moments ago. "The cup was poisoned." With a flick of his finger, the king held her gaze. Next to him, Maaz produced a dagger.

Adrenaline jacked through Owen as the prince flew straight at them. "No!" He dived in front of Leighton even as he heard the woosh of ghutras and an agonal grunt.

With a lethal blow, the prince took Rayan to the ground.

Leighton screamed even as Owen spun her away from the confrontation and held her there. Omen grouped up around them.

"Prince Maaz recently discovered," King Faruq said, "that my nephew has been plotting to take my throne by colluding with the man you witnessed." He sauntered over to the fallen prince and spat on him. Then he moved to Owen and Leighton. "It seems you saved my life today, Nouri."

She swallowed and straightened.

"You may not be my daughter, but al-Zahrani blood *does* flow in your veins because of your mother." He gave a slow, recognizing nod. "For this great mercy you have done me this day, how can I repay you, Leighton Kingslake? Speak and it will be done."

Leighton shifted out of Owen's arms. Stood tall before King Faruq. "Just one thing."

"Name it."

"Swear nobody—not you nor anyone on behalf of House al-Zahrani—will ever again come after me or those I love." She moved closer. "I just want to live in peace." She eyed Owen. "With no more secrets."

EPILOGUE

London, England

W E ARE FREE, UMMI." LEIGHTON SAVORED the hug of the woman who had given her life on a brief stop to share all the news and what had happened with her.

"Oh, my sweet girl," Ummi whispered into her hair. "You are a miracle!" She wept, sobbed. "I never dreamed . . . never imagined this day could be." Slowly, she lowered into a chair. "I do not know how to live without looking over my shoulder."

Leighton caught her ummi's hands and knelt. "We must learn. Together. I would have us visit often." She stared into eyes so like her own. "I want to know you."

"I very much want the same thing." Ummi gave a nervous laugh. "So many dreams coming true all at once. It is too much . . ."

A rap at the door dropped them into silence.

Leighton raised herself, knowing who was on the other side of that wooden barrier. She watched as Gerard went and opened it.

The handsome driver nodded to the new arrival. "Juan."

Juan Navas inclined his head and shook Gerard's hand. His

gaze landed on her, and she noticed how his shoulders tensed. He stilled.

Leighton struggled for a clean breath. *My father.*

Ummi stood again. "Juan," she said with a fondness that saturated the air, "our daughter." Tears ruptured Ummi's calm façade. "Isn't she beautiful?"

The cadence of Leighton's pulse seemed to match his, if the rise and fall of his chest was any indication. The compulsion to rush into his arms was tempered by *his* reserve. The way he held back . . . Was he uncertain? "Leighton," he said tentatively, nervously, his brown eyes searching, hands clenching. As if he wrestled with something.

To keep himself from reaching out for me. Afraid to rush or overstep.

How she knew that, she had no idea. Maybe because it was the same impulse prickling like fire along her nerve endings. The thought threw Leighton toward him, all her misgivings and resentment toward him falling aside as she wrapped him in a hug. "Dad."

"I . . ." His arms encircled her, lightly. His chest tremored. Then his embrace tightened. His face pressed into her shoulder and he sobbed. "*Lo siento. Lo siento.*"

"Don't be sorry," she muffled into his shirt. "It's over. Behind us."

"*Mija,*" he whispered, angled his mouth and kissed her, a noisy one at her ear.

But she didn't mind. It was a piece of the puzzle of her life that had finally fallen into place. They eased apart, and Navas folded his arms over his chest, backing up. Looking at her, tears still falling. He nodded, pursed his lips. Backed up. Then rushed forward, yanking her back into his arms. "I can't let you go . . . not again."

When he released her next, she stayed close and he kept an arm around her. She marveled that this mercenary had a very soft heart beneath the years of hardness.

Ummi laughed as she wiped tears. "Look," she said. "This is the first time we have all been in the same room together."

Leighton then noticed Owen, standing quietly to the side, also with red-rimmed eyes, as if he were trying to hold it together and not cry. "All thanks to Owen. Our hero."

Thank You!

Thank you so much for reading *Apollo*. We hope you enjoyed the story. If you did, would you be willing to do us a favor and leave a review? It doesn't have to be long—just a few words to help other readers know what they're getting. (But no spoilers! We don't want to wreck the fun!) Thank you again for reading!

We'd love to hear from you—not only about this story, but about any characters or stories you'd like to read in the future. Contact us at www.sunrisepublishing.com/contact.

We also have regular updates that contain sneak peeks, reviews, upcoming releases, and fun stuff for our reader friends. Sign up at www.sunrisepublishing.com

READ ON FOR MORE FROM THE

DISCARDED HEROES:
SCIONS

—— SERIES ——

Gear up for the next book in the
Discarded Heroes: Scions series!

WHEN TWO DESPERATE QUESTS BECOME ONE UNSTOPPABLE FORCE

She needs his skills to survive. He needs her secrets to uncover the truth.

For two years, Dillon Jacobs has refused to accept his father's death. He's chased every lead across multiple continents—burning bridges and risking everything to prove Max Jacobs is still alive.

Cove Galtieri is fighting her own impossible battle. Desperate to clear her father's name of corruption charges that threaten to destroy their family legacy, she's gathering evidence to prove the man who raised her isn't the monster the world claims.

After Dillon's hunt intersects their paths in Paris, their worlds soon collide again in gunfire and chaos at the Galtieri estate in Italy. But that collision becomes a revelation: Dillon's missing father and Cove's accused father were photographed together in Yemen. The evidence Cove has been gathering contains clues Dillon desperately needs.

Two quests. One conspiracy. A partnership forged in fire.

Every ally could be an enemy. Every clue could be a trap. Racing across international borders—from Italian vineyards to Greek islands to the dangerous ports of Yemen—Dillon and Cove must navigate a deadly game where trust is a luxury they can't afford and love might be the most dangerous weapon of all.

ONE

Six Months Ago
Paris, France

A RRÊTEZ, POLICE!"
That was his cue *not* to stop as the officer demanded but to break into a sprint across Vendôme Square. Only a fool thought they could get into the Ritz Paris hotel, sneak up to a luxury suite, slip inside said suite, and scour it for a laptop, forgotten phone—a ludicrous hope but one harbored all the same—and exfil without being seen. Or caught.

Maybe the police were pursuing a petty criminal.

Well. Some petty criminal other than Dillon Jacobs.

He checked his six in the sleek black hood of a Bentley Bentayga unloading passengers in front of the hotel. Time to run. Muttering an oath, he monitored for moving vehicles. That split-second recon warned this would be close.

Dillon too late saw the door of the Bentley flinging open into his escape route. Rolling around the obstacle, he noted a beautiful brunette emerging with a handful of shopping bags. A man reached toward her, his hands jabbing into Dillon's corrected trajectory.

Like lightning, he careened between the two. Accidentally clipped the bags from the woman's hands.

Startled at his sudden intrusion into her path, she pitched backward to avoid colliding with him. Staggered.

Dillon caught her shoulders even as she bumped against the tail of the luxury car with a yelp. Was she hurt? "You good?"

Molten, hazel eyes—no, they were more than that, much more—slammed into his. Her perfect pink lips parted. Holy wow, she was beautiful! This had to be fate.

The thought rattled him as a flurry of French erupted from the man. The beauty scowled at Dillon and jerked from his grip. Her gaze struck something behind him—the way things were going, probably the police—and she pushed him away.

Already off-kilter, Dillon stumbled away from her, feeling like destiny was being ripped out of his hands. *Hey, idiot—cops, remember?* He glanced back and found them surging in his direction.

Exfil now!

"*Arrêtez*! Police!" they shouted again.

Calm, cool, collected façade abandoned, Dillon winked at the woman and muttered an apology, then bolted across Vendôme Square. A horn blared. Brakes squealed. He thudded against the vehicle, rolled over its hood, and kept moving on the other side. Cursed himself for being sloppy as he whipped around the bronze central column—which looked more green than bronze, even at this late hour and lit by floodlights. Had to respect that Napoleon replaced the statue of himself with a monument made of 1,200 enemy canons—a powerful statement—but the iconic sight stood in the gaping middle of an open square that left Dillon wide open.

"*Arrêtez*!"

Sorry, dude. Not happening. Heart pounding in cadence with his shoes, he pushed himself hard. Could not afford to get strung up *this* close to answers. The thudding of pursuit was slower but not slow enough.

Get moving!

He cleared the square, banked right onto the side street, and sprinted for all he was worth, knowing every second mattered if he wanted to escape. Once past the first building, he plastered himself into the slightly recessed area of the second structure. Effectively hidden from the corner view of the street, he had seconds before being discovered. Shadows concealed him as he seized advantage of the classic architectural style to scale the walls. The limestone ledges were perfectly spaced to create handholds.

Parkour skills had served him well on this mission to find his dad. Hearing the clap of the officers' boots on the street below, he didn't look down but instead focused on a cat-to-cat move, hiking up onto the ledge of the second story. Climbed on the balcony's iron rail and leapt up, grabbing the third-story overhang. He repeated the move to gain the rooftop. Caught it and hauled himself onto the roof.

Pulse jagged, he wanted to lie there, catch his breath, but the beam of the cop's torch traced the edge. They weren't going to give up easily. While the distinctive architecture of the Haussmann-style homes benefited his ability to reach a high vantage, the roofs were another matter. Between skylights, dormers, vents, and chimneys, he had his work cut out for him. Navigating the tricky surfaces, he trained his ear on the street. Heard shouts moving down the street on a parallel course with him.

Anger simmered. Every building and rooftop he cleared meant more distance between him and his target. Gritting his teeth, he paused on one of the rare flat roofs and looked toward the green column of Vendôme Square, still visible in the night sky. He itched to go back, but if he did and got caught . . .

Get him tomorrow.

Right. Couldn't do that if he was locked up.

Sighting the parking garage he'd scouted previously, Dillon slipped and slid toward it. At the overhang, he hopped out into thin air, rotated his body, and as he plummeted, snagged the ledge, breaking his descent. Gently landed on a balcony rail. Released himself. Caught the next one, the impact vibrating the wrought-iron rail against his palms. Once more. Then, with a check down the length of his body, released the first-story residence's rail. Dropped to the street and pitched himself in the direction of the parking structure. Pulling into the shadows, he sprinted down the street. Aimed right just as headlamps and swirling lights swung onto the narrow road, cluttered on the left with café tables.

Dillon bolted down the cobbled street, banked left, and found a duck-through alley. *C'mon, c'mon*, he mentally prodded the police, *just give up. Nothing to see here.*

The high-pitched *nee-ner nee-ner* of the siren proved relentless.

But Dillon hadn't come this far, spent the last fifteen months chasing down leads, finally ended up in the same city as Massimo Galtieri to end up in cuffs. Pushing himself, he drove his body as hard as he could, working to increase the distance between him and the authorities. Stayed in the shadows. Headed toward the Seine.

By the time he reached the park stretching out before the Louvre, he appreciated the burn in his lungs. This years-long endeavor had built him into the best shape of his life. Even if food was scarce and the nights long, he'd find Dad. Prove wrong every single government entity that had declared Max Jacobs dead. No way a Jacobs died like that, without a fight. Without a body to bury.

Calves tight and side cramping, he slowed to a walk. As he wove beneath some trees, he shrugged out of his black jacket, moving deliberately toward the next road that crossed the famous river. He turned it inside out and threaded his arms back through it. The green wouldn't be too noticeable in the night light, but at least it wasn't black, which authorities were no doubt looking for now.

From the pocket, he pulled out a black ball cap and tugged it on. It was a simple but hopefully effective way to deter first glances.

The faint *nee-ner* swelled for a second—along with his heart rate—then faded again. He nailed the next right and crossed the Seine.

Blue lights swirled.

Jaw tight, he tugged the cap down, glanced over his shoulder before changing to the other side of the road, and spotted a police car emerging from a side street.

Good night, they were relentless.

Head down, Dillon debated running. That would def draw attention. Every step felt leaden as he homed in on the densely packed residential buildings, certain he could lose them there if—

Tires pealed. Blue lights swam toward him.

"For the love of . . ." With a grunt, he threw himself down a side street with little light and worse line of sight to be seen. He broke into a sprint again, anxious to increase the distance. Darted around a corner, effectively plunging into darkness on the narrow alley-like road with no streetlamps. Perfect for concealment. Not so much for navigating. As he jogged, he eyed rooftops, searching for a quick place to hide. Moving, he clung to the buildings and shadows, working in his favor. Right turn.

This time of night, most people were in their homes. Which meant he wouldn't have many witnesses, but it also meant he would be the standout lone wolf prowling the streets.

A baby's wail jerked his attention to a woman pulling a writhing, howling child from the car. Bags of groceries hooked over her arms, she lost grip of what looked like a diaper bag. Stared at it for a long second but then hurried up the steps, unlocking the door.

Swirling blue lights crawled the buildings, tracing them, as if searching for the bug-bitten superhero. The police car glided onto the narrow street.

I must be cursed.

To change up his appearance, Dillon shrugged out of his jacket and folded it under his arm as he reached the woman, still wrangling the screaming child as she stabbed a key at the lock. Her flat door finally swung open.

Dillon snagged the diaper bag from the sidewalk, hustled the five steps up to her stoop, watching as she set down the groceries inside the door and flicked on the foyer light. Not wanting to alarm her, he pushed pleasantry into his voice. "*Voilà, madame.*"

She turned and, finding him on the step, started. Almost simultaneously came the anticipated explosion of light from the police car that blinded her. Shrinking, the thirtysomething woman shielded her eyes.

Dillon did the same, holding his hand up—an effective way to protect not only his eyes but his identity—as he looked toward the car. Y'know, as if he were any other Joe. Because what criminal would just stand on a doorstep and look at the very authorities he was trying to evade?

He checked the woman, realizing she hadn't taken the bag yet.

In her eyes radiated concern and uncertainty that had paralyzed her. Still proffering the diaper pack, he silently begged her not to shout or scream. That look on her face said she had connected the dots and guessed the police were patrolling her street, so he touched the babe's head. Hoped it didn't make him seem like a creeper.

"*Merci,*" she finally murmured, the thanks lost amid the baby's wails. Her gaze bounced between him and the police.

"*Voilà,*" Dillon said as he casually reached around her, depositing the bag inside the foyer. Stepping back, he hated the way she'd tensed and glanced askance at him, as if he were the criminal the authorities thought.

She wasn't wrong, but he didn't have to like it. In fact, he hated it. But this mission was necessary. When he noticed the wash of blue vanish from the walls, he retreated to the narrow sidewalk. "*Bonne nuit.*"

Her reciprocal "good night"—which sounded uncertain but relieved—scampered after him as he headed in the direction the cops had taken, wagering they wouldn't backtrack. At least this way, he'd be behind them, able to eyeball and anticipate their direction. But when he hit the main road, the blue lights were gone. Donning his jacket again, he switched the baseball cap for the warm beanie, hunched into the jacket, and continued down the street.

After another twenty minutes passed without incident, he spotted a flat-topped roof and scaled up to it, the surface still warm from the long-gone sun. He lowered himself against a chimney, folded his arms over his chest, and burrowed into the corner. Tilting his head back, he grunted at the smudge of black overhead, wishing for the canvas of stars. But in even that he was defeated, thanks to the City of Light's ever-present illumination.

Elbows on his knees, he hooked his hands over his head and scratched his shorn hair. Man, he'd screwed up tonight. He'd been so close to Galtieri. Took a risk he shouldn't have. While he'd gotten away, it'd been close. Too close. Cost him time. Maybe got his face on some feeds. Now the Ritz would be on alert tomorrow night for Galtieri's dinner party.

Gut rumbling with hunger, he felt his ribs poking out. Being on the lam didn't make for fattened calves or a full stomach. Clenching his jaw, he pinched the bridge of his nose. His gut grumbled again, hunger gnawing at his insides. In the morning, he'd grab something to tide him over. How much did he have left? He reached in his pocket for his money . . . and faltered when he felt only the fabric lining. His heart skipped a beat, but maybe he'd put it in the other pocket. He checked. Nothing. Empty.

No no no.

It wasn't just the money that had taken a week of tourist trolling to accrue. It was the device. The one Helios had sent so Dillon could pair with Galtieri's phone.

"Augh!" Dillon smacked his head back against the chimney. Again. Again. He jabbed the heels of his hands into his eyes as he growled his frustration. Without the device, being here in Paris—which had taken him weeks to effect—was pointless. A waste of time and resources.

But Galtieri was here. If he didn't figure something out, the billionaire connected to—*responsible for*—Dad's disappearance would leave the city. No guaranteeing he'd go back to his Italian villa, but even if he did, it'd take weeks or months before another opportunity presented itself.

Frustration soaked his muscles, making them heavy, aching. Like his soul. Now he had to find more money. Republic Square was the place to do that. If he could get money, maybe he'd be able to reach Helios in time. But the chances he could get another device before tomorrow night were pretty much nil.

God, I need a break. With the way things were going, he should add a qualifier. *And just so we're crystal, not a limb.*

Ronie Kendig is a bestselling, award-winning author of over forty books. She grew up an Army brat, and now she and her Army-veteran husband have returned to their beloved Texas after a ten-year stint on the East Coast. They survive on Sonic runs, barbecue, and peach cobbler that they share—sometimes—with Benning the Stealth Golden and AAndromeda the MWD Washout. Ronie's degree in psychology has helped her pen novels of intense, raw characters.

To learn more about Ronie, visit her at roniekendig.com and follow her on social media.

BESTSELLING AUTHOR
RONIE KENDIG

WITH **STEFFANI WEBB,** **JJ SAMIE MYLES,** & **VONI HARRIS**

We solve the problem of what to read next.

WE THINK YOU'LL ALSO LOVE...

Fire Department liaison Allen Frees may have put his life back together, but getting the truck crew and engine squad to succeed might be his toughest job yet. When a child is nearly kidnapped, Allen steps in to help Pepper Miller keep her niece safe. The one thing he couldn't fix was the love he lost, but he isn't going to let Pepper walk away this time.

Expired Return **by Lisa Phillips**

Infiltrating a dangerous militia to save her troubled brother, Jamie Winters finds herself kidnapped. Only Logan Crawford, the man she once broke, can rescue her—but he demands a promise in return. As they navigate peril in the Alaskan wilderness, their unresolved feelings spark a chance for love and redemption.

Burning Hearts **by Lisa Phillips**

When an attempt is made on Grey Parker's life and dead bodies begin piling up, suddenly bodyguard Christina Sherman is tasked with keeping both a soldier and his dog safe... and with them, the secrets that could stop a terrorist attack.

Driving Force **by Lynette Eason and Kate Angelo**

We solve the problem of what to read next.

WHERE EVERY STORY IS A FRIEND,
AND EVERY CHAPTER IS A NEW JOURNEY...

Subscribe to our newsletter for a free book, the latest news, weekly giveaways, exclusive author interviews, and more!

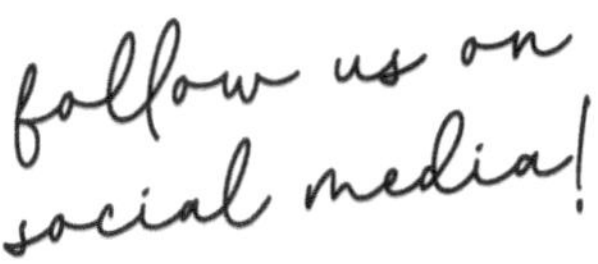

Shop paperbacks, ebooks, audiobooks, and more at
SUNRISEPUBLISHING.MYSHOPIFY.COM